The House
in the
Old Wood

Book One of The Day Magic Died

IAN FALLIS

Second Edition

DEDICATION

This book is dedicated to my dad, who gave me key advice at an important
crossroads of my life:
"If you want to write, write."

ACKNOWLEDGMENTS

My wife, Julie, put up with numerous rounds of reading and proofreading, and endlessly encouraged me to keep working on this book and those that follow in this series. If not for her, this book would not exist. I can't tell you how many times she has given a positive answer to my question, "Yeah, but do you really think anyone is going to want to read this?"

My daughter Jackie made some great points after reading early drafts of this book and the next in the series. Her comments led me to remove major distractions from both books.

Chris Holland took my humdrum cover design and made it sing. At the very least, she made it stop humming and drumming.

Kristen Lang, based on my horrendous sketches, drew a beautiful map for this second edition, which appears on the next pages. A larger version without a page split is available on my author blog, **ian-tallis.com**

The cover photo was taken by the author along the St. Francis Trail in the Ocala National Forest near DeLand, Florida.

Download a printable version of this map at: **ian-fallis.com**

CHAPTER ONE

Karia, glancing back as she pushed through the brush, crashed into a clearing. She fell, her left shoulder slamming hard into the ground and almost knocking the wind out of her. She lay still for a moment.

Battling the feeling of fear tingling at the back of her neck, she lifted her head and listened. Hearing Narck crashing through the brush was no problem. She needed to figure out how close he was. When the rustling stopped, she knew.

"Oh, poor Karia," he called out, taunting her. "Left your shoe wedged under this root, did you? It's hard to run with just one shoe, isn't it? You stay right where you are, and I'll bring it to you!"

Now she heard only an occasional crack and a gentle swish of leaves. She decided that meant he was now moving more slowly, deliberately, following her trail. From the start, she had pushed directly into the bushes and shrubs and vines instead of sticking to the paths. She knew she could fit through places Narek could not, and more importantly, slip through small spaces between the vegetation without leaving much of a trail.

It's not that Narek was large. Karia was thin. Thin to an extreme. She wasn't particularly tall for her age, but since she had also shot up in the last year or so, and was now taller than most of the boys her age, she felt too tall. Combined with her thinness, she felt very awkward and clumsy. In her mind, she was a stick.

But that wasn't all. She was pale. Not just fair, but pale. Her dad had taken to calling her *Tsilinki*. It was a play on the pet name he had for her as a child, *Tsil*. Her mom told her once that it was short for an Inamali word, *Tsilinakaya*, and that it meant something like "hope." She wasn't sure why

1

her dad called her Tsil, but it was his special word for her and she liked that. On the other hand, tsilinki was the name of the grain her family grew – a pale plant with only a hint of green, which grew up straight and tall, rod-thin, to five or six, or sometimes even eight feet, before it ever started filling out and coloring, budding and setting grain. A pale, thin stick.

Thanks, Dad. She hated her new nickname.

At the beginning of this chase her slimness worked out for her. She fit through the gaps in the brush, and was confident she could elude Narek. Then the brush closed in and she had to press her way through. It snagged on her dress and tugged at her long auburn hair. It had snatched off one of her shoes, and more than once she accidentally let a branch snap back across her nose – *my ugly little sharp nose* – or into her very blue eyes, which were starting to water a little. No, she wasn't crying. Her eyes were watering. At least, that's what she would say. Karia did not cry.

But the worst part was that she was now leaving a clear trail for Narek to follow, and he seemed to be catching up.

She rolled onto her stomach so she could push herself up onto her hands and knees, unconsciously digging her fingers into the sandy soil. Still looking down, she silently cursed herself for letting Timbal kiss her when he found her the last time the three of them played hide-and-seek. She whispered a curse at Narek for spying on them. Losing her temper, she loudly cursed Timbal for telling Narek he could have a kiss if he caught her this time. At least, she tried to. She didn't recognize the word that came out. But she had no time to think about it.

"What was that?" Narek called out. "Did you call for me? I'm coming, Karia!" He laughed.

Her fear had turned to anger and now embarrassment burned into determination. She had to escape, but where? And how? Already the bottom of her right foot was bruised and throbbing. Her shoulder was sore and she was still trying to catch her breath.

She could not run. She needed to find a place to hide.

She lifted her head and looked around, and her fear returned. For this was the one place in the forest that she dreaded more than a kiss from Narek.

She was looking down a dirt lane wide enough for a horse-drawn carriage, hard-packed and rutted as if from past use, now covered with silt, dirt and dust from misuse. It ran no more than a hundred feet, ending abruptly in trees and brush at one end, where she was, and at the opposite end. All along the lane on her left grew a neat, orderly hedge, several feet thick, with tiny round waxy leaves and, in spring, fine white flowers that had a sour scent. It was late summer now, and the flowers had become tiny beads of green, some already ripening into the yellow berries that the birds left alone. She had sniffed one once, crushed it and sniffed it again. It smelled sour, like the flowers. *I wouldn't eat them either.*

The hedge even had a wide opening and a stately gate sculpted in some kind of grayish-white metal that did not rust, attended by two square lamps in similar patterns – like interlocking vines – and apparently wrought from the same material. Beyond the hedge, where there should have been at least a cottage – if not a manor house, judging from the majesty of the gate – was only forest.

And now she recognized the feeling at the back of her neck for what it was – not fear of Narek catching her, but that feeling that always crept up her neck near the hedge. The hedge and lane by themselves would have been strange; the sensation on the back of her neck told her there was dangerous power here – though how she knew that, and why Timbal and Narek had never felt it, she did not know.

Here on her hands and knees, she saw something she had never noticed before. A short distance up the lane, on her side of the gate, she could see a space to crawl under the hedge. A dark space – a place she could hide. It looked inviting.

She did not question why she had never seen it before. She did not wonder why the place that had repulsed her in the past now seemed to draw her. She reasoned, quite simply, that she needed a place to hide and had found it.

Swiftly Karia crawled to the space and under the hedge, the shadows growing deeper as she crawled. She was about to question how she could still be crawling under the hedge for so long, when suddenly she was not under the hedge anymore. She was inside a room.

Amazed, still on her hands and knees, she looked up and around. The room was perhaps eight feet square and equally high, the walls white with plaster or whitewash. Narrow windows very high on the walls bathed the room in light. A doorway in front of her opened into what looked like a parlor beyond.

She wanted to explore – even felt compelled to look around – but she also felt wary. The feeling at the back of her neck was acute, and had spread to a tingling in her scalp.

She looked left to a desk made of thick, dark wood, carved with winding knots of snakes and with a lighter colored writing stand atop it. She could tell it was carved as well, but the carving was so fine and intricate it was difficult for her to make out what it was from where she was. A quill was still in an inkwell, as if someone had stopped writing just a moment ago. Behind the desk was a bookcase set into the wall, its top shelf filled with a large number of books, some quite big. Because of the desk, Karia could see only the top shelf, but she had never before seen so many books, or books so big.

She turned to the right, and saw there was a coat rack on the wall. *Odd,* she thought. *Who would use an entryway as a study?*

Her eyes scanned almost to the corner when she saw something that took her back from curiosity to fear again. The rest of the coat rack had been empty, but there, on the last peg – or was it the first? – almost to the corner, nearly touching her right shoulder, was a deep brown robe, edged in red, and a very broad brown cap. The kind of robe and cap only a great sorcerer wore.

The stories she had been told as a little girl flooded back to mind. *A sorcerer wanders the forest,* she remembered Grantik, the dry goods shopkeeper, saying. It wasn't the first or last time she heard that. *He eats little children,* his wife added, seeming to find pleasure in Karia's reaction. *Never play in the forest,* her mom told her. *It's dangerous.* When she pressed her mom, she would only say, *There's magic there, Karia.* Somehow not knowing anything more specific was even more scary – and tempting. And now she was growing up, and she was old enough to start thinking they were just stories adults used to keep children in line, and keep them from playing in the forest, where some had gone lost.

But no – what they said about sorcerers and magic was no story. She knew that now.

All that flew through her mind and she was now terrified. She spun on her knees and launched herself toward the hole she came in through, and saw only a whitewashed wall hurtling toward her. She realized in a split-second that the wall was actually standing still and she was hurtling, but not in time to stop before the hurtling, whoever was doing it, came to an end. A sudden, painful end.

And everything went black.

CHAPTER TWO

For as long as she could remember, Karia lived on the farm at the edge of
the Old Wood. Timbal had always been her best friend, and Narek had
always been the third wheel. The butt of their jokes. The one who always
lost at their games. Sometimes he lost because he was smaller and rather
pudgy; sometimes it was because Timbal cheated. And sometimes, well, it
seemed like he lost just because Karia wanted him to lose. It was probably a
lot more than sometimes, but Karia didn't see how that was possible so she
mostly tried to ignore it.

Karia called Timbal's parents Uncle Avar and Aunt Heather, and Timbal
called her parents Uncle Reva and Aunt Failean. But they both called
Narek's parents Opa and Nana, because they were old. She didn't
understand how a couple as old as Opa and Nana had a child her age.

You see, the families celebrated the children's birthdays all in a row.
Within this month, first it was Timbal's fifteenth birthday, then Karia's two
days later, and a week later, Narek's. Karia reasoned that, fifteen years ago,
Opa and Nana must have been young enough to have a child, but she was
never able to convince herself of that.

Even though fifteen was an important birthday – it marked Timbal and
Narek as men and Karia as a woman – those days had gone mostly
unmarked. It was always difficult to make time to celebrate their birthdays
since they usually coincided with the best time to plant tsilinki, and that was
backbreaking work from sunup to sundown. In fact, this playtime in the
forest was the first break the children had taken in weeks.

This year, the families had talked about doing something special for
their birthdays, like a Big Gathering of all the farm families and perhaps
even folks from the village. But somehow those ideas made it all that much
harder to put something together, and nothing happened. Karia and Timbal
took it in stride. Narek still whined now and then. Though Karia had hoped
for something special this year, she found solace in the fact that the Fall
Gathering would come soon.

5

Planting and harvest had not always ruled their lives. Before coming here, the three families lived near Talitakaya, the capital city, before the fall of the Inamali. In the chaos that followed, with the three children scant weeks old, they had moved together far, far to the south and west, past the Dentanal Mountains and almost to the rugged and appropriately named Wrecked Coast.

Here they settled on a farm that had been abandoned long ago. It wasn't easy at first; only Opa and Nana knew anything about farming, but they taught the others. Soon, thanks to their hard work, the farm produced a rich crop of grain. In time, with the help of the children – or sometimes in spite of the help of the children – they were able to grow enough to pay the tax imposed by the Dr'Zhak conquerors, and even to pay off what they owed from previous years.

It was a calm life, a life that – apart from the tax – was much like life had been for the families and the rest of the Teneka for centuries before the Inamali fell. Far from Talitakaya, the influence of the victorious Dr'Zhak was rarely felt, and Karia had never seen an actual Dr'Zhak herself. Narek said he had, but Karia and Timbal didn't believe him, and when they told their parents, the three were ordered to never speak of it again.

Contrary to their parent's direction, and sometimes because of it, the three children often played in the forest. Six years ago, deep in the densest part of the woods, they had found the lane. Timbal and Narek simply thought it was odd. Perhaps even funny. Neither felt what Karia felt. When she told them of the sensation on the back of her neck, and the feeling that there was some kind of power at work there, Narek laughed at her and made fun of her.

Until Timbal threatened to throw him over the hedge.

Perhaps they too felt there was something strange at work here after all.

CHAPTER THREE

Karia's eyes opened slowly. It's not that she opened them. It just sort of happened as she woke up. She was overwhelmed with the smell of dust – it seemed to fill her nostrils and mouth – but picking her head up off the dusty floor was not easy. Her head felt heavy, very heavy, and like it was being squished, and every inch she lifted it, it grew heavier and the pressure increased. Then she felt like she was yanking her hair out.

She turned her head – painfully – and saw that her auburn hair was stuck to the ground, covered in a dark brown mass of drying blood mixed with dust on the floor. She pulled again, and when it came free – most still in her scalp, some stuck to the floor – Karia felt like her brain was loose and painfully rattling around in her head. She brushed her hair back out of her eyes. The blood – her blood – was still tacky. From that, she thought she had been out for a while. But she had no idea how long.

She sat up – her head hurt more than she could ever remember – and felt her forehead. It was a little sticky and gritty and it hurt to touch it. She pulled her hand back and looked at her palm and fingers. They were bloody, or actually blood-muddy, covered in sandy grit from the roadway, now coated in dust, and she began to realize that the floor – along with her hands and her knees, and her side where she had fallen – was thick with years of dust.

She began to look about – painfully – and found focusing a struggle. The light coming into the room made her head hurt more. *Good,* she thought, looking down again, *it's still day*. But then she wasn't so sure. It could have been the next day. *I hope Mom's not worried about me.*

Looking up again, eyes half-closed, she noticed the thick layer of dust on the desk, on the books, on the coat rack and on the robe and cap. The only markings on the dusty floor showed where she had crawled in, spun, flung herself into the wall and fallen. She looked at the wall, where she was sure she had come in. She saw only wall. A plain, whitewashed wall with a dent, a tiny chip and a small reddish-brown stain. She felt the wall, and ran her

7

fingers over the indentation, and it did indeed feel the same way it looked: solid. A little of the whitewash came off on her fingertips.

Seeing all the dust, Karia felt safer, more certain there was no sorcerer here that she needed to fear. She turned her attention back to the doorway and the parlor beyond. She could hear something she had not noticed before. What was it? Soft … like someone whispering perhaps. She was not sure what she should do, but she did not want to just sit around in the dust.

She tried to stand, but felt herself sinking dizzily back to the ground, and her stomach seemed no happier than her head. Three times, then four, her body heaved and she felt she was going to vomit, but nothing came out. Each convulsion sent more pressure toward her head, which responded with waves of crushing pain that made her more nauseated. "OK," she whispered, trying to control her breathing. "OK, calm … down …"

She did not cry. The pain most certainly brought tears to her eyes, but she fought them back. Still kneeling, she focused until she got her body back under control, then crawled toward the doorway. Each knee fall and each hand fall sent a wave of pain through her head. She stopped halfway and listened again. The sound was still there, steady. Not a whisper; almost rhythmic. *Oh good, not a whisper.* On she crawled. She realized she was shaking and her control was slipping, so she stopped and tried to focus again.

She braced herself on the doorway and carefully, slowly pulled herself up the doorframe. She felt faint and dizzy, and fought back the compulsion to vomit. She leaned on the frame and waited for the nausea to pass and for her head to clear. She did not remember her right foot was bare and bruised until she planted it on the ground. Wincing, she felt tears coming to her eyes again. She fought them back. *I don't cry!* she thought. She looked around. *Too fast,* she thought. She had to wait for her head to stop spinning.

There was indeed a small parlor here. Situated around a small fireplace were two high-backed chairs upholstered in a gaudy orange pattern so ugly that it was revolting even under a layer of dust. Their dark wooden framing and legs were carved with what appeared to be lizards. Between the chairs was a short table. Its top was marked in squares, and there were small pieces of wood in varying shapes and sizes. It looked like a game. In fact, it looked like a game in progress. She was startled by that, and looked around again to see if anyone else was there.

She looked left, and a saw a short hallway. Another short hallway, that seemed to lead to the source of the sound she was following, was to her right. Midway down each hallway was a door in the same direction as the parlor.

She looked at the floor, and could tell from the accumulation of dust that no one else had been here in a long time. She calmed down again. She settled her breathing and stopped shaking. She looked back at the game. There were only two chairs, but the board seemed to be set for four players. She tried to figure the game out, but could do little more than take note of what pieces were where.

Leaning against the wall to her right, shuffling and limping, she again followed the sound. It seemed to be coming from behind a closed door at the end of the hallway. Stopping before the door, she finally recognized the sound of falling water.

Karia reached to the doorknob, and found it turned freely. The door opened away from her, smoothly and quietly, as if it had just been oiled. And there she saw a marvel.

Of all the wondrous things in the stories her mother told her about Inamali houses, nothing fascinated Karia more than the waterfall rooms where the Inamali would bathe. She would often daydream about having a waterfall in her own house, and being able to use it whenever she wanted – instead of skinny-dipping in the muddy creek near her house when she needed to. As she grew older, she knew the whole thing was pure fantasy. Where would so much water come from, and where would it go?

Yet here before her was just such a wonder.

This room, like the study, was no more than eight feet square, and the rear half was a cascade of clear water. She could not tell where it came from, nor could she tell where it went. She stepped into the room, and saw to her right a rack with a towel and a robe. She felt them; they were dry and plush, luxurious and soft – not at all like the worn, rough towel she used on the farm. A light, pleasant perfume filled the room, and her head already felt better. It made her feel, strangely enough, at home.

To her left was a silver mirror, with a small cabinet underneath. She barely recognized her reflection. Her hair was wild, except on the left where it was matted with blood, apparently from a cut on her forehead, mixed with dust from the floor. Her forehead was bruised, and she had a black left eye. Her left eye was half-closed – she had not noticed that – and her right pupil was surprisingly large. She could barely see the bright blue of her eyes, the blue that sometimes made people who had never met her before stop and stare. She noticed something white was stuck in her hair; she plucked it out and saw that it was a tiny chunk of plaster. *Oh,* she thought. *That's where the chip from the wall went.*

She looked at the waterfall and remembered how much she wanted one as a little girl. She closed the door and took off her overdress. She was able to slip it off her shoulders and step out of it. Then she peeked out the door again to assure herself that she was alone. She took off her chemise. This was more trouble. She needed to lift it over her head, and it seemed to hang up on her chin and ears and nose and hair, each time sending a jolt of pain through her head.

As she slipped off her one shoe, she realized the floor here was free of dust. Perhaps because of the waterfall, she thought, looking up. She was about to step in when she remembered her locket, and caught herself.

She looked down at the locket hanging around her neck. Looking down sent a fresh wave of pain through her head, so she picked the locket up and held it before her eyes. It looked like some kind of cheap metal; it was more of a mottled grayish-white than shiny silver or gold. It looked like the same metal the gate and lanterns along the lane were made from. She wondered why she had never noticed that before.

She could barely make out the simple pattern of three interlocking rings on the front of the locket. Worst of all, it was broken. She couldn't open it, no matter how hard she tried. But she smiled. She treasured the locket. *Your father gave you that,* her mom had told her, and she was most definitely her daddy's little girl. Even now, when he sometimes did things that made her angry and frustrated – like calling her Tsilinki – she couldn't help but love him. For Karia, there was no better way to go to sleep or to wake up than being held in her dad's powerful arms, with his thick, long fingers running through her hair. If she had to define love, it would probably be the way she felt when he held her.

A fresh throb of pain almost made her knees buckle, and she remembered what she was doing. *You must never get the locket wet,* her mother had said. *It would be ruined.* She wasn't sure how much more ruined it could get, but she dutifully took if off. She winced as it momentarily snagged on her blood-matted hair, but it came free and she hung it with the robe. She stepped into the waterfall.

It was soothing and warm, and she found that she no longer needed to lean against the wall. Her head was feeling better, and she rinsed the blood from her hair and her face.

She wasn't certain how long she stayed in the waterfall; she lost track of the time and simply enjoyed feeling clean after crawling through the dust. No, there was more. She felt like she was supposed to be here, supposed to be bathing here. And it was so much nicer than the creek. Not only was that sometimes muddy, but she was certain that Narek spied on her sometimes. She shuddered.

When she finally stepped out of the waterfall, she turned to the mirror and, pushing her hair aside, looked at her bruises.

Mom is going to kill me, she thought.

She ran her fingers through her hair, trying to deal with the knots. Lifting her wet hair, she saw a cut. It was surprisingly small for all the blood that she had seen.

Curious, she opened the cabinet. Four small, simple jars held creams – one amber, two a milky white, and the fourth blue. Each had a label. She couldn't read it, but she knew the writing. It was Inamali. She was still looking at the delicate letters when she realized her hand was around the blue one, lifting it. Slowly she pulled it toward herself and looked closely at it.

She put her left hand on the lid, and felt that she should open it. It was more than curiosity; she felt she was being told to open it. *No,* she thought, more like encouraged to open it. This scared her a little, but still she twisted the lid off and slowly brought the jar to her nose. A pleasant aroma similar to the one she smelled when she entered the room wafted up, and she breathed deep. What was left of her dizziness and headache disappeared. She looked back to the mirror and realized that her left eye was fully open now and her pupils were both the same size and normal size. And blue. The blue of a still mountain lake on a sunny morning, a blue that's almost alive. A blue not far removed from the blue of the cream in the jar.

Now she was more scared. How had she known which jar to open? *Coincidence,* she thought, putting the lid back on and placing the jar in the cabinet. Her curiosity stirred.

"I wonder what this one does," she said, lifting the jar with the amber cream. She opened it, and a more sharp smell stung her nose. It looked like the ointment her mom used on a bad cut. Smelled like it, too, but quite a bit stronger. So she dipped her finger in. It burned slightly, which she found odd because her mom's ointment only burned on a cut.

She put the jar down and lifted her hair. Looking in the mirror, she brought the fingertip of ointment toward her cut and paused. Her mom's ointment stung so sharply that it often brought tears to her eyes. She hesitated. She took a deep breath. Then she touched the amber ointment to her cut – and staggered backwards.

Karia felt as if she had just been slapped – hard – across her forehead. Her vision was blurred and her eyes were watering. Unsteady, she reached her finger into the waterfall to rinse off the rest of the ointment, capped the jar and looked up, pulling her hair aside. She blinked, and blinked again. She still couldn't see the cut, and blinked again to try to clear her vision. Slowly it dawned on her that she was seeing clearly. The cut was gone.

"OK," she said aloud, "Mom's ointment never did that." She thought that perhaps the slap was worth it, and hoped she remembered to sit down if she ever had to deal with a more serious cut.

Now she looked down at the two jars of milky cream. She looked up at herself in the mirror, shifting her head to ponder her bruises. Her black eye seemed to be spreading even across the bridge of her nose, competing with her freckles. She looked back down at the two remaining creams.

"I wonder …"

The creams looked identical, but each bore a different label. She picked up one with each hand. Both were almost full. She tilted them, and the one in her left hand seemed thinner, runnier. But only a little. She put down the one in her left hand, twisted the lid off the thicker one and smelled it.

"Roses," she thought. But that still gave her no idea what it was for.

She put the lid back on and put the jar back. She lifted the thinner ointment out, opened that and smelled it. This fragrance too was familiar, but she could not place it. She dipped a couple of fingers of her left hand into the ointment, and it felt oily. She began to bring it toward her bruises, but stopped short, remembering what had happened when she applied the amber ointment.

She sat on the floor. With her back against the door, she tilted her head back until it was against the door. Then she applied the ointment to the bruises on her forehead and under her left eye. It itched briefly. As she rubbed it over the bruises, it seemed to be absorbed, and ceased to be oily.

Standing, she looked into the mirror again, and the bruises were gone. Standing up also reminded her of the bruises on her right foot, and – hopping to keep from falling, and squirming because it tickled – she rubbed some of the cream on the bottom of her foot. Putting it to the floor again, she could tell the bruises were gone.

Only then did she begin thinking about where she was, and what she was doing, and a hollow, empty feeling began to gnaw at the pit of her stomach.

CHAPTER FOUR

In the oldest stories of Karia's people, the Inamali were the heroes. Twelve feet tall, with flaming hair and magical powers, they saved the Teneka when their land was being ripped apart by earthquakes and volcanoes, rain and floods. They brought the Teneka across the sea to this land, to plains and grassy valleys the Dr'Zhak had willingly ceded because they were hunters and gatherers, not farmers.

The Inamali stayed in this new land as well. The stories said they could not return to their home, but no longer said why, if they ever had. They raised a great mound in the middle of the land's central plain, and built the city of Talitakaya upon it. Its glittering walls could – and still can – be seen from throughout the plain. Indeed, it was said that even people traveling from the far south and west where Karia lived could see it as they passed through the Dentanal Mountains.

The land was very good for farming, and the Teneka prospered and multiplied. But the Inamali kept to themselves, seldom venturing from Talitakaya. If there were disputes among the Teneka they could not solve – which happened all too often among the seven clans – they would bring the case to the Inamali. The judgments were often harsh, but the Teneka had no other court system, and no one wanted to argue with people who were twelve feet tall, with flaming hair and magical powers. Truth be told, they were rather terrifying, and most Teneka were glad these sessions in Talitakaya were about the only time they saw the Inamali.

The stories from this time and later were different from the earlier stories. No longer were the Inamali spoken of as heroes. They were disliked, perhaps even feared or hated. But Karia's mom always seemed to temper that as she told the stories.

The Dr'Zhak grew jealous and bitter at the wealth of the Teneka, about the way the people were able to live well while the Dr'Zhak scraped their living from the forests. When the Teneka began clearing forest to make way for more crops, the hostility became skirmishes.

13

The Dr'Zhak did not fight with honor. A small, heavily armed group would suddenly burst from the forest, often at night, kill and burn, and flee back into the forest before the Teneka could rally. Losses among the Teneka mounted, and they appealed to the Inamali for help.

The first response was not what they wanted to hear. A herald came forth from Talitakaya and proclaimed in Teneka towns and villages: "You should have left the forests alone. They belong to the Dr'Zhak. Withdraw, and let the forests grow back. Then you will have the peace you seek."

Reluctantly, more for fear of the Inamali than anything else, settlers packed up and moved away from the forests. But the Dr'Zhak did not relent; in fact, they seemed emboldened. The stories said it was the slaughter of a great number of farmers and their families in a raid deep into the central valley that stirred the Inamali to act.

Just two of them came forth from Talitakaya, one a woman named Irina. The stories said the man was her brother. She seemed to know where the Dr'Zhak raiders were before they ever emerged from the forest, and she burned them all with fire.

Soon the Dr'Zhak sued for peace, ceded the land that had been cleared, and withdrew farther into the forest. And all would have been well had Irina and her brother simply returned to Talitakaya. Instead she gathered the leaders of the seven Teneka clans and told them their boundaries. Only fear kept the clan chiefs from open rebellion then and there. She warned them of terrible consequences if they encroached on the lands of the Dr'Zhak, or mistreated each other, and it was not long before some from the Teneka Miru clan discovered what those consequences were. Irina came suddenly and unexpectedly upon a party of men clearing forest and ordered them to leave. When they refused, she burned them to cinders, leaving one alive to go and warn others.

It is unwise to refuse to listen to someone twelve feet tall, with flaming hair and magical powers.

For two hundred years chief after chief of the Teneka lived and died under what the stories called the Harsh Yoke of Irina, and though they saw her less and less, she never seemed to age. Whenever their fears would wane, she would give them a new reason to fear her.

But the Dr'Zhak were not stupid, nor were they happy. Trading with the Teneka brought them news of discontent. This their envoys massaged, and soon the Teneka Miru and their northern neighbors, the Teneka Hawe, declared themselves allies of the Dr'Zhak and independent of the Inamali.

The other clans watched to see what would happen. Nothing did. Another, and another, and another clan declared their allegiance to the Dr'Zhak, and still there was not a word from Talitakaya. In time, only the Teneka Sil were loyal to the Inamali. Talitakaya was within their borders, and they had always had the closest relations with the Inamali. It was said the Sil were the only people among whom the Inamali freely walked. They were even said to worship Irina.

When the Dr'Zhak and their allies decided to take Talitakaya, they declared their intentions to the Sil and told them to stand aside. The Sil would not, and many died to protect Talitakaya. Still there was no sign of life from the great city, and the Sil could not hold out long against the armies of the Dr'Zhak and the other six clans. The armies halted at the gates of Talitakaya, and issued a challenge.

Nothing happened.

Entering the city, they found it empty. It appeared the Inamali had simply left. But it was said that a scroll in the judgment room held a message for the conquerors: "We will return."

CHAPTER FIVE

Karia realized with fresh shock and fear exactly where she was. This was the secret home of an Inamali. Perhaps they had not really gone; perhaps they had been here all along, watching, waiting for their time to reassert their rule over the Teneka and Dr'Zhak.

She reached down to grab her clothes to dress, but nearly gagged on the cloud of dust that arose from just picking them up. Holding them away from herself, she reached them into the waterfall, moving them around to rinse the dust off. Now she held them, dripping, unsure of what do with them. She didn't want to put them back on the floor.

She held her clothes in one hand while taking the towel off the rack with the other hand. Draping the towel over her shoulder, she put her chemise and dress on the rack, spreading them out but keeping them away from the robe. Then she used the towel to dry off, surprised how dry she already was. Dropping the towel on the floor, she first put on her locket, and then the robe, which was far too big for her.

Of course, she thought. *They're twelve feet tall.* But she stopped when it dawned on her how illogical this was. A robe for a twelve-foot-tall Inamali would not simply be far too big for her. It would envelop her and drag on the ground behind her. And the ceilings and doorways in this house were not big enough for someone twelve feet tall. If anything, they were a little lower than the ones in her house.

Slowly, pondering this, she finished wrapping the robe about herself, then spread her chemise and dress on the rack that had held the robe and towel. And once again, for what seemed like the tenth time since she entered this house, she was not sure what she should do and decided to do something anyway.

Karia opened the door and stepped out into the hall. She glanced down at the dust powdering, then coating, now blanketing her feet, and shrugged. She grew up on a farm. It felt good to get clean, but she knew it couldn't last.

17

She tried the door on her right. It was locked. She listened at the door and heard nothing. She bent down to peek through the keyhole, and then saw that there wasn't one. She tried the door again. It would not open.

So she walked down into the parlor and looked about again. This time she was surprised by something she didn't see. The fireplace was so small that there was no hanger for a cooking pot, and no cooking pot. This fireplace was simply for warmth – something she had never seen before.

She glanced back into the study, looking at the blank wall where she was sure she came in. It was still just a wall. She walked over and touched it again. It was solid.

Still giving the robe and cap a wide berth, she walked behind the desk. She picked up the quill, and felt a tingle go through her fingers. She dropped it immediately. Hesitantly, she picked it up again, and felt the tingle again. Ink dropped from the tip onto the dusty desk, and again she dropped the pen. It hit the desk, nib-first, splattering ink on the desk and onto her robe before dropping to the ground.

"How …?" she asked aloud. If this inkwell had been here, uncapped, long enough for this much dust to settle, it should have been dry. Dry and dusty.

Bending down to pick up the quill, her shoulder brushed against the writing stand, nudging it. When she stood again, she saw that on the stand, under the dust, was a piece of paper with some writing on it.

She put the pen back in the inkwell, picked up the paper and blew the dust off.

The writing was Inamali. She recognized the slender, fine characters. At the top, she saw a familiar word:

It was the only word she could read in Inamali:
"Karia."

CHAPTER SIX

Karia's mom had taught her to read, and Karia read and read again and read over and over the few books the three families had. She read all the books she could get a hold of in town as well, which weren't very many. The Teneka were not exactly a people of literature, and the Teneka Fra among whom they lived even less so. Most of the books were about weather and farming and animal husbandry – which Karia found fascinating but kind of gross.

Then one day she found a book in the mending pile. The sewing for all three families had become her responsibility as she approached fifteen, because, her mom and Aunt Heather and Nana told her, at fifteen she would be considered a woman and it wasn't right for a woman to be working in the fields. They didn't tell her why, but the twinkle in Nana's eye hinted to Karia that they would talk more about all this growing-up stuff later

Deep in what had been her mom's sewing pile, so deep in the mending that Karia thought it had probably been forgotten, was a thin book. It was filled with a fine, very vertical script that just seemed to flow. She couldn't read a word of it, but her heart thrilled to scan it. Even looking at it was like reading poetry.

Her mom walked in on her and they were both startled. They looked at each other a moment, as if neither of them was sure what to say. Then her mom walked over to the desk. She opened the inkwell and picked up a quill, dipping it and tapping it deftly against the side to get rid of excess ink.

She drew out a small piece of paper and fluidly ran the pen across the surface. It looked more like she was sketching than writing, and then she put the quill down and turned the paper toward Karia.

Karia saw three graceful, flowing characters on the page, and before her mom could say anything, blurted out, "That's my name!"

Her mom didn't seem surprised that Karia could read it. "Yes," she said.

"What language is that?" Karia asked.

"It's Inamali."

"How can I read it?"

Her mom paused. She seemed about to say something. She stopped, and then, apparently changing her mind, said, "It's your name, dear. Of course you can read your own name."

Karia studied her a moment. She knew her mom would say nothing more. So she held up the book. "Teach me to read this."

Tears welled in her mom's eyes. She looked down and folded the paper with Karia's name on it. Looking back up, she quietly said, "Perhaps. It's forbidden, Karia. That's the only one I kept. Your dad thinks I burned them all. But I couldn't …"

Karia didn't mean to make her mom so sad. They both stood there for a while, neither knowing what to say. But Karia grew curious.

"Why not?" she asked.

"Why not what?" her mom said.

"Why couldn't you burn it?"

"I … couldn't. Not now, Karia. Put the book back."

"Mom …"

"Please, Karia, not now." Her tone was stern, though not harsh. Karia knew not to push this issue any more. "Put the book back."

Karia put the book back in the mending pile. But every so often, when she was sure her mom and dad weren't around, she would sneak the book back out of the pile and go through page after page. And though she could not read a word of it, it was as if the book fed her soul.

CHAPTER SEVEN

Karia stared at the paper in her hands. The paper in Inamali. With her name at the top. It was a message. A message for her. But the only word she could read was her name.

She ran her eyes over the rest of the text, but it wasn't like the book or the way her mother had written her name. The script was ragged, hurried, tense. It was urgent.

She turned to the books behind her, and scanned the spines. All the words were in the flowing Inamali script. But Karia noted that this script, too, was different from her mom's book. It seemed deliberate, precise, and it made her feel stronger.

She turned back to the desk and put the letter down. Turning again to the bookcase, she selected a large brown book with silver writing and placed it on the desk. She opened it, and it fell open to a page near the back. Flames were depicted on the left page, and Karia began scanning the text on the right, moving her fingers over the letters. Her fingertips began to feel warm, then hot. The sensation moved up her hand, to her wrist, and swiftly toward her elbow. She pulled her hand away from the book and willed the heat to stop. It did not go any farther, but it did not go away either.

She stepped away from the desk and toward the doorway. Without thinking about what she was doing or why she was doing it, she pointed her hand toward the little fireplace and pushed the heat out. Flames briefly kindled in a few embers left in the fireplace, then went out.

I should have pointed at those ugly chairs, she thought.

Before another thought could enter her mind, the room began to shimmer, then grow hazy. Her knees buckled and all went dark.

She did not know how long she slept on the floor, but awoke with her mind focused on what had happened just before she passed out. She had played with magic. Inamali magic. And not for the first time. That's what the ointments were. Magic. And now she had used fire magic.

Which meant she was subject to the death penalty.

21

Karia knew little about magic, but she knew fire was a very powerful type of magic. She knew it was not as powerful as earth magic, which even the Inamali forbade, but she knew nothing about that kind of magic beyond the name. She also knew that the Dr'Zhak seemed to fear magic, and expressly forbade making fire, perhaps because they had been on the receiving end of it so many times.

Karia was awed not simply by the power of the spell, but that she had been able to work any magic at all. She had never before heard of a Teneka woman working magic. In fact, she didn't think they could. And come to think of it, the only Inamali woman she had ever heard of using magic was Irina.

She had heard of Teneka men doing magic, but she had also heard that they were just pretending to do magic – doing tricks and illusions that fooled people. Once she had heard a farmer in town say he thought Teneka who did magic were really just Inamali in disguise, but when she asked her mom about it later she wouldn't talk about it. Was she now in the house of a real Teneka sorcerer? Or an Inamali disguised as a Teneka sorcerer? Whoever it was, he used Inamali books to work Inamali magic. And now, so had she. She thought that perhaps all it took was a few books and some ointments, even for a woman. It seemed so easy. Maybe that's why it was forbidden. If anyone could do it, then everyone could do it – and what a mess that would make!

She stood, still somewhat weak and dizzy, and stepped back to the desk. She closed the book and put it back. That was enough of magic. She picked up the letter and folded it, putting it inside her robe.

Then she walked back through the doorway into the parlor. She walked to the closest of the chairs and blew some of the dust off. She immediately regretted that. She could tell the chair was made of some sort of shiny leather, orange mottled with black and green and indigo, and she could see that it was even uglier than she thought before.

She turned and started down the hallway opposite the waterfall room, and stopped before the door on her right. This doorknob turned and she swung the door open. A small trestle table was near the door, with two wooden chairs. Against the wall opposite the door was a large fireplace with cooking pots. Cabinets were to the right and left; Karia assumed that, like the kitchen in her house, these contained the pantry, along with pots and pans and cups and bowls and the like.

Stepping back out into the hallway, she closed the door behind her and walked to the door at the end of the hall. This too was unlocked, and as she opened it she saw light streaming in and plants beyond. Realizing the door led outside, she closed it quickly. She wasn't going outside in a robe.

She walked briskly to the waterfall room and took off the robe. The letter, momentarily forgotten, fluttered out and she caught it just before it drifted into the water. She picked up her clothes, and was surprised to find they were almost dry already. She dressed, tucking the letter into her dress, then picked up her left shoe and walked to the door that led outside.

Opening the door, she stepped through and heard it close behind her. She turned back quickly, and found herself staring at a tree trunk. There was no sign of the door. She felt around, and it was, as far as she could tell, just a tree trunk.

Turning back around again, she saw Timbal staring at her.

"Where did you come from?" he asked.

Ian Fallis

CHAPTER EIGHT

Karia started at seeing Timbal, and at realizing where they were.

Timbal was a little shorter than Karia, with dark brown hair. He was slim compared to most boys his age, but nowhere near as slim as Karia. He had begun filling out and growing muscles. And facial hair, though it was still more like fuzz punctuated by a few brave whiskers. He was standing by the other odd thing in this forest, the Liliki tree. The old stories said the Inamali brought a Liliki seed from their home, planted it in Talitakaya, and then spread seedlings throughout the city. But she had only seen them in a painting of the city in her mom's room, and had never heard of them being anywhere else. Until they came across this one, near the eastern edge of the forest.

Tall and slender and graceful – like the writing of the Inamali – the Liliki tree reached up at least fifteen feet before it branched out. In the spring it had massive red flowers, which ripened in the fall as red fruits the size of a grown man's head. The children couldn't reach them, but once – and only once – they tasted one that had fallen. It had a smooth and pleasant texture, but the taste was something altogether different.

Narek compared the flavor to dung, and Karia thought that if any of them would know what dung tasted like, it would be Narek.

Because the tree was unique and relatively close to their fields, they used it as their "safe" spot when they played hide-and-seek. Karia suggested it because, unlike the hedge, the tree made her feel safe.

Now she took two quick long steps, almost leaping, and tagged the tree. Timbal caught her by the shoulder and turned her toward him. He leaned in toward her as if to kiss her. Karia dropped her boot. She was just starting to lift her hand to slap him, when he suddenly stepped back as if he had been pushed.

Timbal stared at her.

"What did you do?" he asked.

"Nothing," Karia said, surprised. "I did nothing."

25

"You pushed me."

"I didn't touch you."

"I know you didn't touch me. But you pushed me. How did you do that?"

"I didn't."

"But you wanted to."

"No I didn't."

"Yes you did!" he insisted.

"No, Timbal, I did not!" Karia shouted. "I wanted to slap you." Her anger building, the words poured out. "I wanted to slap you for trying to kiss me again. I wanted to slap you for telling Narek he could kiss me if he found me. I wanted to slap you for letting him see us kissing. I wanted to slap you for kissing me." She realized her eyes were watering. No, she wasn't crying. She didn't cry. She couldn't cry. She wanted to glare at him, to show him she was angry. To make him apologize. *Maybe even*, she thought, *to give him an opportunity to make up with me.*

Timbal looked confused, as if he didn't know what to do, or what to say. Apparently he decided he had to say something anyway. "How was I supposed to know he was watching?"

"You should have known! You're supposed to protect me. How can you ever expect to marry me if you can't protect me?"

Now Timbal looked seriously confused. And he wasn't the only one. *Wow, where did that come from?* Karia thought. *But it's not like he shouldn't have been thinking about that. We are both fifteen already.*

"Marry you?" Timbal asked, his voice as high as it had been a few years back.

Karia picked up her boot and threw it at him. He ducked aside, and she turned around. She could feel tears, wet and hot, on her cheeks, and felt her chest heave. She struggled to regain control. *I do not cry!*

"Karia …" he said.

"Shut up. Shut up shut up shut up."

He said nothing for a while, and without realizing what she was doing, Karia channeled her hurt feelings into anger at him. Apparently the silence was too much for him, and he began to say, "But …"

"SHUT! UP!" Karia shouted.

Karia could hear him moving behind her, and saw him deposit her boot next to her. She leaned against the tree and looked up, trying to clear her head. She didn't cry, but she didn't like to stay angry, either. She saw a rumpled bird land on a branch in front of her. It was like a crow, but a bit smaller, and with a longer, thinner beak. It looked as if it had been black, but now was weathered to shades of dark brown and charcoal gray. Its feathers looked disturbed; it looked ragged.

Rumply, Karia thought, trying in vain to remember ever seeing a bird quite like that before. Looking into its green eyes, she realized it was staring at her.

Her attention was stolen by Timbal calling out from behind her, "Safe! Narek, we're safe!" She turned enough to see his hand against the tree, then turned back. The bird was gone.

A few seconds later he called again. He put his hand on Karia's shoulder. She shrugged it off and stepped away from him.

He waited a short time longer, and called again. "Safe! Narek, we're safe!"

"OK, OK, I heard you already," Narek called from one of the trails leading to the tree. Soon Karia heard him say from behind her, "How did you do that?"

She said nothing, but wiped her cheeks and turned toward the boys, defiance – and not tears – on her face. Narek stood before her, holding her other boot. He was just shorter than Timbal, also with dark brown hair. If his muscles were filling out, Karia could not tell. She thought of him as plump, though he was only plump compared to Karia and Timbal.

"What did she do to you?" Timbal asked Narek.

"What?"

"What did she do to you?" Timbal said again.

"Nothing. What did she do to you?"

"She pushed me. She pushed me without touching me."

Narek looked at him like he was crazy. "Right."

"What did she do to you?" Timbal asked again.

"She didn't do anything to me."

"Then why were you asking her how she did that?"

"Because just a few seconds, maybe a minute, before you called out that you were safe, she was over by the hedge."

Karia was stunned. She looked at Narek. "What?"

"You heard me. You were over by the hedge. And then all of a sudden you're here. How did you do that?"

She felt as surprised as he looked. She had been in the house for ... how long? Hours? A day perhaps? She thought it might even have been two days, or more. She was even more puzzled than he was. But even if she had an answer, she wasn't going to give it to Narek. "Give me my boot," she said.

"Not until you answer me."

Karia stood up straight and stared down into Narek's eyes. "Timbal, make him give me my boot," she demanded.

When Timbal said nothing, she glanced over at him. He looked as if he was thinking this over. Karia guessed that he wanted the answer too, but she was counting on him not wanting to mess things up with her. *OK, mess things up any more than they already are.* She was right. "Narek, give her boot to her," he commanded.

Narek glared at him. So he added, "Or else."

"You want to know as much as I do, but you two always stick up for each other. You make me sick." Narek tossed the boot at her feet and stormed off toward home.

Timbal watched as she slipped her boots back on. "I still want to know," he said.

"What?" She tried to act as if nothing had happened.

"How you pushed me without touching me. How you got across the forest – because I know you weren't anywhere near here, and then, there you were. I want to know what you're up to, Karia."

"I'm not up to anything. I didn't push you."

"OK, fine, but how did you get here?"

She ignored him and started toward home.

"Karia?"

"Stop it," she said. She wished she knew the answer herself.

CHAPTER NINE

The next day, after Karia's morning chores were done, she helped her mom clean up after their hearty farm breakfast. This day it was her family's turn to feed everyone, and she helped her mom cook eggs and sausage and bake bread for all three families. As usual, Timbal ate like a horse, and Narek ate like a pig.

Now the men and boys had gone back to the fields, and Nana and Heather back to their houses, and Karia was alone with her mom.

"Aren't you supposed to be sewing?" her mom asked. Karia was making a new pair of pants for Timbal, and wanted to put it off. Right now, she was tempted to make the crotch too tight, or perhaps leave a pin there. Or both.

But she also wanted to talk with her mom. Ducking the question, she said, "Mom, when are you going to teach me to read Inamali?"

"I don't know, Karia. Some day. We have things that need to get done, dear."

"Can you start teaching me today?"

"I don't know …"

"Even a little bit, even for a short time. I need to learn to read Inamali."

"Need to? What's the hurry?"

Karia paused. She had pushed too hard, and didn't know what to say.

"Karia, what's the hurry? What are you up to?"

"Why does everyone keep asking me that?!"

"Who else is asking you that?" her mom asked.

Again Karia paused. *Nymph's wake!* Why did she always end up telling her mom a lot more than she wanted to?

"Karia, tell me what is going on. Now."

Karia reached into her chemise and pulled out the letter. She'd kept it close to her ever since finding it. She held it out to her mom.

Her mom took it, unfolded it and looked at it, scanning back and forth as if she was reading it. First her eyebrows lifted. Then her eyes grew wide, and began to water. It looked as if her mouth was beginning to quiver. *She's terrified.* And that scared Karia.

Suddenly her mom packed the letter into a ball and threw it into the fireplace. Karia shrieked and stepped forward, reaching toward the tongs, but her mom grabbed her around the waist and stunned Karia by picking her up, carrying her a large step back from the fire and putting her down solidly. She stood between Karia and the fire.

Karia looked around her and saw the letter unfolding in ashes, and cried out through tears, "Mom, that's **my** letter!"

"No! There was no letter. You will never speak of it again."

"What did it say?"

"Nothing. It was nothing."

"You read my letter," Karia said, now yelling. "What did it say?"

"Karia, you will not raise your voice to me. You will not defy me. There was no letter. Never speak of it again." She stepped in closer. "Go do your sewing."

Suddenly Karia saw a glint of light from her mom's hand – her ring, she realized – and felt herself pushed a step back. Her mom glanced down at her ring, then up at Karia, and the look of terror was on her face again. "You … you tried to push …" She stepped back, and back, as if she was in fear of her daughter, as if Karia was some kind of monster. *Did I push her? I … I wanted to …*

"Mom …" Karia pleaded. *What have I done?*

"Never," her mom said, backing toward the doorway. "Never do that again. Go do your sewing. Now." She turned, and Karia watched her run out the door and down the front steps.

Karia walked to the fire. The letter had become a small, wispy lump of ashes, dancing atop a flaming log. She thought, *I want my letter back.* She reached out her hand, and leaned down, and before she realized what she was doing, picked up the lump of ash. She stood back up and looked down at her hand. She was not burned. She could feel something like the heat from the book – but not as orderly. This was chaotic, perhaps even malicious and angry. It filled her hand, and moved up to her wrist, toward her elbow. And as she watched, the ashes began to gather and solidify.

She felt the heat move past her elbow, up to her shoulder, but she was focused on the ash becoming more and more like a crumpled piece of paper. The heat spread across her chest and back, and still she watched. The paper was whole again, not even singed, but Karia's chest and back, both her arms, and now her face and her entire head, burned as if she had a fever. She reached to open the paper, but missed and saw it fall to the floor and roll away. She felt dizzy, and her vision blurred, then dimmed and went dark.

CHAPTER TEN

Before Karia was awake, before there was even a thought in her mind, she felt hot. Very hot. As her mind began to work – sluggishly – she knew her mom was with her. She was always able to tell when her mom was near. It comforted her, especially when she opened her eyes and found she could not focus. She felt something cool on her face, but her mouth was dry, so dry she found it difficult to speak.

"Wa ... wa ... wad ..." she said.

"Water, dear? You want water?" It was her mother's voice.

"Ye ... ye ... uh-huh."

She felt a hand behind her neck, gently lifting her head. She saw something coming toward her face – a hand – and could only make out two things about it. One was a whitish circle, which she took to be the rim of a glass. The other was a strip of whitish silver metal with a pale green dot. *Mom's ring,* she thought. She remembered playing with it, spinning it on her mom's finger, when she was a little girl. *Mommy's giving me water,* she thought. She felt like she was six again, but not in a bad way. Not like she was being treated like she was six, which she sometimes felt her mom and dad did. But like she was being cared for like she was six – safe and secure and loved.

The hand moved the rim of the cup to her lips, and she felt it touch. Water dripped gently into her mouth. Some ran down her chin as well, but she didn't mind. It felt good.

After a few sips her mom took the cup away from her lips, and lowered her head back to the pillow. Karia closed her eyes and felt herself drifting away again.

"Karia," she said. "Can you hear me?"

"Uh-huh."

"Are you awake, dear? Can you talk with me? I need you to talk with me, Karia. Wake up, dear."

31

Karia felt very tired and very hot. She wanted to go back to sleep, but she tried to wake up for her mom. "Uh-huh."

"Karia, did you ... did you do something with the fire, dear? Something ... you know ... like when you pushed me? It's OK, you can tell me, dear. You're not in trouble. But ... did you?"

Karia opened her eyes and looked at her mom, struggling to focus. She could tell she was not in her room, but did not know where she was. She thought she saw fear in her mom again, and wondered if her mom was afraid of her, or afraid for her.

Reluctantly, slowly, she said, "Uh-huh." Her mouth was dry again, so dry her tongue was sticking to her teeth and the roof of her mouth.

"Karia, you must listen to me. I will try to help you." She was crying now. Karia couldn't see it, but she could hear it in her mom's voice. "But you mustn't ... you can't ... not with fire. Fire ... you need years of experience, and the right training ... you can't just ... with fire ... do you understand?"

Karia had no idea what her mom was talking about. But she said, "Uh-huh."

"And if you keep ... I mean, if you do that kind of thing, we can't protect you, and they won't just hurt you, they'll take the others, and you don't want that to happen, right?"

Who'll take whom? she thought, though since no one was watching her grammar in her head, it was really *Who'll take who?* "Uh-huh."

"OK, then, dear, I'm going to try to help you. I don't have much ... I mean, I really can't, and I don't, but a little ... so you need to really concentrate, really think hard. Can you do that with me?"

Again, Karia wasn't sure she understood what her mom was trying to say. Concentrate, sure, but with her? "Uh-huh."

She saw her mom fiddling with her left hand, and realized she was taking off her ring. Then she felt her mom lifting her arm.

"OK, dear, I have your hand and it's pointing to a safe place. Get ready. I need you to think hard about the fire coming out of you, and I'm going to ..."

Fire coming out, Karia thought. Suddenly there was a loud whooshing sound and Karia felt cool again, but even more tired. She caught a glimpse of the fireplace in the kitchen, aglow, and thought perhaps she was on the couch in the parlor. She felt her mom let go of her arm abruptly, and Karia, jolted back to sort of awake, looked toward her. She had stood up and stepped back from Karia. Again she looked afraid. Perhaps she looked afraid of Karia. It registered to Karia, but just barely. She was mostly relieved.

"Thanks, Mom," Karia said weakly, and then began to fall asleep.

It seemed as if, just before Karia went out, her mom softly said, "I didn't do anything."

Ian Fallis

CHAPTER ELEVEN

Karia woke up feeling fine, but quite thirsty. She looked up, and saw that she was in her room. A cup of water and a pitcher were by her bed, so she drank deeply. It was much later than she usually woke up – on the farm, all three families were busy before dawn, carrying out chores before gathering for breakfast. It looked to be about mid-day, and she fussed at herself for being such a baby and sleeping in.

She rose and felt weak and dizzy, but pushed through it. She thought that perhaps she had slept too much, and was still waking up. She had to steady herself on her rickety old table as she ran her brush through her hair, then went out of her room. Her room opened directly into the large room of their house, as did her parents' room. On the left of the large room was the cooking and dining area, with a large fireplace with two small ovens built into the brickwork, a trestle table for both food preparation and dining, and two large sideboards for cooking gear and the pantry.

On the right of the large room was a couch, a couple of chairs and some pillows. The right was the parlor, but they usually called the whole room the kitchen, and spent more time on the left than on the right.

Her mom was preparing the noon meal. Each family usually ate the noon meal apart. Evening meals were also taken apart, except for once a month, when the three families got together to eat and drink, and usually to swap stories. Often there was music, and music led to singing and dancing. Once in a while folks from a neighboring farm would join them, and once in a great while they would go to someone else's farm to gather with one or perhaps two other families.

About every three months their get-together was supplanted by a large Gathering, when all of the farm families, and usually most of the folks from town, got together at a farm or on the village lawn for dancing and singing, eating and talking. The big ones were the Spring and Fall Gatherings, which almost everyone made an effort to take part in.

At a few of the recent Gatherings Karia thought that perhaps some of the boys were noticing her, since she was almost fifteen. But she dismissed that, since she did not consider herself at all attractive, and, anyway, she had eyes only for Timbal.

Right now, she and her mom were alone.

"Karia!" her mom exclaimed with a smile as she came into the kitchen. "How are you feeling?"

"I feel fine, Mom." But she didn't. She put her hand on the doorframe to steady herself. "I'm sorry I slept so late. At least I didn't sleep through our turn at breakfast yesterday."

"Dear, our turn for breakfast – when you ate with us – that was three days ago. Two days you lay with the fever, and then …" She stopped.

"Karia, everyone thinks you had Ylintera fever. I told them that so I could keep everyone away from you, in case I was right about … the fire." She paused again.

"Then you slept all the rest of that day, and last night, and this morning. You mustn't speak of what happened, and above all, you must not … you understand, with fire, right?"

Karia vaguely remembered the odd sort-of conversation with her mom, but it still wasn't making much sense. "Sure, Mom."

Her mom went back to preparing the meal.

That was when Karia felt like the floor in front of her tilted upward violently. And how was she supposed to keep herself upright when the doorframe she was hanging onto violently shifted in the other direction? She slammed into the floor face-first.

"Karia!" her mom shouted. She tried to help Karia up, but helping Karia up required that Karia try to get up. She felt like a stalk of tsilinki that's been without water for too long – she flopped around limply, and didn't seem to have the strength to do anything about it. Karia finally managed to grip her mom's arm, and her mom helped her to one of the dining room chairs.

Karia leaned against the back of the chair, and steadied herself with a hand on the table. The room seemed to be moving still, and she didn't really trust the floor right now, but it was beginning to dawn on her that her spill wasn't really the floor's doing.

"Are you OK here, or do you need to lie down again?" her mom asked.

"I'm fine," Karia said.

"OK, because I should knead the bread, and I don't want you toppling over again," she said. "Are you sure?"

"Yes, Mom," Karia said. Her mom walked over to the side of the table near Karia, reaching into a bin for some flour and sprinkling it on the table.

Then she got a lump of dough from a large bowl, where it had been rising, punched it down and began to knead it.

"Mom?" Karia said. Her mom looked up. "What happened to my letter?"

A stern look came across her mom's face. She looked at Karia and stopped kneading. "There was no letter, dear. Remember that. There was no letter. And you had Ylintera fever. And you must not … do that … with fire. Remember these things." She turned back to the dough, folding it, pressing it and turning it a little more vigorously.

"Mom …"

"Karia," her mom said, in the tone that told Karia she had pushed too hard – a tone she was hearing far too often these days. But then her mom's tone softened. "Karia, your life depends on this. My life depends on this. The lives of your dad, and Uncle Avar and Aunt Heather, and Opa and Nana, and Timbal and Narek – they all depend on you. There was no letter. You had Ylintera fever. And do not … By Gnome's Arm, Karia, not wild fire! You can't!" She wasn't angry. She was struggling to keep herself from crying. "You could have died!"

Karia was confused. She had no idea what her mom meant about the fire, or wild fire, or how that could kill her. But she knew she had hurt her mom, and worse, had scared her. That hurt and scared Karia. "Mom, I'm sorry, I just … I don't understand. So much has happened …"

"Don't try to understand, dear. Just be you. Do the things you're supposed to do. Live on the farm. Marry a nice boy. Work hard. Be happy. Have children … children of your own."

Her mother dusted the flour off her hands, then picked up a dishcloth and wiped her eyes. "Please, Karia. Just be my Karia. My little girl." She laughed slightly, then leaned down and hugged Karia. "I mean, my young lady."

"Yes, Mom," she said. Karia felt a little better, hearing her mom talk that way. She toyed with her mom's whitish silver ring, turning it so the small pale green stone was on the inside of her mom's hand. Her mom – just as she always did when Karia was little – stepped back, chuckled and turned the ring around again.

Karia decided to try to brighten the mood, to go along with her mom. "I think I've found a nice boy, Mom."

Her mom stood and went back to folding and pressing the dough. "Oh?" she said, folding the dough. "And who would that be, my dear? Who do you have your eyes on?"

"Oh, you must know, Mom. Timbal."

Her mom pushed down so suddenly and hard on the dough that a cloud of flour flew up in every direction, settling all over the table, as well as her.

Karia looked down and saw white spots all over her dress. When she looked up again, her mom was pushing two lumps of dough together again. Apparently she had ripped the bread in half.

"Oh. Ah. Um … my dear, Karia, really, not Timbal … no … ah … dear, we'll … let's … ah, talk later, shall we?"

Karia felt like her whole life was like that lump of dough. In just two days – at least, it seemed like two days to her – it was slammed and broken, and she didn't know why. She just had to try to put it back together. If she could.

CHAPTER TWELVE

All the rest of that day Karia's mom kept her occupied with sewing. She still felt weak, but she was able to sit on her bed and mend. She regretted not being able to spend any time with Timbal.

When her dad came home early to wash up and change, she realized it was the night for all the families to get together. She hoped Opa would play his hurdy-gurdy, because she wanted to dance with Timbal. Sure, it would just be a small Gathering, and almost any instrument was better than a hurdy-gurdy, but that was all you really needed to dance, and Karia could already picture it. *As long as the floor behaves itself I should be fine.*

"I think Karia and I should stay home this evening," her mom said to her dad, shattering the picture.

"What?" Karia said.

"You've just gotten over your illness, and I think you need to stay in and get to bed early, dear."

"I feel fine!"

"Now, Failean," her dad said, "she seems to have bounced back nicely, and everyone will be eager to see her again."

"Yes!" Karia said.

"No," her mom said. "Ylintera can be tricky. You may feel fine now, but if you overdo it, and so soon after getting over it, you might have a relapse. Remember this morning? So off to bed with you now."

"I haven't even had supper," Karia protested.

"I'll bring you some soup later," her mom said.

"Failean, are you sure that's necessary?" asked her dad.

"Oh, yes. Very."

"Oh, please, Daddy, can I …" Karia began to whine.

"That's enough, Karia," her mom interrupted. "To bed. I'll bring soup later."

"I won't be able to sleep," she grumped.

"That's fine. Just lie in the bed and get some rest."

Karia knew she wasn't going to get anywhere. "Yes, Ma'am." She went to her room, striving to pretend the floor wasn't moving so she could prove she was fine. She closed her door, wobbled and regained her balance, then slipped off her dress and shoes, and climbed into bed, sulking. She wasn't going to cry. She didn't cry. But she was upset.

She could hear her mom and dad talking quietly in the kitchen, but the only word she thought she could make out was "Timbal." For a long time she tried to hear what they were saying, but lying still and listening hard were more work than she thought, and soon she had drifted off to sleep.

When she awoke, her first thought was, *I'm hungry*. Her second was, *Oh, no, I've slept through breakfast again*, for the sun was already up. She hopped out of bed, brushed her hair and hurried to the kitchen, but no one was there. She heard something on the porch, and stepped out to see her mom doing the wash, her hands hard at work deep in the sudsy water.

She smiled, but her mom looked surprised. "Karia," she said. It sounded like her mom was scolding her, and for a moment she thought she was in trouble for oversleeping. Then her mom added, "Get back inside and get your dress on!"

Now Karia was surprised, but she backed away, went inside and closed the front door. She didn't think of herself as a little girl, but she didn't really think of herself as a woman either. She didn't think she needed to put on a dress to go onto the porch. To town, certainly. *Oh, gosh, yes*, she thought. She almost definitely would have put one on to go to one of the other family's houses, but it didn't seem like it was that long ago when she had not. So now she had to put on a dress even on her own porch? *It's so confusing to feel — and look — like a girl, when I'm supposed to be a woman*. She went to her room and put her dress on. She thought about pulling her shoes on, too, but decided she didn't need them. Then she stopped and wondered if she really did. "No," she said aloud, and stood up.

As she did, the floor misbehaved again. She grabbed the doorway to her bedroom. "Stop that," she said. She closed her eyes and took a deep breath. Everything seemed fine when she opened them, so she walked across the living room and stepped back out onto the porch. "Sorry, Mom," she said.

"It's OK, dear. It's just that you're getting older, and you don't want the boys to see you like that."

Well, it was true that she wouldn't want Narek to see her like that. She didn't like the way he looked at her sometimes.

Her mom's voice snapped her out of her thoughts. "I didn't wake you because you needed your rest. You were surprised how quickly you fell asleep last night, weren't you?"

"Yes, but I don't see why I need to sleep so much. We both know I didn't have Ylintera fever."

"Quiet! You must not speak of that. Yes, you're right but you … you had something that can take a lot out of you, just like Ylintera fever. You needed the rest. And you likely still need more. I have never even heard of any girl your age, with no training, no experience, surviving what you went through. Wild fire is very dangerous."

Karia was surprised again. "Really?"

"Really. But that's enough of that." She lifted a shirt from the sudsy water and put it on a bench. "Help me dump this so we can rinse."

They dumped the water on the scraggly grass in front of the house – unlike Nana, Karia's mom was not one to grow flowers. Oh, she tried, and Nana helped, but the plants were all stunted and never flowered. "Remind me never to ask you to help in the fields," her dad had joked, and Karia laughed. Then her mom cried, and Karia felt terrible. She didn't like to make her mom feel bad. And she wasn't going to do so this morning, so she pitched right in. She wasn't about to tell her mom that the porch was misbehaving, rocking and swaying. She kept that to herself, and kept herself upright, though she did feel queasy.

They refilled the basin from the rain barrel, rinsed the clothes and hung them to dry. By then it was lunchtime.

After lunch, when Karia would have done some sewing and then gone to play, her mother made her rest again. But soon she was up and out of bed, finishing the pants she was making for Timbal.

She pushed the needle through for the last stitch, knotted the thread, then knotted it again – just to be sure. She cut the thread, and held them up to look at. Pants were quite an accomplishment. Sure, they looked like the pants just about everyone else wore – Karia used the sturdy brown fabric that the seamstress, Silla, sold to a lot of the farmers. But she knew that shirts and chemises, dresses and skirts were a breeze compared to pants, and she felt a great sense of accomplishment.

She quickly checked the crotch to make sure she'd taken all the pins out. And to make sure she hadn't put any more in. She put away her needle and thread, thimble and scissors. She picked up the pants and headed for the door.

"Where are you going?" her mother called.

"I'm taking Timbal his pants," Karia said, proudly holding them up for her mother to see.

"Those look very nice, Karia." Her mother was beaming; Karia was so glad to see that again. Her mom was proud of her. "Tell you what, I need to talk with your Aunt Heather, so why don't I take the pants over?"

"Well, sure, but … could I come along?"

"No need, dear. Get a whetstone from the shed and sharpen the kitchen knives."

"Can I please give Timbal his pants myself?"

"No, dear. You stay here."

"Why?"

"Karia," her mother said, her tone even, "you are staying here and sharpening the knives, because I have told you to stay here and sharpen the knives. Do you understand me?"

"Yes, Ma'am," Karia said, and she went to the shed for a whetstone. Frustration put a bit more vigor in her sharpening than usual.

CHAPTER THIRTEEN

After Karia sharpened all the knives, her mom had her sit at the table and polish all their pewter. And after dinner she was sent straight to bed. At least she was feeling less and less dizzy and lightheaded all day, but that only made her a bit more cross to be sent to bed early.

She awoke before dawn, and thought from the soft footfalls beyond her door that it must be morning because her mom and dad were up. To Karia, that proved that she was fine, and she resolved to get right back into the routine of farm life.

She quickly arose and slipped on her shoes – she wasn't sure anymore whose turn it was for breakfast – and was about to open the door when she remembered her dress. She slipped her ratty old farm dress over her head. *I'll need to make a new one soon,* she thought. Fully dressed, she opened the door. Her mom and dad were already outside. She assumed her dad was headed for the fields, and her mom was going to help either Aunt Heather or Nana with breakfast, so she hurried after them across the great room, opening the door and stepping out onto the porch.

She rushed down the steps, and was about to call out to them to wait for her. When she noticed the moon, the words caught in her throat. Nana had taught her to tell the seasons and the time – day or night – by the positions of the sun and moon, and she knew immediately that it was most assuredly not morning yet. It was not much past midnight, and her parents were walking down the short, hard-packed path to Opa and Nana's house.

After stopping to gather her thoughts, she decided to follow, staying quiet and sticking to the shadows as much as she could. They went around the corner to the front of Nana's house – for each house faced south like all the houses of the Teneka Sil – and she hastened to keep up. She was about to go around the corner herself when she realized from the voices that they were outside, on Nana's porch. She stopped short, then heard the crunch of shoes on the path behind her. Someone else was coming!

Karia dove under the porch, but her dress snagged on a nail and ripped.

"What was that?" her dad said. She heard him walk across the porch until he was standing over her. Apparently he looked around the side of the house. "Oh, here are Avar and Heather."

Avar and Heather came around to the front, and Karia could tell from their greetings that all six adults were there. She heard chairs scraping as they sat. Then they all got quiet. She heard Heather say, "Failean, you need to tell everyone what you told me."

The silence was long. Karia's heart was beating so loudly she was certain they would hear it, and if not, they'd surely hear her breathing. She thought she sounded like a pig snuffling for food, she was breathing so loudly. But they did not hear her. Finally, her mom spoke. She smiled as she realized that she knew exactly where her mom was before she said a word.

"Karia ... Karia can work magic," she said.

She heard a deep laugh. It was Uncle Avar. "Meadowstars!" he said. "Girls can't do magic."

"She's not really a girl anymore," Nana said. "She's become a young woman. If you haven't noticed that, your boy certainly has." Karia blushed.

"Wait, what?" Opa said.

"In a moment, Opa," Nana replied.

"OK, OK," Avar said, his voice rising. "A *woman* can't do magic either."

"Keep your voice low, Avar," Opa said. "You'll wake Narek."

"Right," Avar said, quieter now. "Though I wouldn't doubt the little sneak is already listening."

"Let's get back on track, shall we?" It was the voice of her dad. Quiet but strong. How Karia loved him. They seldom talked, not like she and her mom. But each of them made her feel secure and loved in their own way.

"Women can do magic," Karia heard her mom say. "I ... I have some small powers."

All went silent. Again, Karia felt like she was a beating, snorting beacon, just below their feet, sure to be discovered any moment. *My mom can do magic?*

"Reva," Opa finally asked. "Did you know about this?"

"No."

"This puts us in danger," Avar said.

"Hush," said Heather. "Hear her out."

"Start again, dear," Nana said.

"Karia can do magic," her mom said. She was quiet again.

"Why are you looking at me like that?" Avar asked.

"She masters fire," her mom said.

"Nym'chin!" Avar shouted.

"Avar, watch your language!" Nana scolded. Karia jumped. She had heard the term only once or twice before – it was short for "Nymph on a chain" and was a strong curse word. She never could figure out how that could be a curse word, but then again, there were expressions she used a lot – Nymph's Wake, Meadowstars and Fires and Ashes – that didn't make a lot of sense to her either.

She knew how to use them, of course. Meadowstars was a way of saying something was ridiculous; Nym'chin was a much cruder way of saying much the same thing. Nymph's Wake was something you said when you found yourself in a bad spot. *Fire and ashes?* she thought. *I guess it's just something you say.*

"And keep your voice down," Nana continued, "or should we just invite Narek, Timbal and Karia to join us?"

Lowering his voice again, Avar said, "Few Inamali men, with years of experience and training, can master fire, and you expect me to believe Karia – a Teneka girl – can?"

"Shall I go wake her and have her come here and light your shoes?" her mom asked. "Maybe set your chair on fire?"

"That'd be my chair, dear, and I'd rather you didn't," Nana said.

"She didn't have Ylintera fever," her mom continued. "She must have done something with the fire because of the letter, and took it into her."

"Letter? What letter?" her dad asked.

"Oh, my, well, I'll have to come back to that," her mom said. As much as Karia loved her mom, she had to admit that she was the worst storyteller Karia knew. "I found her next to the fireplace, and Reva helped me get her to the couch in the parlor. I thought at first she actually did have a fever, but it came on so suddenly. And then I noticed that the fever radiated not from her chest, but from her right arm. She had fire inside her – wild fire – and didn't know how to get it out."

"That's usually fatal, dear," Nana said.

"Meadowstars. I hear that any idiot with a tiny bit of magic can get fire in them. In fact, it takes a Tenner to mess with fire like that. That's not mastery of fire," Avar said.

There was a pause. Karia could imagine her mom's eyes almost burning a hole in Avar. Especially since Avar had basically called Karia a Tenner – a curse word for something worthless, or a waste. And she'd certainly seen that look.

Then her mom continued. "So I kept trying to wake her, and finally on the second day she stirred. I got her to take some water, and I tried to explain what we needed to do, and how I could help her. And then she just did it herself."

"Did what?" her dad asked.

"Sent the fire out of her body. Herself. She didn't need to concentrate. She didn't need my help. I'm not even sure she was fully awake. All I did was tell her to think about the fire coming out of her, and she sent it out."

There was a pause, and then Nana said, "Wild fire."

"What?" Avar asked.

"Wild fire," Karia's mom said. "It's one thing to make magical fire using a spell book. It's quite another to expel wild fire."

All were silent again, until Opa said in a hushed voice, "This puts all the children in danger."

"It puts all of us in danger too," Heather added. *She sounds scared,* Karia thought.

"Dear, let me just make sure I understand this correctly." It was Nana's calm, soothing voice. "You say she took fire in, and sent it out. But she didn't actually make fire, right?"

"I can't see how she could," Karia's mom said. "She'd need to read a spell book for that, wouldn't she? And she can't read Inamali. Anyway, where would she get a spell book?"

Where indeed, Karia thought.

"You never taught her Inamali?" Nana asked.

"No."

"Not one single word of it?"

"No … not really."

"What's that supposed to mean?" Avar asked.

"I wrote her name for her."

"And she could read it," Nana said.

"Yes."

"Then she doesn't need to be taught to read a spell book to use a spell book," Nana said. *"Inamali ili, Inamali kri."* There was a pause. "You don't still have any spell books, do you, dear?"

"No. We all agreed to get rid of all the spell books."

"Not exactly," Opa said. "We agreed to get rid of all the Inamali books. Period. Because even one book could expose us to the Dr'Zhak, and even more, any one book could stir Inamali in the minds of the children. Do you have any Inamali books at all, Failean?"

There was another awkward silence. *Stir Inamali?* Karia thought. *What's that mean?*

"You kept it, didn't you?" her dad asked.

"Yes," her mom said quietly.

"Kept what?" Avar asked.

"Her grandfather's diary," her dad said. *He's angry with Mom,* Karia thought, trying to remember the last time she had heard her dad get angry with her mom.

She heard a sharp intake of breath all around.

"You didn't tell me about that!" Heather said. "Do you know what you've done?"

"She's killed us all, that's what she's done," Avar said.

"Not yet, my dears, not yet," Nana said.

"It's only a matter of time," Opa said.

"Well, we'll just have to work it all out, now, won't we?" Nana said. "We pulled it off once, and we can do it again. But there's more to this story still, isn't there, Failean?"

It was quiet; Karia assumed her mom nodded. *Pulled what off?* Karia wondered.

"Tell us about the letter, dear," Nana continued.

"Just before she got the fever, she was pestering me to teach her to read Inamali. I pressed her to find out why, and she showed me a letter. It was in Inamali, and it was addressed to her."

Three voices rose at once.

"What did it say?"

"Where did she get it?"

"Who was it from?"

"I don't know how or where she got it," her mom said. "It was signed by her father."

My dad? Karia thought, as she heard banging on the porch and more than one person saying, "What?!" She assumed someone, or more than one person, had gotten to their feet. *My dad can't write Inamali, can he? And why would he write me a letter?*

"What did he want?" It sounded like her dad's voice, and that shocked Karia. It didn't make any sense to her. "What did her father write to her?!" *Yes,* she thought. *That was definitely him.* Karia was having trouble breathing. *My dad? My father?* She couldn't form in words what was going on in her mind, but she was certainly figuring it out. Tears started streaming down her face. She choked back a sob. She was thankful her mom began talking again.

"He wrote that he knew she would find this place. He told her to use the books, but to be careful and start at the beginning. He also told her she could take her time, because the place was *hiklinikra.*"

Again, several people spoke at once.

"What place?" "What books?" "What's *hiklinikra* mean?"

Her mom did not answer. After a pause, Nana spoke.

"We have to assume," Nana said, "that the place is the place she found the letter, and the books are the books of her father's trade – magic."

"What's *hiklinikra?*" Reva asked.

"I have heard of places where time does not pass," Opa said. "Places enchanted by great sorcerers."

"Like her father," Avar said.

"That's what I thought, when Failean came to talk to me yesterday," Heather said. "And that's why I thought everyone should know, since it concerns us all."

"Why did you keep this from us?" Avar said angrily.

"Watch your tone toward my wife, Avar," Reva said.

"She's kept secrets from you, too," Avar said. "Secrets that put us all in danger."

"Oh, my, I'd better go put some tea on if we're all going to sit here and holler at each other," Nana said. "Or can we just try to figure out where we go from here?"

"Do you suppose," her mother said softly, quietly, "we could have some tea **and** try to figure out where we go from here?"

"Well, that sounds like a very good idea, Failean. Let's you and me and Heather go inside and get some started, and let the men bluster about out here until it's out of their system."

Karia heard chairs scraping and the front door opening and closing.

The men were very quiet for a long time. She could hear the women speaking softly, but could not tell what they said. She heard clinking and tinkling, and she thought of the fine china tea set that Nana had. She loved to drink tea with Nana from the tiny cups with the pink flowers. "Just us girls," Nana would say, as they talked about how to make tea and how to grow flowers.

Finally Avar broke the silence. "If she can really master fire … if she really does have access to spell books … there's only one thing keeping her from making some changes around here."

"Helena would sooner die herself," Opa said. Karia assumed that was Nana's name. She'd never heard it before. All these years everyone – even Opa – had simply called her Nana. Then again, she hadn't listened in on the adults talking before. *Not often anyway,* she thought.

"It's their way," Avar said.

"It's the old way," Reva said. "It's what they used to do. Our way is to hide and till the ground."

"We could bring back their ways," Avar said. "She could."

"Fire and ashes, Avar, you dream a fool's dream," Opa said. "The past only seems bright because we forget the hardships."

"And I could never – never – ask Karia to do that," Reva said. "I love her no less than if she were my own daughter."

There it was then. Reva was not her father. Someone else – a great sorcerer – was her father. Karia fought to keep from crying out loud. But she told herself that Reva was still her dad, and she loved him no less. She told herself that, but she didn't fully believe herself.

The men were silent again.

Ian Fallis

CHAPTER FOURTEEN

The door opened and Karia could hear the tea service tinkling on trays, and the footfalls of the women walking back onto the porch. From the scraping of the chairs and sounds of footsteps, it seemed to Karia that they all stood, poured and fixed their tea, then sat down again.

"Where do we start?" Opa said.

"Well, there's still one more thing we need to talk about," Nana said. "Failean and Heather tell me that Karia is quite smitten with Timbal."

"And," Heather added, "Timbal admitted to me that he and Karia kissed."

Karia blushed. *He told his mom?*

"Do you mean," Reva asked, "that he kissed her, or that they kissed each other?"

"He said they kissed, and I pressed him on that very point. I'm not having my son push his affections on anyone, but he said it was mutual."

Oh gosh, Karia thought, *can this get any more embarrassing?* Even though no one was looking, she put her head down.

"He also said she expects him to marry her."

Yes. The answer is yes, she thought, burying her face in her hands. *It can get more embarrassing.*

"That's the impression I got from her as well," said Karia's mom.

Thanks, Mom. Ugh. Maybe I'll just live here under Nana's porch from now on.

"I've kept them apart since I found out, but that's not a long-term solution, with them living right next door on the same farm," her mom said.

"We could tell them the truth," Avar said.

"And Narek?" Nana asked. "He's trouble enough as it is. It would only get worse if he knew the truth, and we can't exactly tell them and keep it from him. Even if we tried, he'd find out."

"Let's not assume we know how Karia and Timbal would react either," Reva said.

"But all this is just muddying the waters, isn't it?" Avar asked. "Now that we know what Karia is, the children should be told the truth, and Karia needs to …"

"Don't you say it," Nana hissed. "Don't you even, ever suggest that. The old ways were cruel and harsh and irrational."

"Irrational?" Avar said. "Irrational? Can anyone here tell me that the third one is not evil? Can you?"

"He's just a boy," Nana said. "You can't judge the man he will become by the boy he is. I remember a certain brown-haired mischief-maker named Avar."

The conversation paused. Karia's head was spinning. *The truth? What truth? There's more than, 'Gee, Karia, the man who you thought was your father isn't'? And, now that they know what I am? What is that supposed to mean? And what would my dad never ask me to do? What made Nana so angry?*

Finally, Nana spoke again.

"This is an awful lot to digest," she said. *Digest? It's moving so fast I can't even get a bite out of it!* "And tempers are running a bit hot. Let's resolve together to keep Timbal and Karia apart, get some rest and talk again."

"Agreed," said Reva.

"Yes," Heather and Failean said at the same time.

"Good," Opa said.

"Avar?" Nana said.

After a pause, he said, "OK."

Karia heard the chairs sliding again, and the tinkle of Nana's delicate tea service being put back on the trays.

"Let me help you," Heather said, and Karia heard the door open and the two women's footsteps go into the kitchen. Then it sounded as if Opa went in and Heather came out, and the door closed. She saw Uncle Avar and Aunt Heather walk past her hiding place, and then her mom and Reva. *My dad. Not Reva. My dad. He raised me. He loves me.* She was still trying to convince herself.

She waited a while, listening. She thought she heard Uncle Avar and Aunt Heather's door close, and then the door to her house close. She crawled out from under the porch, and still kept to the shadows and stayed quiet, just in case, as she walked to her house. At the porch, she took off her boots and tried to walk silently up the steps and across the porch. She hit that one loud board – of course – and stopped to listen. She heard nothing.

Slowly and carefully, she turned the doorknob and opened the door. She saw that the door to her parents' room was closed, and she stepped in and tried to close the door silently. It still made a slight snick, and she glanced quickly back to her parents' door. Nothing.

Karia tip-toed across the floor to her room. This she also tried to open quietly, and she stepped in and closed it. She climbed into her bed and felt somewhat relieved. But not at home, and not safe. It was like her insides were moving around. She quietly cried herself to sleep. She never used to cry.

Ian Fallis

CHAPTER FIFTEEN

She awoke feeling fingers running through her hair, and she knew before she opened her eyes that her dad was there. That's how he always woke her up when she was little. She looked up at him, and it was like last night never happened, like the last several years had never happened, and she was little again and warm and safe and loved.

She sat up and threw her arms around his large, strong sturdy frame, and hugged him tight. She hadn't done that for a long time. She was surprised her arms were now almost long enough to reach all the way around him.

"You aren't going to make a habit of sleeping in, are you, Tsilinki?" he said. When he spoke while she held him, it was almost as if his deep voice rumbled inside her. She liked the way that felt. "This is a farm, you know."

Sunlight was already streaming into her room, and she knew she should have been up hours ago helping her mom, but none of that mattered. At this point, she didn't even mind being called Tsilinki – at least, didn't mind it much – as long as he held her. She just wanted to be Daddy's little girl again.

"Oh, Daddy," she said, still holding him, and started to cry.

"Hey, what's this?" he said. His voice was so kind, so concerned. "They keep telling me you're becoming a woman, but I think sometimes you still need to be a little girl, don't you?"

Karia let go of him and lay back in her bed, wiping her tears. "I'm sorry, Daddy." *Daddy.* Looking into his deep hazel eyes, between his prominent forehead and cheekbones, she knew now that she really felt it, really meant it.

"No, no, nothing to apologize for." He rested his large hand on her forehead a moment, then ran his big, thick fingers through her hair again. "Are you alright, Tsil?"

"Oh, yes, Daddy. I'm OK."

"We missed you at breakfast again, and all morning I couldn't stop worrying about you. I finally realized I was so worried I wasn't getting anything done. Or at least, done right. You and me, we do things the right way, don't we, Tsilinki?"

Karia winced at the name, but nodded.

"So I had to come back to check on you, and your mom said you were still in bed."

"I'm sorry, Daddy."

"Oh, you stop that apologizing. I just want my little Tsil back – even though I know she's growing up. Just like the tsilinki out in the fields."

Her dad completely blocked Karia's view of the doorway, but she knew her mom had come in. She could feel her presence.

"Daddy," she said. "Please ... don't call me Tsilinki. It makes me feel ... ugly."

She heard her mom's voice: "I've been telling you that, haven't I?"

"I was just kidding," her dad said. Now he sounded and looked hurt.

Karia sat up again and put her arms back around him. "I know, Daddy, but ..."

"OK, Tsil." She gave him a squeeze. "But you listen to your mom, and you get the rest you need."

"Yes, Daddy."

She let go of him and lay back, and he got up and walked out. She started to get out of bed, and her mom hurried over, her hand up.

"Hold on there, young lady. I'm not so sure you should be out of bed yet."

"Mom, I feel fine." She swung her legs to the side of the bed, and truth be told, she did feel faint. She heard the front door close; her dad must have gone back to the fields.

"That's what you said two days ago, and I let you get about your chores, and you slept even later this morning."

"Maybe it was because you kept me busy all day with chores. Maybe I need some time to play."

"Karia ..."

"Why can't I be with Timbal, Mom?"

"Karia, you lie back down ..."

"No!" she said sharply. "No." She stopped short. She had intended to threaten to walk out and go to Timbal's house right then and there, to force her mom to answer her. But as the second "no" came out of her mouth, the look on her mom's face stopped her. She knew that was wrong. She kept hurting her mom, and she didn't know why. She didn't want to. "I'm sorry, Mom. I just want to see him. You understand that, don't you?"

"Yes, dear, I do. But," she said. She stopped and looked at Karia a moment. She got up and walked to the bedroom door and closed it, and came back and sat next to Karia on the bed. "Nymph's wake, Karia, I don't even know where to start."

Both were quiet for a while. Then, looking down and speaking softly, tentatively, Karia said, "You could tell me the truth."

Her mom raised her voice. "There are reasons you haven't been told everything, facts you're not old enough for, dangers we want to protect you from," her mother said. "You would do well to not go hiding under porches and listening in on things you're not supposed to hear."

Ian Fallis

CHAPTER SIXTEEN

Karia was horrified and embarrassed. *Did she really say … how did she know?* She turned to her mom, unable to mask the shock on her face.

"You're a smart girl, Karia," her mom said. "Put aside everything else. Focus on the important thing. How did I know?"

"I … I … you …" Karia stammered.

"Don't you always know when I'm near, Karia?"

"Yes," Karia said.

"Don't you think I can tell when you are close?"

Oh gosh, Karia thought. *Stupid stupid stupid. I should have known that.*

"Do you know why you can feel me and I can sense you?" her mom asked.

Karia was stumped. She hadn't ever thought about it. It had always been that way. She just thought everyone could just tell when their mothers were close. So that's what she said.

"That's not why," her mom said. "I could feel my dad, and like you, I just thought everyone could. But I couldn't feel my mom. Timbal can't feel either of his parents, and Narek can't either."

"Because they're boys?" Karia asked.

Her mom laughed. "Well, men can be dense at times, but that's not the reason. You know Litara, don't you? From the farm down the river?"

"Yes." *The old maid*, Karia thought. *Seventeen, almost eighteen, and still no suitors.*

"She can't feel her mom. Very, very few girls can."

That must be a very lonely feeling, Karia thought. She remembered the time a few years ago when her mom had left for "family matters," whatever that was, for a couple of weeks. *Yes, lonely.*

"Karia?"

"Sorry, Mom. But I don't understand. Why can I feel you, and you can feel me?"

"What do we have that very few women have, Karia?"

59

"We can ... we can do magic?" Karia asked. "So people who can do magic, can feel each other?"

"Well, not exactly. It's more like, we can feel each other and we can do magic for the same reason."

"Huh?"

"It's the same reason you could read your name in Inamali."

Karia just stared at her mom. She had no idea where this was going. She had no clue why she could feel her mom and other girls couldn't. She had no idea why she could do magic. She couldn't even begin to guess why she could read her name in Inamali.

"Karia ... you and I ..." Her mom stopped. "You wanted the truth. I hope this is the right thing to do.

"You and I are Inamali, Karia."

CHAPTER SEVENTEEN

Inamali? Karia thought. *Oh no. No! That's why I've been growing so tall. I don't want to be twelve feet tall! I'm already a little taller than Timbal.*

Karia jumped to her feet. "I don't know any boys twelve feet tall!" she blurted out. "I'll never get married!"

Her mom started laughing so hard she almost fell off the bed.

"Mom! It's not funny! This ruins my **whole life!**"

Her mom appeared to be fighting to keep from laughing. "Karia," she said. "I'm sorry. Keep your voice down, dear." She giggled. "Karia, you're not going to be twelve feet tall. You're probably going to grow more for a few years, but only a couple of inches, and you'll also start filling out and looking a lot like other women. A lot like me, probably. I'm not twelve feet tall, am I?"

"No," Karia said, calming down again.

"Oh, my little Karia," her mom said, smiling so sweetly that Karia couldn't help but smile back. "I tell you that you're part of a great and mighty people, and the first thing you think of is boys."

They both laughed at that.

Karia sat back down next to her mom, and they put their arms around each other.

"Karia," her mom said, getting very serious, "none of the other adults wanted you to know this. You must keep this secret, between us."

"OK."

"Not even your father can know that you know."

"You mean Reva."

"Fifteen years he's raised you and cared for you and sacrificed for you — and loved you just as if you were his own little girl," her mom scolded. "He's your father and your dad and pretty good at both."

"I know that. But I also want to know who my father is."

"We'll get to that, Karia, first …"

"I don't want to get to that. I want to know. I have a right to know who my father is."

"Was. I'm sorry, Karia, that you never got to know him, but he's gone."

Karia suddenly discovered a hollow spot inside her that felt like it could never be filled. She didn't feel like she had lost anything, but she felt like there was something she needed that she could never have.

"Tell me about him."

"I will, Karia. But not now."

"Was he Inamali?"

"Yes, Karia, but …"

"And you're Inamali?"

"Well, not fully, dear, but …"

"So I'm not fully Inamali?"

"Karia, can we come back to this? There are other things we need to talk about."

"So I'm not going to be twelve feet tall because I'm not fully Inamali?"

Her mother was silent.

"Is that why, Mom?"

"Karia, I wanted to tell you about your heritage, about your family. The others forbade it. And I came to think they were right. I guess I wanted to ignore what I knew was true, and maybe it would go away. But now, with what you're doing … I feel like I've left you unprepared. I still don't know what I should tell you, or where to start.

"But … well, because you are Inamali, and … well, I still need to sort out what to say to you, but it's important that you try to forget your feelings toward Timbal."

Karia was puzzled for a moment, then assumed her mom did not want to her to marry Timbal because he wasn't Inamali. *She wants me to marry an Inamali. But why?*

"If I marry an Inamali, won't that be sort of like intermarriage for them?"

Her mom looked as if she didn't understand what Karia was saying.

"Mom? Isn't that right? You're not fully Inamali, so neither am I, so why should that stand between me and Timbal?"

"No, dear, you've got things a little confused."

"But why is it so important that I marry an Inamali?"

"Meadowstars, Karia, that's not even what I was talking about."

"What's the problem with me and Timbal? You're not fully Inamali, so that means I'm not fully Inamali, so what does it matter if I marry a Teneka?"

Her mom looked frustrated, and looked her in the eyes and said, "Karia, there are very few pure Inamali left, and you're one of them." She instantly looked as if she regretted saying that.

But Karia barely noticed her look. She was stunned. *Mom isn't fully Inamali … but I am … then …*

Karia's head was spinning. She couldn't breathe. The hollow inside her was expanding and she felt like she was just going to be a shell. A hollow shell.

"You're not my mother," she said. She wasn't angry; she said it as a statement of fact, because she was still processing it. "You're not my mother. My dad's not my father, and you're not my mother."

She stood up. Her mom tried to take her hand, but Karia shook her hand free. "You lied to me. I don't know you. I don't even know who I am. How could you do this to me?"

"Karia …"

Karia threw open her door, then bolted to the front door, swung it open and ran out. Her mom ran out behind her, calling her name, but she did not stop. It must have been nearly lunch time, because Timbal was coming in from the field.

"Timbal, stop her!" her mom shouted.

Timbal ran toward her. He may have been shorter, but working in the fields had made him fast and strong. He caught up with her a full field before the forest and grabbed her around the waist.

"Karia!" he said.

But Karia – deliberately this time – pushed him away, hard. Without touching him, she flung him back. He lost his balance and landed with a solid thump. Karia stopped and looked at him. His eyes were open, and he was gasping for breath. She believed the wind had just been knocked out of him, so she again ran toward the forest.

Ian Fallis

CHAPTER EIGHTEEN

The small, thin man abruptly stood up from his noon meal, squinted and pointed his hawkish nose off into the distance.

"Yes," he said. "Yes, he's close now." He pointed a long, bony finger toward the southeast. "That way. I am certain." He turned to the hooded figure next to him. "You see? I have led you well. We are close."

"Perhaps, *Chti'iki*," the hooded figure said in a breathy voice. "Perhaps. But I still have only your word for it."

"A week and a half out from Talitakaya, across the mountains, into this accursed backwater, and you had better be right," said a taller, stockier man in armor.

The small man ignored them. "A map, Hinar!" he shouted to the armored man. "A map!"

Hinar turned to a young man lounging against a tree, chewing on a piece of grass. "Jiraki, up! Bring a map!"

Jiraki lazily took the grass from his mouth and looked up. "Which map?"

The hooded figure stood and turned to Jiraki. *"Zhkar ki'atitchi tanikhi!"* he shouted.

Jiraki jumped to his feet and turned to Hinar, looking close to panic. "What'd he say?"

"I'm not sure. It was either, 'You know what map, imbecile,' or it was a spell to make your manhood shrivel up. Might've been both, actually. Get the map!"

Jiraki ran to a nearby tent. They could hear him rummaging through papers, and then he emerged with a rolled-up map and ran to the table. He began trying to spread the map in a small clear spot on the table, but the small man abruptly swept away all the lunch plates and opened the map fully. He turned to Hinar.

"Orient it," he said, and then he turned back to face southeast.

Hinar took out a compass and turned the map until north on the map lined up with north on the compass.

The small man turned back to the table. "And where are we?" he said.

Hinar pointed to a small forested area about halfway between the mountains and a town, just off the road. The only town anywhere near them.

"We go there," the small man said.

"He's in the town?" Hinar asked.

"I don't think so. I feel he's farther on, but I don't know how much farther."

"Or you seek a soft bed for your tender buttocks," the hooded figure said.

Hinar pulled the small man aside. "I'm not sure how the people this far out will take to a troop of cavalry riding into town," he said. "Or him," he added, motioning to the hooded figure.

"My people have very good hearing, Hinar," the hooded figure said. "And the hood amplifies your words."

"Sorry, but I was going to say, it seems best if we wait here and send the Seeker."

"No," said the figure. "If the *Chti'iki* even tries to leave, I must kill him."

"How about sending an escort – a couple of men – to keep an eye on him?"

"No. Where the *Chti'iki* goes, I go."

Hinar stepped closer to the hooded figure and lowered his voice.

"I doubt many in this area have ever seen any of your people," he said. "And some may not like you. There could be trouble."

"Then we will all go, and we will kill anyone who causes trouble. They're all *gru'cheti'iki*."

Hinar knew enough of the language to know that was a very crude term, and that it was a very crude term for all the Teneka, including Hinar and his men.

"No need to talk like that," Hinar said. "I just think we should try to avoid making trouble. If he gets wind that we're on his scent, he may stop using magic and run."

The hooded figure knelt down, bowed his head and fingered the white crescent at his collar.

Hinar knew better than to disturb him. He and the Seeker stood and waited for about fifteen minutes. Then the hooded figure arose and said, "I do not see trouble ahead." He turned to the Seeker. "I also do not see success. If I am correct, you will pay with your life."

As if on some warped cue, someone began playing a giddy tune on a fiddle. It sounded as if it was coming from the road that led to town. The

66

three men walked to the edge of the forest and looked down the hill to the road. A carnival procession was making its way down the road, its colorful wagons bouncing along the rutted track. A fiddler, seemingly oblivious to his precarious situation, stood on top of one of the wagons, smiling as he played.

"I think I have an idea," Hinar said.

Ian Fallis

CHAPTER NINETEEN

Karia ran all the way to the hedge without ever slowing. A little past the gate, she dropped to her hands and knees to crawl under, crawled until she was inside the house again, then leaned back against the wall she had just come in through. Exhausted, she began crying again, sobbing, and, despite the turmoil in her heart, fell asleep.

It was daytime when she woke up. She wondered if perhaps it was always daytime inside the house; if the house was, as Opa said, a place where time does not pass.

But she didn't think about it long. She didn't really think. She just felt hollow, and numb. Thoughts came and went, or rather, fragments of thoughts. Nothing fit together, nothing connected. And she felt so tired, so very tired. She sat there like that for what seemed like hours.

It was finally hunger that broke the spell. She stood up and took one step toward the kitchen, then stopped. She thought that if there had been any food left there, it was spoiled by now. *But then again,* she thought, *if time does not pass here* …

She walked across the dusty floor to the kitchen, opened the door and went in. She walked over to the cupboards on the left of the fireplace, and discovered pots and pans and cups and bowls, knives and spoons, and other kitchen implements, some familiar, some not. She picked up an odd utensil with a short wooden handle and three fine blades, puzzling over what it could be for. *Oh, right, sure, this must be for torturing carrots that refuse to talk.* She smiled at her joke and put it back.

She walked to the cabinets on the other side of the room. First she opened the leftmost top cabinet and was thrilled – but hesitant – when she found a dozen ten-inch wheels of cheese, still in wax. She picked one up and felt the outside, and it felt fine. She took it across the room and put it on a cutting board. She used a knife to cut a wedge from it. Inside the whitish wax was a pale yellow cheese with a few tiny green veins. She had never seen a cheese like it before, and feared it had gone bad.

She picked up the wedge and put it near her nose. It smelled strong, but she didn't think it smelled bad. She broke a tiny piece off the tip of the wedge and tasted it. It was indeed a strong cheese, and didn't taste like it had gone bad. In fact, it tasted quite good, savory even. She took a larger bite, and realized quickly that was a mistake. It was difficult to eat a strong cheese like that on its own.

I need a piece of bread, she thought. *What are the odds of that?*

She put down the cheese and walked back across to the pantry cupboards. In the next top cupboard were several tall bottles with corks sealed in wax; she guessed there were twenty. She went back to the cabinet on the left side of the room and got a corkscrew. She opened one of the bottles and sniffed. *Wine*, she thought, and tipped it back to take a sip. *Good wine*, she thought, and took a drink.

She walked over and put the bottle by the cheese. She took another bite, a smaller one this time, and then another drink. Then she went back to the pantry.

The next cabinet contained more bottles, probably another twenty. She opened one – these were only corked, not waxed and corked, like the wine. She sniffed it and wrinkled her nose. *Vinegar.* She worked her way through more of the bottles. A couple were vinegar, but most were oil. That was far more oil than would be found at her house. She poked her little finger into one of the bottles of oil to taste it. *That's better oil than we have at home too.*

She opened the final upper cupboard and found a dizzying array of dried herbs hanging from a rack, with a number of small ceramic jars sealed with corks underneath. She uncorked a few and saw that they were a variety of spices. Just the aroma made her feel good – but hungrier.

She went back for another small bite of cheese and another sip of wine, and knelt down to look in one of the three large lower cabinets. Inside were burlap sacks of grain. She recognized tsilinki, but also the anarka that was so popular in the central plain, because it produced such fine flour and light bread. She found hinarka, too, which could also be used for flour but was mostly cooked with water and eaten. Oh, and there in the back she found jiki, tiny red beans, and kariki, the larger dark red beans her dad liked. *Reva likes*, she corrected herself. Then she corrected herself again, *Daddy likes*.

She remembered all the times he would push back from the table when times were tough and they were eating their tenth or eleventh or even twentieth meal in a row of boiled hinarka and kariki. He'd smile and say, "Failean, if all I have for the rest of my life is hinarka and kariki and you and Karia, I'll be a happy man."

And her mom would always reply, "Well, Reva, one day Karia is going to have a family of her own, and you're going to eat up all the hinarka and kariki, so I hope you'll be OK with just me!"

She laughed out loud at the memory of them smiling and kissing, then drawing her into their embrace. She wished it was all so simple again.

My family isn't my family but it's still my family, she thought. Puzzled a little, she thought through that again. *No, that's right. My Mom, my Dad and me. We're family, even if we aren't related by birth.*

She stared at the grain for a moment, sighed and turned her attention to the middle cabinet. Here she found potatoes and turnips and onions. She felt them, then picked them up and smelled them, and they seemed good.

She selected a turnip, stood up and chose a leafy herb and a bottle of oil, and took them to the cutting board. After a little more cheese and wine, she peeled and chopped the turnip, then got out a frying pan. She put a splash of oil in the pan, then the turnip. She crumbled the herb over the turnip. She stepped toward the fireplace, and put down the pan.

She found split logs, but no kindling and no matches. She put a couple of logs on the fire, then looked around for a small hatchet so she could make some kindling, but could not find one. She looked again for matches, and could not find those either.

She looked down at the frying pan. "I am most certainly not eating oily raw turnip," she said.

But she wasn't sure what she was going to do. Back again she went to the cheese and wine, and then she remembered that she had not looked in third lower pantry cupboard. She was certain there would be a hatchet and matches in there, and was disappointed to find only a small ceramic crock and two small sacks.

She stood up and turned toward the fireplace, putting her hands on her hips. *What am I going to do?* she thought. *Oh …that's right.*

She stepped back, held up her hand, closed her eyes and thought very, very hard about sending fire. Her hand suddenly felt very hot, and then she felt something fly from her hand with so much force it rocked her backward, accompanied by a sound like a very strong wind.

She opened her eyes and looked at the fireplace.

"Oops," she said. The only thing on the grate, where the logs had been, were a few smoldering embers.

She knelt down to put a couple more logs on the grate, but first needed to stop and catch her breath. She felt tired and dizzy. Balancing carefully, she placed the logs and stepped back again. She held up her hand, closed her eyes and thought just about sparking a flame. She felt the same heat in her hand, and felt it leave with a soft *whoosh*. When she opened her eyes, she saw a small fire crackling away. A quick wave of dizziness washed over her, then passed.

Karia set a grate over the fire, and put the pan with the turnip over the fire to cook. She would normally have waited until there was uniform heat

71

and less smoke from hot coals before starting to cook, but she was quite hungry. After some more cheese and wine, she went back to inspect the ceramic crock. She hoped she knew what it was, and hoped it too was still good, and when she opened it she knew her hopes were met. She smelled the pungent aroma of leaven, and looked in and saw it merrily bubbling away.

She found the sacks by the crock contained salt and sugar.

She took a pinch of salt for her turnip, finished cooking it and ate it straight from the pan, along with more cheese and wine. Then Karia ground some of the anarka. She looked around for a water barrel and found none, so she took a pitcher to the waterfall room to fetch some.

She went in and held the pitcher under the water. She turned to exit, and then stopped, surprised. The towel and robe – which she had left on the floor – were back on the rack. She put the pitcher down and checked them. They were clean and dry.

She stepped back to the doorway and looked at the floor. She saw only her tracks in the dust. "Magic?" she said.

Picking up the pitcher, she went back to the kitchen. She put most of the flour she had just milled on a board, sprinkled in a little salt and about three times that much sugar, mixed it roughly and made a well. She poured in some water, then scooped out some leaven and mixed it with the water.

She mixed the little bit of the reserved flour and more water into the leaven, then put the crock back in the cupboard.

Seeing the leaven already bubbling away in the well on the board, she mixed in the dry ingredients, then kneaded it. She turned, folded and pressed it until it was smooth and uniform and elastic, then set it aside. She oiled a bowl, and put the dough inside and put it under a towel to rise on the pantry sideboard.

Now, she thought, *it's time to read.*

CHAPTER TWENTY

Karia walked to the study and took down the top-left book. She opened it to the first page, and scanned down the letters. She scanned it again and again. She turned the page and scanned the markings there. She could understand nothing. She felt nothing. She flipped through the first dozen or so pages, and still nothing. She slammed the book shut.

What did the letter say? she thought. *Use the books. Use the books. What does that mean?*

She reasoned that if someone put down a book in Teneka in front of her, and told her to use it, she'd read it. And the letter was in Inamali, so her father expected her to be able to read Inamali. But she could not.

She kicked the desk, and instantly realized that kicking a desk while barefoot was perhaps one of the less intelligent things she had ever done. Hopping on her left foot, holding her throbbing right foot, she turned to face the bookcase while leaning on the desk. She was looking toward the bottom of the bookcase now; she had only looked at the top before. And something looked familiar about some of the books on the bottom row.

Almost – but not quite – forgetting the pain in her foot, she reached down and pulled out one that looked very familiar. Opening it, she realized it was about farming. And she knew she had read it before – in Teneka. She'd read it so many times she almost had it memorized. Either this was a translation of the Teneka book, or the Teneka book was a translation of this one.

She started on the first page, trying to figure out what the Inamali letters said from what she remembered about the book. After a few minutes she was utterly frustrated, and slammed that book shut as well.

"I wish I'd never found this place!" she yelled at the top of her lungs. *Fire and ashes!* she thought. Kissing Narek sounded like a great idea compared to what she'd been through in the last – what was it? – a week? Two weeks? She wasn't sure. She'd kiss him now – gladly, and again and again – if it could just undo this mess. *Well, maybe not gladly.* She thought a moment more. *Maybe not again and again either. Ew.*

She thought about just going home. *They'll all be so angry with me. Mom and Dad. Timbal for sure, and after what I did to him, Uncle Avar and Aunt Heather. Opa – he and Nana won't be happy either. Narek too, but he's always angry with me, and I don't care.*

It suddenly struck her that she'd always been very mean to Narek, and it didn't really matter how much she felt like he deserved it. She should have treated him like family. But … family? What is that? She had no family. Her father was dead, and the only thing she knew about her mother was that she was Inamali. But Karia had the horrible feeling that if Reva and Failean had taken her in, her mother was dead too. And she never got the chance to even meet her mother or her father.

Her tears began to flow. She yelled, "I don't cry!" and picked up the book and threw it across the room. Its spline slammed into the opposite wall, and it flew open, landing cover-up and pages-splayed, with a loud thud in a cloud of dust.

Karia slumped down against the wall again. Her thoughts were again an incomplete jumble. Again she didn't know how long she was there. It could have been a few minutes, or hours. And once again, she might have fallen asleep. She was drifting, lost. Until in the stillness of the house, she heard that sound she had first mistaken for whispers.

She pulled herself up and discovered she once again could not put much weight on her right foot – the one she had kicked the desk with. It wasn't quite supposed to be that large, or those colors either. She limped to the waterfall room, and went inside and closed the door. As before, something about the smell of the room said "home" to her, and that comforted her greatly. She undressed and took off her locket, and paused, looking at it. *Did my father give me this, or my dad?* She had no way of knowing. She wasn't sure it meant anything to her now. She hung up the locket and stepped into the waterfall.

Like the time before, being in the waterfall was like a dream to her – pleasant and timeless. Soothing and healing. Her thoughts coalesced. She was determined to figure out the books. She toweled dry, then limped over to the cabinet.

She picked up the blue jar and smelled it, and still her foot hurt.

She picked up the thinner of the two white ointments and rubbed it on her foot, and while the swelling and bruising decreased, it still hurt.

"Oh, goody," she said. She picked up the amber ointment and sat on the floor. She carefully unscrewed it and got some of the amber ointment on her finger, then leaned forward and rubbed it on her foot. Immediately her foot felt driven upward, slamming her knee into her shoulder and her shoulder into the door.

"Ouch!" she cried. *This stuff could hurt you worse than what ails you!*

She put her foot back down and was about to rub her shoulder, but remembered to rinse the amber ointment off first. Then she stood. Her foot felt better, much better, but not fully healed. Her shoulder would be OK. She put on the robe.

"Back to the books," she said.

Ian Fallis

CHAPTER TWENTY-ONE

Karia, walking with less of a limp, went back to the study and picked up the farming book she had thrown. She brought it back to the desk and tried to smooth out and clean off the pages that had gotten creased and dusty when she threw it. That was when she saw the illustrations.

She had forgotten about the drawings. In the center of the book were hand-drawn, color illustrations of different types of crops, here annotated in Inamali. She found tsilinki, and looked at the legend on the illustration. Excited, she grabbed the quill and found a piece of parchment inside the writing desk. She copied the Inamali characters, and stopped. She stared at them. This made no sense. She thought tsilinki was the name of the plant in Teneka and Inamali, but there were only three characters in the Inamali word.

She turned to the next page and here was anarka, and hinarka, but she was not sure that helped much because she was not sure if those names were the same in Inamali and Teneka. She wrote them down anyway — three characters each. She flipped through the grains and came to the legumes, and there were jiki and kariki. She was almost certain those were the same in Inamali and Teneka, but again she was perplexed. They were only two characters and three characters.

She wrote them on her paper anyway. But this was getting her nowhere.

She tried to remember how to write her name in Inamali. She was surprised when it just flowed out as she put the pen to the paper. She looked at it, and realized it was only three characters. *Wait*, she thought, *do I have a different name in Inamali? Meadowstars, nothing is working!*

She put the pen back and was about to crumple the paper when she noticed that her name and kariki looked almost identical. In fact, the first two characters were the same. Only the third was different. She said them aloud. "Karia ... kariki ... wait ... ka, ri, ya ... ka, ri, ki ... oh, that's it! Those aren't letters! They're syllables!"

Smiling now, she scanned the other words. There were ki and ka, and ji. She could identify an, ar and hi. And other symbols she recognized as tsi and li. She may not know what the words mean – yet – but this was a start. She could start sounding words out, and find more words she knew and identify more symbols for more syllables.

Energized, she scanned through the farming book and discovered she knew a lot more words than she had thought. She filled four pieces of paper with Inamali syllables and their pronunciation in Teneka. She discovered that she was wrong about anarka being made up of an, ar and ka. It was a, nar and ka. It seemed as if every syllable ended in a vowel or an r.

She turned to the bookcase and excitedly began trying to sound out the titles on the spines.

None were making much sense to her, but now she was getting a definite feeling from each word she read. She sounded out the books on the top row, and the next, and moved methodically across the middle row.

"Tsi … li … don't know … ka … ya. Tsili, kaya. What's that symbol?" She shuffled through her papers, and there it was. Nar.

"Tsilinarkaya?" Suddenly it just hit her. "Oh my. Tsilinakaya."

CHAPTER TWENTY-TWO

Karia pulled the large book from the case and examined it. It was ornate, almost gaudy, with a leather cover embossed with flowers and leaves and geometric patterns, enhanced with what looked like gilding. She turned to put it on the desk but bumped her right foot on the desk leg, and it hurt so badly she nearly dropped the book. Closing her eyes and taking a deep breath, she put the book on the desk and opened it.

She scanned the first page, and the next, sounding out words here and there, but couldn't make any sense of it. *These words are so long!* She couldn't even get a feeling from it. She closed the book.

This is so frustrating, she thought. She had figured out how Inamali writing worked, and figured out how to sound out words. *I guess that means I can read Inamali. Sort of.* But where did that get her? She still didn't know enough to get anything out of the books. She still didn't know the language.

Yet she was able to master fire after just scanning a spell, before she could even pronounce the words. Her eyes moved back to the top shelf, and she scanned what she believed were spell books.

Then again, her father wrote *use the books*, not, *use the spell books.* Did they all have a purpose? Her eyes went back to the bottom shelves. *Do I really need to read about animal husbandry in Inamali too? Gross.*

And what were the books in between? History? Poetry? Novels? *Joke books. I could use a good joke book. If I could get the jokes.*

She felt tired. She had no idea how long she had been here, and realized she had only had a nap, maybe two, while sitting on the dusty floor. She needed to sleep. The bench in the kitchen didn't sound appealing, nor did the chairs in the parlor. She shuddered just thinking about them. They were so far beyond ugly they gave her the creeps.

She thought that the locked room was probably a bedroom, but who could be sure in a house with a waterfall, an entry for a study – *or is it the other way around?* – and one door you came in and another you went out, neither which was actually a door on the other side?

She limped back to the locked door and tried it again. It still didn't budge. She bent down and looked at the knob, and could see no lock. *A magical lock?* She stepped back and thought, *Open.* Nothing happened. Just in case, she tried the door again. Still locked. *Aargh!* She didn't need a puzzle. She needed to sleep.

She mustered all her will and pushed the door like she had pushed Timbal, but this time she pushed as hard as she could. The door gave a little, then splintered and flew into the room. "That worked."

She stepped in, expecting to find a wizard's bedroom, her father's bedroom. But it was not. Unless he was very strange, and she really didn't want to think about that.

All along the wall to the left was a series of three wardrobes, constructed from a light wood with little grain, almost a light golden color, carved to resemble a field of tsilinki. In that type of wood, it looked like it was harvest time, a very pleasant time to Karia. Harvesting meant hard work with a great reward, which made the farm girl happy. The center wardrobe was open, revealing a pair of dresses more beautiful than any Karia had ever seen before. They were in several pastel colors, made like ball gowns, with ruffles and bows that looked like they would not be out of place in Talitakaya – but most definitely would be out of place anywhere close to here.

Directly before her was a canopy bed that Karia thought would be suitable for a princess – at least, it would be once she picked all the wood splinters out of it. She sighed. *The only bed and I've filled it with splinters. That probably wasn't the way I was supposed to open the door.*

An ornately turned pillar at each corner held up the canopy, reaching to within a foot or so of the ceiling. The underside of the canopy was richly embroidered to resemble a field of spring flowers – Karia recognized most of them – and this was reflected in the carving of the headboard. The bedspread – the splinter-pocked bedspread – was sewn together in shades of brown, and reminded Karia of looking out over newly planted fields.

On the right side of the room was a dressing table – with a mirror and, she saw with excitement, a hair brush! Karia realized she hadn't properly brushed her hair in too long. On each side was a large dresser. These were in the same golden wood as the wardrobes, with the same tsilinki carvings.

She decided she'd look in the dressers and wardrobes later. She went to the bed and peeled the bedspread back, thankful that it seemed to catch up all the bits of wood she had sprayed across it. She put it on the floor at the foot of the bed. She pulled back the covers and started to climb in. But while it was great to wear the big, fluffy robe around the cottage, it bunched up uncomfortably as she tried to get into bed. She just could not get comfortable wearing the robe in the bed.

Reluctantly, and looking around even though she knew she was alone, she took off the robe and climbed into the bed. The sheets felt so comfortable, that she was asleep almost as soon as she covered herself.

Ian Fallis

CHAPTER TWENTY-THREE

Karia awoke sharply. She was not startled or suddenly awakened by something else. It was as if she had the rest she needed and awoke, her mind sharp and her thoughts clear.

And the thoughts! Not the random jumbled thoughts of the night before – or whenever that was – but crisp, clean thoughts, important thoughts. Thoughts she needed to capture.

She let out an excited little shriek, leapt from the bed and ran to the study. She rifled through her mess of papers from last night – or whenever that had been – and found a clean sheet of paper. She grabbed the quill – noting for the first time that she never needed to shake excess ink from the nib – and began writing quickly:

> *My father built this house for me. He was the sorcerer in the Old Wood, and he was here to do this. Here he put everything I need for all that is expected of me.*
>
> *Revu and Tuilean are my dad and mom and they love me very much. And I love them. Avar and Heather and Timbal, and Opa and Nana and Narek are also part of my family. They are all part of my destiny.*
>
> *I am not a girl anymore. I am not a woman yet. I am being prepared for the future set before me.*
>
> *The bread ...*

She let out another little shriek. "The bread is still rising!" She started running toward the kitchen, still holding the quill. She turned and ran back and put it in the inkwell, then ran into the kitchen.

There on the pantry sideboard was the sorriest mess. The bread had risen well past the edge of the bowl she put it in to rise, and then sort of deflated. It now hung over the sides of the bowl, past the small towel that was supposed to keep it from drying out.

Working quickly, she removed the towel and felt the edges. They were not very dry, so she gathered the dough back into a ball and punched it down and kneaded it a while. When the texture was smooth and even again,

83

she shaped it into a simple round loaf and put it on a baking sheet. She took a sharp knife and cut into the top the pattern her mom had always cut – a cross, and then a cut from the top end of one slash to the right edge of the other. She put a towel over it. She knew it would be fine; she had seen her mom do this before.

She went to the fireplace and knelt. She put a few more logs on the hearth and kindled the fire, to preheat the small oven over the fireplace. And as she put her hands on the floor to get up, she let out another small shriek.

She stood with a start and looked all over the kitchen floor. It was clean. There was not a speck of dust.

She ran out into the parlor and – "Oh, my eyes!" – the chairs were clean, as was the floor and everything else. Stepping to the study doorway she looked down both halls and into the study. The dust was gone. She looked down at her feet, and they were clean.

She suddenly felt embarrassed that it wasn't just her feet that were bare. She ran into the bedroom to where she had left the robe, but it wasn't there. "Right, it'll be hanging up again," she said, and ran to the shower room. There it was, in its place on the rack. She grabbed it and hastily threw it on, and breathed a sigh of relief.

"Wait a minute," she said, turning to the rack. There was the towel, clean and dry as usual. But where was her chemise? She had left it on the rack to dry. She checked under the towel, and looked under the rack, but it wasn't there.

She walked back to the bedroom. She briefly admired the gowns, thinking, *I wouldn't have anywhere to wear those*, then went to open the wardrobe nearest the door. Or rather, nearest the doorway with splintered wood hanging from it, which caught her attention. She looked at the wood and her dad's words came to her: *'Karia, there's usually more than one way to get a job done. You and me, we do it the right way.'* She winced. She had found a way to open the door, but not the right way.

She turned back to the wardrobe and opened it. She almost expected to find her chemise here, as if the house was picking up after her. But her ratty old threadbare chemise was not here. There was a new chemise in the same simple style that a farm girl would wear. A plain, unbleached linen chemise. But – luxury of luxuries! – beside it was a second chemise just like it! Karia was excited. She had never had two chemises before.

Beside that was something she at first took for a very fine dress, but she looked closer. It was another chemise, of the nicest and whitest and richest fabric she had ever seen. It also had, well, some shape. It wasn't just a sack with arms, like her chemise and the others in the wardrobe. It was a woman's chemise. She looked down. *If only I had a shape.* She looked at the chemise again, and thought about the sheets. The sheets in the bed were silky and smooth beyond anything she had ever felt, but this! This felt like the surface was oiled, and it sort of shined like that too. She could not resist.

She took off the robe and put on the silky chemise. It felt light and airy and cool. She spun in place and laughed. This was a wonderful morning.

Then she looked at the two very practical chemises, and she knew that she had work to do, and this most certainly was not a chemise for working. Anyway, it sort of bagged where she was supposed to make it full, and that was embarrassing, perhaps even disappointing. Reluctantly, she took it off and hung it back up, running her hands over it one more time before picking up and putting on one of the tan linen chemises.

She walked over to the other closed wardrobe and opened it. Here were two simple dresses like she usually wore, but also brand new, and in very nice linen. And two again! Karia had never owned more than one dress at a time. She picked up one of the dresses. It was deep green, with darker trim. She liked it. She held it and looked at the other one. It was blue, a striking blue. Not a navy, not a medium blue, nor light blue. It was bright blue somewhat brighter than medium blue.

It was the color of her eyes.

Ian Fallis

CHAPTER TWENTY-FOUR

Karia put the dress back. No need to get something that nice dirty while she worked around the house. As she did she noticed something hanging on the back of the wardrobe, behind the two dresses. She dug into the wardrobe and saw there were two things: A stout travel cloak and a sturdy haversack. Well, she didn't need those.

She picked up the robe and said to the house, "Sorry for making you pick up after me." She stopped suddenly. Had the house said something back to her? She looked around and listened, but saw and heard nothing. She decided she was just imagining things.

As she picked up the robe, she noticed two pairs of shoes in the bottom of the closet. One pair was nice and sensible, sturdy and comfortable, much like her own farm boots but a little shorter. The other pair was almost like slippers, embroidered and beaded. She decided she'd check them out later.

She walked back into the waterfall room and hung the robe in its place. Then she looked at the waterfall. It was so inviting. But right now she was hungry.

She walked back to the kitchen and couldn't resist checking the bread. It was too early to tell if it was going to rise properly.

She fried up some potatoes and onions, and cut another wedge of cheese. There was a good deal more wine in the bottle she had opened, but this time she poured herself a cup. She served up the potatoes and onions on a plate and sat down at the table, using proper manners as she had been taught.

She got up from her meal and realized there was no washbasin. She looked down at the frying pan on the sideboard. It was the same one she had used for the turnip. She hadn't thought to wash it because her mom never washed their skillets. She simply wiped them out. But Karia remembered she had not even done that, and the skillet had been clean this morning. She rubbed her finger against the outside of the skillet and it came away clean. *Even the soot from the fire is cleaned off,* she thought.

87

"Well, what am I supposed to do?" she asked.

Study, she supposed. Learn Inamali.

She put her plate and the cup on the sideboard, and went back to the study. There was the paper she had written this morning. She picked it up and began reading it again.

"All that is expected of me? My destiny? The future that is set before me?" Those parts of the note jumped out at her. She couldn't remember writing them. The things about her father, about her mom and dad, about who she was, those made sense. She knew she wrote those things. And there in the same flowing hand were those other words.

"All that is expected of me. My destiny. The future that is set before me."

In the same flowing hand. In the same graceful, fine characters. She had written – and was reading – Inamali.

CHAPTER TWENTY-FIVE

Karia moved papers aside until she could again get at the large, ornate book she had left on the desk. The one with Tsilinakaya on the spine and what appeared to be the title page. She turned to the first page and began scanning the words. She remembered what many of the syllables meant, and consulted her papers for the others, so she could sound out the words.

But still it made little sense. She knew too few of these words; they were very long and they didn't seem to be in order.

She closed the book and thought a moment.

She put the book back on the shelf and reached again for the book on farming. She hefted it from the bottom shelf to the desk, and opened it to the first page. Then she began reading. And she was reading. She knew these words. These were words about farming, words she had read before in Teneka. She still had to sound out a few syllables and sort out some meanings. Here and there she came across words or even whole sentences that baffled her, but she kept moving forward.

She discovered that often, the words were not in the order she had expected them to be. For a while this confused her, but she began to sort it out. Words about time, or phrases about time, seemed to almost always come first in a sentence. And if a sentence started with a time word or phrase, the next word was the action word.

But then there were the sentences where the time phrase came second. The first words were long – four or five or even six characters. Then she saw that almost all of those first words had the same second and third characters – li and na. They were all action words, with lina inserted in the middle. This was really confusing; in Teneka, the action word came first only in commands, as in "Fetch some water." As she puzzled through it, she noted that the times in those sentences were always in the future. *Is that – lina – future tense in Inamali?*

Oh gosh, reading this is so much more than just sounding out the words. I need to learn all these words, and how they change in different situations. And I need to know how they put the words together into sentences.

But that's not all, she soon discovered.

She turned and got out the big book she had put back earlier, and opened it to the first page. She couldn't quite puzzle out what even the first sentence was saying, but she pushed on to the next one, and the next one, and the next one.

It is all out of order, she thought. *It's like it's backwards.*

She knew few of these words, so she could not be certain, but it seemed as if the first sentence of the book could not be understood until you read the rest of the paragraph.

She looked back at the farming book, and the sentences were in the order she would have expected them to be. She stopped and rubbed her eyes.

Enough, she thought. She left both books open on the desk and went to check on the bread. It had risen nicely, so she put another log on the fire and put the bread in the oven. When she straightened back up, she felt an ache in her back. *Standing is great for writing, but I need to sit down if I'm going to keep reading.*

She went back to the study and gathered her syllable papers. She tucked them into the farming book and carried that into the parlor. *No, I am not sitting in those ugly chairs.*

Anyway, the kitchen table was a better place for study, and she could keep an eye on the bread. She took the farming book to the table and opened it, spreading her syllable charts to the left. Then she went back and got the ornate book – the book she was beginning to think, only half-jokingly, was about her, because it bore the name Tsilinakaya.

She laid it on the table, open, to the right of the farming book, and sat down with the farming book on her left and the ornate book on her right. She glanced from book to book.

The words in the ornate book were so much bigger. She knew so few of them. She began to again despair of ever figuring out Inamali. She stood and stretched. She walked over and grabbed another nibble of cheese. She went and peeked through the vents at the bread. *Wait, I just put that in*, she thought, yet it was a nice golden brown. *The fire's too hot. It's just going to be dough in the middle.*

She felt terrible wasting the fine anarka flour, but there was nothing to be done about it. She fetched a paddle from the cupboard and opened the oven. She slid the paddle in to bring the bread out, and took it over to the sideboard. She went back and closed the oven, then put the paddle away and sighed.

Best be sure, she thought. She took a towel in her left hand and lifted the loaf, and then tapped on the bottom. It sounded hollow, telling her that the bread was properly baked.

Either that's a magical oven, or I've been looking at these books a lot longer than I thought.

Or maybe she just didn't understand time here. She had just assumed that time did not pass outside when she was here, and passed normally here. But was that right? What if time just passed more quickly here than outside? Or what if it passed differently here depending on what room she was in?

Karia closed her eyes and took a deep breath. She could almost hear her mom's voice in her head: *'You're a smart girl, Karia. Put aside everything else. Focus on the important thing.'* She realized she did not have enough information to figure out how time worked, and she was just guessing. And that wasn't the important thing. The important thing was learning Inamali. She had to read the books.

She went back to the books and scanned again from one to the other. She turned the pages and scanned, left and right, book to book. Something was right in front of her. She was missing something. On and on she went. She would look at the farming book, and it made sense, mostly. Then she'd look at the ornate book, and it was a jumble of mostly unfamiliar words, and the words she understood were in strange places. She didn't understand why, but she felt like she was right on the verge of getting it. Yet she wasn't getting it.

She glanced up and noticed the fire was out. She thought she had just put another log on. *No, that was when I put the bread in.* Even so, it should have been burning still. She walked over and put her hand above the remnants of the logs. They were still quite warm, so the fire had not been out for long.

She considered adding another log, but she wasn't sure how long she would be in the house and didn't want to use up all the wood when she didn't need a fire. She picked up the fireplace shovel and scraped the embers together to keep them warm longer so it would be easier to kindle a fire later. Karia leaned in too close and jumped back as a few small flames licked up, and then she laughed.

"Like I really need to keep the fire going," she said.

She went over to the bread and, as she now expected, it was cool. The wedge of cheese she had cut for breakfast was almost gone, so she finished it and cut another wedge, and sliced the bread. There was still a good cup of wine in the bottle, so she poured the rest of it into the cup she had used, and put some bread and cheese on the plate she had used. She took them to the table and sat on the opposite side of the books.

As she ate, she looked over at her syllable charts. She had not needed to consult them recently; she was able to sound out all the syllables without them now. Now she knew by heart that there were some variations in the way the characters were pronounced. The one that looked like an elaborate h could be na or nar, and the one she called the boat could be mi or ni, for instance. She puzzled over "tsilinki." It was the only word she had found where li and ki were pronounced like linki. *Maybe it's just linki in Teneka, or the pronunciation changed over time.*

She moved on, continuing to glance at the books as she tipped her head back to take a drink, and saw something. She put the cup down and got up and walked to the other side of the table, so she was looking at the books right-side up. Again she looked from one to the other, again and again, but now with growing excitement.

They're the same words.

CHAPTER TWENTY-SIX

Karia continued to scan from book to book. She was correct, mostly. A lot of the words in the ornate book were the same words as in the farming book, but they had other characters added to the front, or the back, or even in the middle, just like the future-tense action words had lina or linar as the second and third characters.

She decided to go back to the beginning. Without meaning to, she flipped all the way to the title page. She was about to turn to the first page of text when the title caught her eye. It seemed so familiar – and not just because it was her nickname. There was something else.

She went and got another piece of paper and the inkwell and quill, and came back to the table and wrote the word out. Tsilinakaya. She was about to cross out a couple of characters, but then it seemed almost blasphemous to cross out anything in Inamali. Instead she wrote the word again without li and na. Tsikaya. No, that still didn't make any sense.

She looked at the characters a while longer. She glanced over at the farming book, and her eyes settled on the word *krikaya*. She knew that word. It meant storehouse. She looked at it again. There was something else about that word. She wrote it down under the other words. She thought hard. She closed her eyes; that helped her think, and also helped her sore eyes, but she was getting a headache.

Opening her eyes again, she realized she was not just tired, but frustrated. *I thought making pants was hard work.* She walked back over and finished her lunch, and tried not to think about it.

She cleared her plate and cup from the table, then swept the crumbs into her hand and tossed them in the fireplace. She walked back over and looked at the books. She knew something was right in front of her, but she couldn't figure out what it was.

She thought she had had a good night's sleep, but now she felt very tired again. Perhaps she had been working longer than she thought. Maybe she was still weak from her ordeal with fire, or from making fire just now. *Or hours ago.* At any rate, learning to read Inamali was certainly hard work. She went back to the bedroom to lie down.

She remembered how good the sheets felt, and considered undressing. She immediately scolded herself. *What kind of a girl are you?* Then she thought, *I'm the kind of girl who's alone in a house with a bed that has soft, comfy sheets.*

Still feeling somewhat guilty anyway, she blushed as she took off her chemise and put it on the floor, where she hoped she would find it in the morning, and climbed into bed. As before, she fell asleep almost instantly.

CHAPTER TWENTY-SEVEN

Again Karia awoke sharply. She felt both fully rested and fully awake. Her thinking once more was clear and crisp, and there was just one thought in her mind this time. She threw the covers back and stood up, and remembered to look for her chemise. But it wasn't on the floor; it was back in the wardrobe. She threw it over her head and ran to the kitchen.

She took up the quill and under *krikaya* she wrote *krika*. Krikaya was storehouse. Krika was an action word, to store. Then she wrote *tsikaya* without the final ya: *tsika*. That word she knew. It meant to pledge or to promise. So did tsikaya mean a promise place? She looked back at the top of the paper, at Tsilinakaya. *A place of promise in the future? Why would Daddy call me a place of promise in the future?*

This had felt like a breakthrough, but now it seemed like just another puzzle.

Burn, she thought. *Riki. And fire is rikiya. It's not place, but ...* She could not think of words to express it. She settled on "thing." Fire is the burn thing, and storehouse is the storage thing. *So he called me promise in the future thing?*

She rifled through the farming book. To grow was *lili*, and a farm was *liliya*. She wrote those words. But what was farmer? *Right, that's lakima*. She wrote *lakima* on her paper, and then wrote *laki*. Of course — harvest.

But that was ma, not ya. And then there was the action word for smithing, *kraka*, and the word for a smith was *krakama*. She knew those words because the three families used them. In fact, many of the Inamali words she knew because the three families used them, which sometimes confused the people in town and on the other farms.

"We're Teneka Sil," Opa had explained to her. "Our clan had much more to do with the Inamali, so we use a lot more Inamali words on the farm. Best for you to learn and use the Teneka words, Karia."

And that had indeed turned out for the best, because now she knew some words in both languages, and they started spilling out onto the paper.

95

Bake and oven; drink and cup; wash and washbasin – each object word was the action word with ya on the end. *Ikrili and ikriliya*, she thought. "Hug and arm!" she said with a laugh. Of all the action words the Inamali could have used for arm, they used hug. Karia smiled. *Maybe they aren't all so scary after all.*

Then she thought about eat and plate, and her expression grew serious again. That was *seka* and *sekarai*. Stand and floor, and walk and ground, and run and lane – those all used rai.

So now she had ya, ma and rai as ways to make action words into objects. Maybe that's all they did. But she still felt like she was missing something.

She looked back at her paper. It was starting to look like just a jumble of characters that meant nothing. She ran through more object or person words in her head – she was surprised she knew so many. A lot of them ended in one of these syllables, but some did not follow this pattern at all.

She got up and rubbed her eyes. She noticed the dirty dishes and looked again for a washbasin to put them in. Again she could not find one. She looked at the cup and the plate. *Rikikaya* and *sekarai*. Drink and eat. *In and on!*

She went back to the paper. *Yes, you bake in an oven, and you burn in a fire.* "So what's a promise for the future in?"

The answer jumped into her head so sharply and clearly that she said it aloud.

"Me."

CHAPTER TWENTY-EIGHT

Karia's knees felt weak. Her eyes began to water. She was most certainly not crying. She had to sit down. She realized she was taking short, sharp breaths, and her heart was racing. She closed her eyes and took a deep breath.

I hold a promise for the future.

The words she had written in Inamali came back to her:

All that is expected of me. My destiny. The future that is set before me.

Fire and ashes! Again, there's something I'm missing! Something familiar about those words, and I can't remember what it is!

She took another deep breath and opened her eyes. She blinked to clear the tears, then got up and used a towel to wipe her face. *I don't cry.* She still felt unsteady on her feet, weak and somewhat dizzy, so she leaned against the sideboard.

Her thoughts were getting jumbled again. It was as if disjointed, incomplete sentences were dancing a ragged jig in her head. She could almost hear the tune – a happy tune. Certainly not a refined one. It was simple. Fresh and clear. It was almost as if she caught a fleeting glimpse in her mind of a big tree in a huge meadow, but then it was gone, lost in the thoughts swirling inside her.

One thought jumped to the front. *My dad called me Tsil, short for Tsilinakaya. Someone who holds a promise for the future – if I'm understanding that correctly. Maybe I'm not. Maybe … no, back to the point.* If her mom called her that, her mom, who was Inamali like she was, and could do magic like she could, had called her that, it would make more sense. But her dad? What did he know that he had not told her?

She was taking short, sharp breaths again. She closed her eyes and stopped her breathing, then took a deep breath and held it. She exhaled slowly, then took another deep breath and exhaled. She opened her eyes.

She looked around the room. She was not used to eating alone, to cooking for just herself. She had seldom been alone, and never for this long. She began to feel very lonely. She missed her mom most of all. She

97

thought about the last words she had said to her mom, and she was ashamed. No, Failean was not the woman who gave birth to her. And she had not told Karia the truth. But in spite of everything, she was Mom. Karia missed the feeling of her presence, and wanted to tell her she loved her for all she had been for her. *My family isn't my family but they're still my family,* she reminded herself.

I need to go home.

She had learned so much here, but she felt like the answers she needed now, she needed from her mom and dad.

She took the books and papers, and the inkwell and pen, back to the desk. She put the books away and made a neat stack of the papers on the desk.

She went back to the kitchen and spread the ashes in the fireplace so they would cool harmlessly. She glanced around, and felt all was as tidy as it could be. But she hated to waste the bread and cheese. There was still more than half a round of cheese and most of a loaf of bread. *Oh well.*

She walked to the bedroom and drew out the green dress. Then she thought of seeing Timbal again, and put the green dress away. As she did, she noticed the haversack, so she took it out and put it on the bed. She pulled out the dress that matched her eyes, put it over her head and smoothed it down over her chemise. She glanced longingly at the embroidered slippers, but picked up the sensible shoes and put them on.

She took the haversack to the kitchen, but then went back to the bedroom. She made the bed, except for the bedspread. This she moved to the side, by the dressers, and she realized she had never looked inside them. *When I come back,* she thought.

Walking past the dressing table mirror she caught sight of her hair. Wild was an understatement. She sat and brushed it. At first, that was more like beating it into submission, but soon she had the knots out and her mind was on her reflection: the auburn hair that matched a few freckles across the bridge of her nose, her vibrant eyes and the dress that matched them. *I'm pretty,* she thought. That surprised her. She usually thought of herself as a stick-girl. She thought her nose was too small and too sharp. She thought people stared at her eyes because they were strange. And she most definitely did not think freckles were attractive. She couldn't recall any time she had ever thought of herself as pretty.

She looked at her reflection again. She was still a stick. Her nose was small and sharp. Her eyes were a color of blue that no one else had. And freckles – oh my, she certainly had freckles. But altogether, she realized, she wasn't looking at the awkward little girl, someone boys would consider a playmate. She was a young woman – though she thought, *I'm becoming a young woman.* It scared her and thrilled her at the same time.

Am I really pretty? she asked herself. She stared into the mirror, and could not answer that. She thought, *Maybe,* then caught herself staring at her own reflection. She was embarrassed. She felt like she was acting vain. She put down the brush and hastened to the kitchen. She picked up the haversack and was about to open it when she noticed a pattern on the flap of leather that folded over to close it. The pattern was worked in the leather and hard to see. She ran her finger over it to trace it, and jumped back when the pattern glowed and made her finger tingle.

The whole pattern briefly shone like hammered gold for a moment, then faded back to the color of the rest of the leather. It was a pattern she had seen before: a vertical cross, with a line connecting the right and top bars, sort of like a backwards numeral four. It was the pattern her mom had taught her to carve into the top of a loaf of rising bread.

She gently touched it again, and nothing happened. But as she rubbed her finger across it, again the whole pattern glowed and her finger tingled. *Magic,* she thought. *Wonderful.*

She opened the haversack, put the cheese and bread in, and went to the door at the end of the hall. She braced herself to go home. She knew it could be difficult. But she took a deep breath, opened the door and stepped through.

Into her own home's kitchen.

Ian Fallis

CHAPTER TWENTY-NINE

Karia looked around the kitchen, surprised. Then she heard a commotion outside.

She put the haversack on the table, went to the door – which had been left open – and looked out. She was just in time to see Narek leading the men toward the forest. *Where is Timbal?* she thought.

Then she heard yelling coming from Aunt Heather's house. She saw her mom backing away from the porch, and Karia stepped back so she was just peering around the door.

"Haven't you done enough harm?!" Karia recognized Aunt Heather's voice, coming from the direction of her house. "Go home! Stay away from my boy! By Gnome's Arm, pray that they never find that witch, or I'll kill her myself!"

Karia stepped farther away from the door. *Witch? What witch?* She was wondering what that had to do with her mom staying away from Timbal, when she heard her mom coming up the steps and onto the porch. She stepped back farther.

Her mom walked into the house and closed the door behind her. Then she turned around and saw Karia – and froze.

"Mom, what's going on?" she asked. "Why wasn't Timbal with the others? And what's this about a witch? Has something happened to Timbal?"

Her mom did not answer, but ran to Karia and wrapped her in her arms. Then she took her by the hand – "Quick!" – and led her to her room and shut the door.

"How did you get here?" her mom asked. She looked Karia up and down. "Where did you get that dress?"

"I'm not sure. I was in the forest. Then I was here."

"Narek told the men he thought he knew where to find you, so they followed him to the forest. Avar is very angry, and your dad and Opa went along to make sure nothing happened to you if they found you."

"Avar is angry?" Karia asked. "Why?"

"Because of what you did just now to Timbal."

Just now? Karia had to think a moment. To her, a couple of days had passed since she went to the house in the Old Wood. But if time did not pass there, in reality, she had only just now run across the field. This was so confusing. First she lost a few days, now she'd gained a few. But what had she done? She just pushed him away. Hard, yes, but …

"I hurt him?"

"Yes, dear, you hurt him. Nana is …"

Karia started toward the door and interrupted, "I have to go to him."

Her mom got in the way. "No, Karia, let Nana take care of him. You and I need to stay away from there right now. Aunt Heather is angry too."

"I'm the witch," Karia said, suddenly realizing what Aunt Heather had meant and stepping back from her mom.

"You are not a witch," her mom said.

"Yes I am — I work magic and hurt people. I'm a witch."

"Karia," her mom said sternly, "you are an Inamali. You still need to learn to control your abilities, but that is different from stealing magic and using it to harm others. A mistake doesn't make you a witch."

Karia lowered her head. She felt confused again.

"Hold your head up," her mom scolded. Karia lifted her head. "I'm afraid this is partly my fault. I'm sorry that there are things I have not told you. I thought I was protecting you. Instead, I've left you unprepared for your destiny, for the future set before you."

"I don't want a destiny!" Karia shouted.

"Keep your voice down. No one must know you are back."

Karia nodded. "But Mom …"

Her mom softened. She reached up and brushed back a lock of Karia's hair that had fallen across her cheek. "You'll find, my dear little Karia, that a truly full life is not about what we want, but about serving others. And you have an opportunity to serve many."

Dear little Karia. Oh, gosh, can't I just go back to being twelve-year-old dear little Karia? I'll even take thirteen or fourteen. That's when the gross stuff had started happening with her body, and what her mom told her didn't make it any better. *Yuck.* But this was worse. Far worse.

"Mom, I don't like all the stuff that's happened. I didn't mean to hurt Timbal; I love him. Why can't you just be happy for me? Why do I have to have some other mother and father? Why can't I just have you and Daddy? Why do I have to be Inamali? Why does it matter? Why can't I just be the wife of a Teneka farmer and have lots of little boys and girls who call you Nana?"

Her mom closed her eyes and took a deep breath. *Is that where I get that from?*

"Would it matter to you, Karia," her mom said, "if you knew that the woman who gave birth to you thought you had an important destiny, and gave her life to protect you?"

Karia didn't know how to answer.

"Does it matter to you that the Dr'Zhak are hunting down and killing the last of your people, and robbing and enslaving the Teneka?"

"And does it matter to you that your father chose to have you raised as a Teneka, so that when your power rose inside you, you would have compassion for your fellow man instead of the superior contempt that we thought raised us up, but actually brought us down?"

Karia just stared at her mom. Her mom stepped closer, put her hands on Karia's shoulders and spoke softly.

"I think those things matter to my Karia. And I think that if I gave her the choice of hiding and living a perfectly normal life as just another Teneka, or creating a place where the races really could live in harmony, she'd choose to create that place, whatever it cost."

Karia looked into her mom's eyes. She saw that her mom was tearing up, but also that she had that same look she had when Karia showed her the pants. *She's proud of me*, Karia thought.

"I don't know where to start, Mom," she said. "I still have so many questions."

"You're a smart girl, Karia," her mom said. "Put aside everything else. Focus on the important thing. What do you know?"

"Not much."

"I know it might feel that way, but let's work through what you know, and then we'll fill in the important gaps."

"OK," Karia said reluctantly. "Where do I start?"

"Let me help you. You know you are an Inamali, and your father was a great sorcerer and your mother died to protect you. You know that Reva and I took you in and raised you as our own child."

"Dad knows too, doesn't he?" Karia asked.

"Knows what?"

"About my destiny. That's why he called me Tsilinakaya, right?"

"Not exactly, dear. You see, we weren't able to have children, so when we were given the opportunity to raise you, your dad and I were overjoyed. Your mother called you Tsilinakaya, and somehow your dad found out and he thought it meant hope, which it sort of does, and he really liked that. But I insisted on keeping the name she gave you, Karia. It wasn't safe to call you by a name that was so clearly Inamali, or to have your dad use it."

"Then why did Dad keep calling me Tsil?"

Her mom laughed and put her hands on Karia's shoulders. It was good to hear her mom laugh. "Do you think I could keep him from doing that, any more than I could keep him from calling you Tsilinki?"

Karia laughed. "No, I guess not. But … Tsilinakaya … that means something like 'container of promise for the future,' right?"

Her mom looked surprised and proud. "How and when did you work that out?"

"In the last couple of days, in the house."

"What are you talking about, Karia?"

"I was in the house – the place my father made for me. Between the time I … I hurt Timbal and ran off into the forest, until just before you met me here, I spent two or three days there."

"So that's what the letter was talking about," her mom said.

"Yes."

"I'm sorry about burning the letter, dear," her mom said. "I was trying to protect you. I didn't think it was time yet for you to know all this. But I think I was wrong. Can you forgive me?"

Karia hugged her mom, and her mom hugged her back. "Oh yes. Can you forgive me for calling you a liar and running off, Mom?"

"Yes, dear. Everything is forgiven. But not forgotten."

"What do you mean, Mom?"

"I've learned the hard way that I cannot shield you," she said. "I've only hurt you. And I think you've learned that running away isn't an answer."

"Yes, Mom."

CHAPTER THIRTY

Karia was about to ask what had happened to the letter when she realized where she'd seen the words about her future.

"You didn't tell everyone everything the letter said, did you?" Karia asked.

"Well," her mom said reluctantly, "no."

"You left out the part about my destiny and future, right?"

"Yes, Karia, I did."

"Why?"

"The others would never have agreed to let you live among them if they knew what the letter said."

"What did it say?"

Karia's mom looked down. "The words your father used – the way he talked about your destiny and the future before you – they're words about Tsilinakaya."

"But I am Tsilinakaya," Karia said.

"Karia, Tsilinakaya isn't a name. Well, no, that's wrong, it is a name. Oh, dear, I'm not sure how to explain it to you."

"Am I a witch, like Aunt Heather said?"

Her mom looked up. "No, dear, no, certainly not! This is nothing bad, it's just … very difficult to explain. And Uncle Avar only thinks he knows. What he thinks is based on old stories the Teneka have passed down – and altered here and there over the years."

"You mean like Inamali being twelve feet tall, with flaming hair and magical powers?"

"Oh, that's all true, Karia," her mom said. "Sort of, anyway. But that's not what we're talking about. No, let me try to explain, but please don't interrupt me, so you don't get the wrong picture from just part of the story."

Karia really wanted to know how the twelve-foot tall and flaming hair part could all be true, but she nodded for her mom to go on. Her mom had a hard enough time telling a story, and Karia didn't want to get in her way.

"The Inamali have no leaders. No kings, no chiefs, no captains or sergeants even. But we have Tsilinakaya. The Teneka think just of the power that person has – magical power, power to lead, power to rule. That's what your Uncle Avar thinks of when he thinks about Tsilinakaya. And I suppose that's all true. But there's also sacrifice and responsibility. The path of a Tsilinakaya is never easy, and it's usually very lonely. And – now, this part would be very controversial, and I'm sure there are Inamali who are a lot more learned than I am who would disagree with me – I think each Tsilinakaya has some very specific thing they need to do. And I don't think any of them got to choose what that was, or even knew what it was. It was just sort of thrust upon them, and they had to respond. I think it's always carried great personal cost."

She paused. "So your mother called you Tsilinakaya, and you're demonstrating that you are Tsilinakaya. But you could not continue to be known as Tsilinakaya. That would have been too obvious. She might as well have named you Irina."

"Irina?" Karia asked.

"She was the last Tsilinakaya."

CHAPTER THIRTY-ONE

"Wait, Irina was twelve feet tall, with flaming hair and magical powers," Karia said.

"Yes," her mom answered.

"You told me I wouldn't be twelve feet tall with flaming hair."

"I told you that you wouldn't be twelve feet tall," her mom said. "I didn't say anything about flaming hair."

"What?!"

"I'm just kidding you, Karia. No, you won't be twelve feet tall with flaming hair."

Karia took a breath and saw her mom smiling at her. "Well, that's good. I'd hate to keep catching pillows on fire. And it'd be really hard on brushes," she said.

They shared a nervous laugh.

"Dear, remember, we know who and what you are by the power inside you. But we don't know your destiny. Our people cannot see the future. That's something only Dr'Zhak prophets can do."

Karia had heard stories about that, but hearing it from her mom was another matter entirely. "I wish I could see the future," she said.

"That certainly sounds nice, doesn't it?" her mom said. "But I don't think it is. How would you ever know if you were right? I mean, if you knew a bad thing was coming, you would do everything in your power to avoid it, and if you succeeded, wouldn't that mean you were wrong about the future? And if you couldn't avoid it, what's the good of seeing the future?

"Gosh, I need to stop rambling. We have a problem right here. We need to hide you from everyone else, and we can't hide you in your room."

"That would be kind of obvious, wouldn't it?" Karia said.

"Yes, dear."

"But Mom, why do I have to hide? Can't we just work all of this out? I know Timbal will forgive me, and then Uncle Avar and Aunt Heather will have to forgive me."

Her mom put her hands on Karia's shoulders. "I know this might be hard for you to understand, but you really scared Timbal. And people who are scared don't act the way you expect them to."

"But Mom …"

"Karia, don't you know that your Aunt Heather loves you too?"

"I guess so."

"And if you heard what she called you, you also know what she threatened to do to you."

'Pray that they never find that witch, or I'll kill her myself,' Karia thought. "Oh." She paused. She hadn't thought about that. "But what about Opa and Nana? They'd reason with her, right? They'd never let her hurt me." Karia wasn't all that certain Uncle Avar and Aunt Heather really did love her, but she was pretty sure Opa did, and absolutely certain Nana loved her.

"They have their own reasons for fearing you right now, Karia. We need to hide you."

"Do I have to hide from Daddy?"

Her mom sighed and smiled. "I'm sorry, dear, but your dad couldn't keep a secret if your life depended on it, and it would. We'd have to keep it a secret from him."

"OK," she said.

"This way," her mom said, taking Karia by the hand and opening her bedroom door.

That was when Nana said, "Secrets got us into this mess, didn't they, Failean?"

CHAPTER THIRTY-TWO

"How dare you come into my house uninvited!" Karia's mom shouted.

"I could toss some sharp words your way too, Failean, but that's not going to get us anywhere," Nana replied calmly. She turned to Karia. "I do have my reasons for fearing you, dear, but I also love you, almost as much as your mom here does, and I'm just as determined to keep you safe now as I was before I knew what you are. Because I also know who you are."

"Helena," her mom said, "how much did you hear?"

"Enough to confirm the suspicions I've had ever since I heard what that dear, sweet ox of a man you married nicknamed Karia."

"You knew what Tsilinakaya meant?"

"Had my suspicions, Failean. Picked up quite a bit of the Inamali language. It's a real brain-tweaker. Can't do any magic, though. Wish I could. Opa sure has gotten wrinkly. Oh, well. What matters is what Karia is, and how we get the others to calm down and take her back in."

"Nana, can I talk with you a moment?" Karia's mom asked.

"Dear, I think the time has passed when we can talk about things related to Karia's future without Karia being involved."

Karia's mom looked at her daughter. Karia realized that if it was hard for her to remember she wasn't just a girl, it must be harder for her mom. "You're right," her mom said. "This is going to be tough for you and her to hear. But it has to be said. Karia's great personal costs could be your great personal costs."

"I understand that, Failean," Nana said, looking sad but determined.

"I'd never hurt you," Karia said to Nana.

"That's very sweet of you to say, dear. But I think you will. You may have to."

"I couldn't!" Karia said.

"You must do what your destiny calls you to do, young lady," Nana said. "No matter what it costs you or the ones who love you. You really don't have a choice in the matter. But there's not time to debate this. Not now, at any rate. The men left before having lunch, so they won't be searching long before they come back for food. Men have their priorities, you know. We need to get you hidden until we can work this out." She turned toward the door.

Karia, remembering that Nana had been tending to Timbal, asked, "Nana, is Timbal going to be OK?"

Nana laughed. "Oh, yes dear. He'll heal up just fine. But it's going to take a while. You broke four of his ribs."

"Oh no," Karia said.

"But I don't doubt that as soon as he's up and about he'll be thinking about you every day."

"You think so?" Karia beamed.

"Oh yes. Probably several times a day. You made the crotch of his new pants too tight."

CHAPTER THIRTY-THREE

Nana made sure Heather was inside tending to Timbal and none of the men were back yet, then she and Failean took Karia up to the hay loft in the barn. They arranged the bales so she had a hiding place. That wasn't a long-term solution, but they thought they could convince everyone to reconsider soon.

It didn't take Karia long to realize she could see the farm through gaps in the barn roof. Narek had been told to patch it. As she looked west over all three houses and sheds – and could even see all the way across their fields to the Old Wood from up here – she was glad for Narek's irresponsibility.

She watched Nana take her mom to Aunt Heather's house, in front of the barn and to the right. She could even see them going up the steps onto the covered front porch. Behind that, mostly hidden behind Aunt Heather's, was her house. Aside from the color of the trim – red instead of green – the little tan box-like houses looked identical.

Nana's house, of which she could see the back on her left, was the only one that was much different. It was the same efficient, inexpensive, simple box – even the inside layout of all three houses was identical – but it was bright green with white trim, and ringed with bushes and flowering plants. Karia smiled. Growing tsilinki was hard work. But Nana's plants made working in the soil fun.

Her smile faded as she saw the men returning across the field. Their faces were set in expressions of concern. Even her dad was lacking his usual smile. And they did not speak. Karia could remember few times when they were not joking or at least talking as they came home across the fields, no matter how hard the labor of the day. But this was different.

They split up and headed for their own houses. She lost sight of her dad, and Opa and Narek, but watched Uncle Avar go into his house. She heard a sharp exchange, but it ended quickly. Her mom and Nana came out, each going to her own house.

111

Karia watched for a short time longer, but there really wasn't anything else to see. She sat down and looked around. She had nothing to do either. She tried weaving the straw, but it was cut too short to make anything. She stretched and lay back, with her hands behind her head. She could just barely see clouds going past through the gaps in the roof. She wasn't sleepy at all, but she had been there for a while now, and she wished she had brought along one of the books from the house in her haversack.

My haversack! she thought, sitting up quickly. *I left it on the kitchen table! What will Mom tell Dad if he sees it?*

She sprung to her feet just as she heard someone on the ladder to the hay loft. *Did they hear me sit up? Did they hear me stand?* Karia was near panic. She froze. Someone was stepping across the loft, coming straight to her hiding place. She thought about throwing the hay loft doors wide open and jumping, but it had to be at least twenty feet down. She had to do something, but she ran out of time.

A man's large hand reached over one of the bales and moved it aside.

"Thanks for the cheese," her dad said.

Karia ran to him and clambered over the bales to give him a big hug. He hugged her back. "I was worried about you, Karia."

"Don't worry, Daddy. I'm fine."

"That's why you're hiding in a hay loft, then."

"Mom and Nana thought it best."

"Well, your mom and Nana worked things out with your Aunt Heather – sort of – and Nana can take care of Opa. So unless Avar wants to take things up with me, I'd say we're all set."

"You mean I can come down?"

"I mean you can come home, Tsil."

They climbed down the ladder from the loft and walked home, her long fine-fingered hand in his big, thick strong hand, just like she used to walk with him. She felt safe again.

CHAPTER THIRTY-FOUR

The three of them ate dinner early. Her mom and dad ate the bread she made and some of the cheese. Karia was rather tired of the cheese, but happy for another slice – or two – of the fine, light loaf she had made. And she was glad that her mom and dad seemed to like the cheese and bread. Her mom also boiled some cabbage with a little salt pork, and that was a good meal by her family's standards.

Karia told them all about the house, and what she had done, and most of all, what she had learned. Her dad seemed to be trying to look pleased, but she wasn't sure he really was. Karia's mom smiled at times, but at others seemed concerned, or perhaps even worried. Through it all, though, she thought she could tell that they were both proud of her, and since, truth be told, she was rather proud of herself too, their looks didn't stop her from going on and on.

After dinner, Karia helped her mom tidy up while her dad went to check the horse. Then her mom asked her to sit in the parlor, lit one of the lamps, and went into her bedroom. Karia felt awkward; they didn't often sit in the parlor. That was where her dad found her, sitting, waiting, when he came back. Her mom returned with her grandfather's diary.

She sat next to Karia and opened it.

"Are you sure that's a good idea, Failean?" he asked.

"I should have done this years ago," her mom said.

Her dad did not look happy, but said no more about it. "I'm going to bed. It's been a long day today, and I barely got anything done, so tomorrow's going to be even tougher."

"Goodnight," her mom said.

"Goodnight," Karia said.

"And goodnight to you two too," he said. "To you two too," he repeated softly, chuckled, then went into the bedroom and closed the door.

Karia turned her attention to the book. She was eager to find out what was in it.

113

But her mom kept it closed and quietly said, "There is one thing you didn't mention about the house, Karia, so I need to ask you about it."

Karia nodded.

"Your father is likely to have put weapons there, and you haven't been trained in the use of weapons. So I need you to tell me if there are any weapons there, even a dagger," she said.

"No, Mom," Karia responded. "The most dangerous thing in the house is the kitchen knives – and, I guess, me."

"OK," her mom said. "Just make sure, if you come across any weapons, even something as small as a dagger – they can be very dangerous no matter how ornate or pretty they are, and you need to let me know, and you should probably even bring them here for safekeeping. OK?"

"Yes, Mom."

"Good," she said, and held up the book. "This is my grandfather's diary," her mom said. "His name was Jiki – yes, just like the bean. He sure got enough ribbing about that! He wasn't an altogether outstanding man, and I'm afraid you won't find this a very thrilling book, but I think that if we work through it together, I can teach you enough to help you read the other books."

They started moving through the book together, with Karia's mom explaining how words were put together and how sentences were formed, and showing Karia different ways her grandfather had written about different topics. It was indeed, as Nana had said, "a real brain-tweaker," and going through the book was hard work. But Karia was enjoying learning, and her mom was having fun teaching her.

Something else was happening as well, something Karia didn't realize at first. Her mom wasn't treating her like a little girl, she was treating her like a woman. They were not interacting so much like mother and daughter, as they were like sisters. Older, wiser sister and younger sister, to be sure. But sisters nonetheless. Karia had never had a sister. *If this is what it's like, I sure wouldn't mind having a sister.*

CHAPTER THIRTY-FIVE

Karia and her mom were so deep into the diary that they were startled when her dad came back out of the bedroom.

"Have you two been at this all night?" he asked.

"I suppose so," her mom answered.

"No we haven't," Karia said with a smile and a wink. "Not yet. And now we're going to stop and make you breakfast." She stood up and hugged her dad. She couldn't get enough of that lately. She was stretching a little each time to see if she'd grown enough to reach all the way around him yet.

"Breakfast is supposed to be over at Avar's this morning," her dad said.

"I'm not sure any of us would be particularly welcome there right now," her mom said.

"I thought you worked everything out with Heather," her dad said.

"Mostly, and that's just Heather. You still need to talk with Avar."

"Ah. Right." It did not appear to Karia that he was looking forward to that task. "Well, I suppose it's just the three of us, then."

Karia and her mom made breakfast, and the three of them ate before her dad went off to the fields and Karia and her mom went to bed.

Karia was having a wonderful dream about fixing the barn roof with Timbal when she realized the hammering in her dream was actually someone knocking on the door. She leapt out of bed, ran to the door and opened it. Narek stood there, and the way his eyes drifted downward reminded her she was in her chemise.

"Hey, Narek, I'm up here!"

He looked up into her eyes and turned bright red, before looking straight down at the porch.

"My mom and dad are making the run to town this morning," he said, "and since you made such a mess of yesterday, they didn't get your mom's list."

She ignored the accusation. "OK," she said, and she turned and headed for her mom's room. Halfway there she turned and – yes, she was right, Narek was eyeing her backside. "Hey!" she said, and again he turned red and looked straight down. She didn't like him looking at her like that; it made her feel dirty. But making him blush was kind of fun.

Karia knocked on her mom's door and went in. She tried to explain why she was there. But her mom didn't really wake up, and handed Karia a small piece of paper from the nightstand. Karia looked at it and smiled. This was no shopping list. It was a love note from her dad. She didn't know he wrote her love notes. *That is so sweet.* But it wasn't exactly going to help Opa and Nana at the store.

She was about to leave when she spotted her mom's ring on the nightstand as well. She never knew her mom took it off at night; she had never really thought about it. She picked up the ring. It was much lighter than she expected, and as she touched it, the green stone flashed. She thought at first it was just the glint of a reflection, but then she noticed that the ring felt oddly sticky. It was as if it was trying to stay in contact with her, and was drawing something out of her. She put it down quickly and the stone dimmed. She backed out of the bedroom with the note, staring at the ring. She closed the door and turned to Narek.

"Just a minute," she said. Head-on, Narek kept his head down. Karia went to the kitchen and put the love note on the table, and found a list on the counter which she took to Narek. He accepted it without looking up and turned to leave. She was about to slam the door after him, but instead mostly closed it so she could look out from behind it.

"Narek," she said.

He turned around, keeping his head down.

"Please don't look at me like that. It's not very nice."

"I ... I ... didn't mean it," he said.

Didn't mean it?! Now she slammed the door.

CHAPTER THIRTY-SIX

Karia tried to go back to bed, but she was angry and couldn't relax. So she went back to the parlor and started reading the diary where she and her mom had left off.

She made slow progress without her mom, and not just because she still needed help reading Inamali. It was also deadly dull at times. Her great-grandfather – *no*, she corrected herself, *my mom's grandfather* – in one span went on for four pages about trimming his beard. Or it could have been his hooves – the words were the same – but she didn't think that was right. After that, she was very glad she didn't have a beard. Or hooves.

She was greatly relieved when her dad came in for lunch. She took the opportunity to give him another hug, and then set about waiting on him. He found the love note on the table, and seemed embarrassed. She thought that was cute, and she told him how it got there. She left out the part about Narek being creepy. She didn't much like Narek, but she didn't want to know what her dad would do if he found out Narek had been leering at her. Maybe she didn't altogether dislike Narek after all. The way he acted, sure. But he was sort of like a brother to her. *My brother, looking at me that way ... ew!*

She looked up at her dad and realized that he probably didn't even know Narek was that sort of boy. He always gave people the benefit of the doubt, and forgave freely and easily. She remembered the price he paid for their horse, and how upset her mom had been. "That horse trader took advantage of you," she said. Her mom could tell the horse was older than the trader had let on.

"He probably just made a mistake," her dad replied. That made her mom angrier, but he just smiled. He did go and talk with the trader later, and Karia went with him, and he was very friendly and kind, but firm. She couldn't understand why he wasn't more upset.

He told her, "Karia, I figure if other people can forgive all the mistakes I've made, I can forgive one or two by them." She had a hard time believing he made many mistakes, but as she thought about all the times in the last week – *or is it two weeks?* – she'd hurt him and her mom, and Timbal and, gosh, just about everyone, she realized that it was very good to live forgiven and forgiving, and to give people the benefit of the doubt.

When he got up to go back to the fields, she stood up and gave him yet another hug. He ran his hand through her hair and said, "Karia, I think you're growing again." He was so happy about it that she smiled back at him, but she did not want to be growing anymore. She was already a tsilinki. A tall, skinny, pale stalk.

She set about clearing the table and after a short while noticed he had left his knife on the bench. She hurried out the door and was down the porch steps before she realized he was already out of sight. But Uncle Avar was just going back. He fixed her with an ugly stare, and she backed slowly up the stairs and into the house.

After she closed the door she was shaking. Her dad was out in the fields and her mom was sleeping. Opa, Nana and Narek were in town. Timbal was bedridden. What would she have done if Uncle Avar had followed her? She looked down at the knife in her hand.

No, she thought. *No, I could never do that. I could never stab another person.*

Then she wondered if she really felt that way, or was just trying to convince herself of that.

CHAPTER THIRTY-SEVEN

Karia's mom got up soon after lunch, and Karia helped her get bread and soup going for dinner. Then Karia went to check on the mending. She knew it was probably starting to pile up.

But before she could start, her mom came and got her. The two of them went back to the diary. She told her mom what she had read so far, and was very pleased to hear that her mom's Grandpa Jiki did not have hooves. They dug back in, and the reading came easier and easier to Karia. By the time her dad came home for dinner, she was reading aloud smoothly and understanding what she was reading, though she needed occasional help with a word here or there that she didn't recognize.

She and her mom were in great spirits, so they were surprised by the expression on her dad's face when he came in. He looked worried.

"Opa and Nana aren't back from town yet," he said.

"They got a late start," Karia observed. "Narek didn't come by for our list until, well, it was about mid-morning."

"Still shoulda been back by now. Wonder if I ought to get Avar and go check the road while there's still light."

"I'll go get Avar," her mom said. "Karia, go hitch the wagon." Karia started for the door. "Karia, for goodness sake, girl, put a dress on." Karia scurried back to her room to put on her dress and shoes, embarrassed to be corrected about that in front of her dad.

She overhead him saying softly, "I keep forgetting she's not a girl anymore."

Karia went to the barn and gathered all the parts for the horse's bridle. She seldom did this, but it was very similar to hitching him to the plow, and that she had done many times before she turned fifteen. She went to the horse, which her dad had named Rosebud.

She remembered the debate that name had started around the dinner table, shortly after they got the huge draft horse. "She's not exactly sweet-smelling," her mom had said.

119

"It's just a sign of affection, so she feels loved," her dad replied.

"I'm not sure you should be showing any sign of weakness around such a great big horse," her mom countered.

And ever since then, she had not been Rosebud to Karia, but the Great Smelly Beast.

Karia bridled her and hitched her to the wagon, then watched with a little fear as her dad and Uncle Avar, looking grim and not saying a word to her or her mom, mounted the wagon and headed off down the road to town.

Karia turned to her mom. "Do you think something bad happened to Opa and Nana?"

"No, dear. Your dad is just being careful. Let's go back inside."

They set dinner out in anticipation of her dad's return, then went back to the book. But Karia could not concentrate. The later and the darker it got, the more she worried. When she heard the sound of wagons, she ran outside ahead of her mom. Her dad and Uncle Avar were back, followed by Opa and Nana and Narek in their wagon.

As she ran to the wagon, her dad dismounted and handed her the reins. "Brush her well, Karia. I pushed her a bit tonight."

Oh, wonderful, she thought. *I get to take care of the Great Smelly Beast again.* She really wanted to know what had happened. And then it got worse. Narek was leading Opa's horse to the barn as well. And he looked excited.

What I wouldn't give right now to be wearing that big traveling cloak on top of this dress, she thought.

But Narek busied himself with taking care of his dad's wagon and horse. He had done it a lot more than she had, and was finished while she was still brushing. She was surprised when he came over and helped her.

"Guess what we saw, Karia!" he said.

"A two-headed purple Dr'Zhak," she said.

"No," he said. He seemed to be seriously considering the possibility that there were two-headed purple Dr'Zhak, so Karia spoke again.

"I was kidding, Narek."

"Oh. Fine. Didn't see one anyway. No, Karia, a carnival's come to town, and my dad talked to some of the other farmers who were in town and decided we'd all have our evening in town the day after tomorrow! It'll be the biggest and best Gathering, in, well, I don't know how long!"

"A carnival!" Karia exclaimed. "With games and songs and foods?"

"And more, Karia – they have storytellers and a magician!"

Karia almost squealed. It was exciting enough that a carnival was in town. The last one came through when she was eleven. She still remembered some of the special foods baked or brought in for that occasion. There were even apples, the big red juicy ones from the cold mountains where the Teneka Dhu lived. She could almost taste them now. The apples, not the Teneka Dhu.

But with a storyteller and a magician? She had heard tales of the carnivals of old, with storytellers and magicians, but those had ceased before she had ever been to a carnival. The Dr'Zhak frowned on the old stories and magic. But she wasn't thinking about that. She was just excited that an old-fashioned carnival was in town, and she was going to get to see it.

Her mom had a few misgivings about going, but Opa and Nana convinced her. And that night it was settled. The day after tomorrow, following morning chores, everyone but Avar and Timbal would head into town. Timbal was not able to travel yet, and Avar was to stay and keep an eye on him and the farm.

They would set their tents in the field by the river, enjoy the carnival into the evening, and come home the next morning. Karia was so excited that it did not even dawn on her that Timbal would not be there with her.

Ian Fallis

CHAPTER THIRTY-EIGHT

The following day flew by, and early the next morning, while the men were in the fields, Nana, Heather, Failean and Karia packed up food and the tents and blankets and loaded the wagons. Aunt Heather gave Karia a wide berth, and did not speak to her. That was fine with Karia; she planned on having a good time at the carnival regardless of who she was with or not with.

When the men came home for a real breakfast, each family went to their own house, but soon everyone was done eating and Narek and Karia were hitching the wagons. She wasn't sure how taking care of the horse suddenly became her job, but right now she didn't mind. She would have taken on almost any chore to be able to go to the carnival.

Everyone started to climb aboard the wagons, but before Karia could climb to the front bench of her parents' wagon, Aunt Heather climbed up and sat next to her mom, taking the seat where Karia usually sat. Her mom looked down and said, "You're riding with Opa and Nana." She began to walk toward the bench when Nana, with a sweet smile, said, "You ride in back with Narek, dear."

She was so looking forward to the carnival that she was not going to let even this dampen her mood. She went to the tail of the wagon, where a canopy had been put up to deflect the dust, and sat down next to Narek.

They fell in behind her parent's wagon, and she glared right back at Uncle Avar as he receded into the distance and soon could not be seen anymore because of the dust. She thought about shooting just a tiny little flame his way, but realized that with her inexperience, they might hit a bump and she'd release a fireball and burn down one of the houses.

And that would keep me from going to the carnival, she thought.

They rumbled down the hard-packed trail that ran through their farm, past their houses, past two rows of fields. Each field was about one *dilitirisi,* or dil, as the Teneka Fra here said. That was about the area one draft horse could plow in a day, some seventy of her dad's big paces on a side. Each

123

row had twelve fields they tended, running from the Old Wood – where the road petered out – to a half-mile short of the Heldasfar River. As always, half the fields were planted with tsilinki, the other half with clover.

After passing a fallow area – for the fields of this old farm had once gone all the way to the road – they turned left toward the big stone bridge over the Heldasfar. Only their farm was this far out of town, and on the far side of the Heldasfar. It was the only way she knew of to cross the river except for a ford some fifteen miles upstream. Below here the Heldasfar met the Orully and flowed wide and deep. Above the ford was a great marsh.

She knew the bridge was ancient, built long before they had come here to farm, because no one would build such a large bridge – or any bridge at all – just to get to their farm. It was nearly seventy feet long, and two or even three wagons could cross it abreast. There had even been a round tower and a gate on the far side, though these had fallen.

Once while playing there, the children had found a skull. After Karia brought it home to show her mom, they were forbidden from playing there again, and since the entire span of the bridge was visible from Nana's house, they had to obey.

Just past the bridge was the intersection with the road from the south. Two other farms were out that way. *Wait, no, that's not right,* Karia thought. *There may be three.* There was a very old hermit who had a small farm well down the road, but Karia did not think anyone had heard from him in years. Maybe he was dead.

Karia thought she could see fresh wagon wheel marks in the dust from the south, which would mean other farmers were on their way to the carnival as well. But she could not be sure the tracks were from this morning.

The road was also a lot dustier past the intersection, so she hitched up her pretty blue dress and her chemise to keep them clean. She noticed Narek look at her legs, then turn away. *At least he didn't stare.*

A lady wouldn't show her legs like that, she thought.

Well, a lady doesn't have to ride in the back of a wagon either.

She looked off to her right, where the soil was rocky and no one farmed, and where she didn't have to see Narek. Only a few scraggly trees grew there. Then she looked back toward the old bridge, but there really wasn't much of a view with all of the dust. Out of the corner of her eye, it looked like Narek was staring at her legs now, so she turned to confront him. It was still shocking to her to see him just staring like that.

She threw her arms atop her legs. "Fire and ashes, Narek, please!" she shouted.

He turned quickly away.

"Is everything OK back there?" Nana shouted over the noise of the wagon.

"We're fine, Nana," Karia shouted back. Then she leaned toward Narek's ear and lowered her voice. "Narek, so help me, if you don't stop that I'll dump you off the back of this wagon and swear to Nana that I never even noticed you were gone!" She leaned back away from him.

He said something, but because he was turned the other way, she couldn't hear it over the creaks and groans of the wagon.

"What did you say?"

He turned and looked her in the eyes. "I said, you oughtn't be showing me your legs like that if you don't want me looking." Then he turned around again.

She was sorry she had asked him to repeat it. She thought about lecturing him about the difference between looking and staring. She considered telling him – forcefully – that she needed to hitch her dress up and that it was quite rude of him to even look. She wanted to tell him how offended she was by his staring. How dirty it made her feel. But she did none of those things. She knew he wouldn't apologize. He'd just make another lame excuse, and then she'd get even angrier, and then she really would pitch him off the back of the wagon.

What a great ride to town this was going to be.

And after she'd decided she needed to try to be nicer to Narek. She was trying to treat him like family, and he was trying to … *ew*. She shuddered. *Ewwww*.

Ian Fallis

CHAPTER THIRTY-NINE

"I can't do *that!*" the Seeker shouted. He turned and paced, but could not go far in the tiny tent that was his dressing room and sleeping quarters at the carnival. He turned back around. "That's a capital crime! And right in front of a cavalry sergeant and you!"

"I'm going to kill you anyway," the hooded figure said. "Make your choice. Refuse and I kill you now, or do as I say and live at least until tonight."

"You need me to find the sorcerer," the Seeker said.

"I told you, I do not see success in your future. If this works, I will not need to rely on your powers. He will show himself."

The Seeker flailed his arms in frustration. In his brightly colored flowing robe and ridiculously tall pointy hat, it looked kind of like a neon duck exploding.

"So you want me to go out there tonight, make fire, and invite people from the audience to try it? Who's going to be that stupid?"

"I believe we are dealing with a neophyte here. It has been too easy to track him. He will be, as you say, stupid. And it will be quite a show. Tonight. After dark. People from all around have come to see you. The fire will be doubly impressive."

The Seeker stared at him a moment. "Are you actually enjoying this?"

"It is a means to an end. That is all."

The Seeker hesitated again. "You do realize I'm not very good with fire, don't you?"

"The worst that could happen is that you take fire in and kill yourself, and I am going to kill you anyway."

"No, the worst that could happen is that I get some sudden nervous jolt of energy from being scared half to death of you and burn the audience to cinders," the Seeker said.

"No. They are nothing. You are somewhat useful. Now go prepare yourself. Pray and meditate."

127

"That's not how it works," the Seeker said.

"Perhaps, since you are not very good with fire, you should try praying." He turned and ducked out of the tent. The Seeker stuck his head out. *Ah, there,* he thought, looking at the young man lounging by the tent opposite him. That would be the cavalryman assigned to kill him if he tried to escape. He went back inside.

CHAPTER FORTY

The wagons reached the rise near Milliken's Farm. This was as far south as the road bent in its journey around the maze of rocky hills to the north that extended all the way to the mountains. Soon after the rise the road would turn back north and east to get to town.

Karia hated being in the back on this part of the road. There was less dust, but only because it was rocky – and that meant it was bumpy. She and Narek bounced around, and she made sure to hold onto the sideboard so she wouldn't have to hold onto him, or even touch him.

Now that she was away from all the dust, she could almost make out the river and the bridge from this point. She knew that if the old tower here was still standing, and so was the bridge tower, you could clearly see one from the other. It suddenly occurred to her that she had no idea who had built the towers. The Dr'Zhak were hunters and gatherers, and built no fortifications that she knew of. The Teneka were farmers, and did not build towers either. And the Inamali? As far as she knew, they had only built Talitakaya.

She was lost in her thoughts – at least, she was when she wasn't struggling to keep from either falling out of the wagon or touching Narek – when Narek spoke to her again.

"I don't believe it," he said.

"Believe what?"

"That you master fire."

"Oh." She really didn't care what he thought, and she was about to tell him so, but she stopped herself. She was trying not to be rude to him. It took more effort when she realized that the only way he could know about her and fire was from eavesdropping.

"You're a girl," he said.

"You're observant." *Oh, great, that wasn't rude at all, was it, Karia?*

"Everybody knows girls can't do magic."

"Oh."

That apparently wasn't the response Narek was looking for. So he took a new approach.

"I can make fire," he said.

"Yes, but how many matches do you have to go through?" *Oh, golly, it's hard to be nice to him after being mean all these years.*

"I don't need matches! I can make fire in my head."

Now there's an enticing picture, she thought. *I'd like to make fire in his head.* Then she caught herself. She didn't particularly like Narek, but she wouldn't deliberately hurt him. *Just with words. And by treating him badly. I have hurt him, haven't I?* She felt bad until he spoke again.

"Did you hear me? I can make fire. I don't need matches. I can just make it shoot out of my eyes!"

Karia laughed, then stopped herself. "That's not how it works, Narek."

"What do you know? You can't make fire. You're a girl."

He turned away again, and she was glad. She just wanted this ride to be over.

CHAPTER FORTY-ONE

Karia heard her dad's wagon start across the wooden bridge over the creek just outside town, and put her dress down over her legs. Then Opa's wagon rumbled across, with her and Narek aboard, and off the road into the grassy field west of town that they called the village green. Several shops on this side of town backed up to the green – most notably, the apothecary and the baker – and most of those shopkeepers made their back doors their front doors during a big Gathering.

Already several wagons were in the field near the stream, and tents were up, and farmers and their families were milling about, talking and playing games. Some were selling produce and handicrafts.

Sikarra, the five-year-old girl from one of the farms close to town, came skipping up behind the wagon and waving to Karia, her long auburn hair and blue checked dress almost floating as she bounded through the grass behind the wagon. Sikarra seemed to think that since she and Karia were the only people she knew with auburn hair and freckles, they must be related. Karia didn't mind her hanging around at Gatherings and the like; she thought Sikarra was adorable. Karia smiled and waved back.

Opa pulled his wagon up alongside her dad's, and Karia jumped down just as her mom went to the back of her dad's wagon. "Karia," she called, pulling a large canvas bundle to the back of the wagon, "help me get the tent up."

But Karia was delayed a moment. Sikarra ran up to her, hugged her and ran off, giggling. Karia looked after her and laughed, then hurried to the other wagon to help her mom. Before she could get there, a boy a little older than Karia – she didn't know his name – came up suddenly and, saying, "I've got that, Ma'am," took the tent from her mom. Karia was getting ready to grab the other end when Drical, Sikarra's 16-year-old big brother, rushed up and said, "Let me take that, Karia." He sounded like he was trying to make his voice sound deeper.

"I've got …" she began. But her mom interrupted her.

131

"Karia, let Drical help." Karia shot her a confused look, but her mom just smiled and nodded at her. "You go along to make sure it gets put up the way your dad likes it."

"Yes, Ma'am."

The two boys carried the tent to a spot Karia directed them to, and then set to work rolling it out, setting aside the stakes and tie-down ropes, and putting up the poles. Karia went back to the wagon for a hammer, then picked up a stake and walked to a corner of the tent. She knelt, positioned the stake, and lifted the hammer.

But she felt the hammer taken out of her hand, and as she turned around Farakis said, "Let me do that, Karia."

"Be my guest," she said, standing and gesturing. She stepped aside and wondered what was wrong with him. She turned and realized Drical was doing fine but the other boy was putting one of the shorter poles where one of the longer ones went. "Um, you, there, what's your name?"

"Kent," he said, beaming. "I'm new in town. Pleased to make your acquaintance, Miss Karia." *Miss Karia? OK,* she thought, *that's a Teneka Dri accent, so maybe they talk like that there.*

"Yes, um, Kent, you need one of the longer poles there."

"Oh, right, Miss Karia. Thank you!" he said, smiling. Karia smiled back, but only because she thought it was the polite thing to do. As soon as he turned away, she quickly turned to see if she could figure out where her mom had gone.

But her turn brought her face to face with Helith, who had come striding up with a big grin on his face and a melon in each hand. Karia had tried to grow melons, and they were nothing compared to the ones Helith and his family grew. She was impressed. "Hi, Karia. Remember me?"

"Yes, Helith," she said, stepping back slightly.

"My dad's got me selling melons over at our wagon, so I can't stay and talk, but he let me go so I could come and say hi to you."

"Hi," she said.

"Hi," he said. Then he just stood there, smiling at her.

After a long awkward silence that probably really lasted only a second or two, Karia asked, "Is there something else?"

"Uh, yeah, … um, these are, they're for you," he said, holding them out.

She took them, almost dropping one. "Thanks," she said. Again he just stood there, looking at her, a blank, dull expression on his face. She raised an eyebrow.

"Uh, oh, sorry, I better get back to the, um, uh, melons," he said, blushing, then hurrying away. She felt a little like screaming, when she heard Drical call from behind her, "How's this, Karia?"

She turned around and looked at the tent. She was surprised it was already up. "Wow, that was fast," she said.

Drical smiled and blushed, and lowered his eyes. "Thanks, Karia."

Why is he blushing? What has gotten into everyone today?

"Did I get all the other poles right, Miss Karia?" Kent said.

"Yes, Kent."

"Are the stakes and lines all good, Karia?" asked Farakis.

"Yes, Farakis, you did well." Now he smiled and looked down and blushed. Karia was feeling like the whole world had gone mad. She spotted her mom and made a beeline for her.

"Mom, everyone is talking and smiling and blushing like idiots and they won't let me do anything," she said.

Her mom laughed.

"It's not funny. I'm gonna lob these melons at the next boy ..."

"Excuse me, Karia," she heard from behind her. She spun on her heels and looked down into the eyes of Jikala – he was about four inches shorter than her, even though he was almost a year older – and spat out, "Not now!" before spinning back to her mom.

"Oh, OK, sorry," he stammered.

"That wasn't very nice, Karia," her mom said.

"I didn't chuck a melon at him. What's wrong with everyone?"

Her mom started to laugh again, but held her laughter in check. "Karia, I'm sorry, I should have talked with you about this, but things have been so crazy."

"Talked with me about what?"

"This is your first Gathering since you turned fifteen," her mom said.

"So?" Karia said. And then it hit her. She was horrified. She had never thought about what this would be like. Teneka customs said boys and girls entered adulthood at fifteen. It was considered highly improper to make an advance toward a girl before she was fifteen, and boys who made advances before their fifteenth birthdays were laughed off.

My first Gathering since I turned fifteen ... fine ... but this is ridiculous.

"But why are they all coming to me?" Karia asked. She winced because it sounded like she was whining, and she hated whining.

Again her mom laughed. "Karia, you're a smart girl. Why do you think they're all interested in you?"

"I'm strong?" she said. "I can sew? OK, maybe I can't sew. But I cook, and I can make bread. Is that it?"

"Karia, there's not a boy here makes any of those a priority when he's looking at a girl. And you know that." Her mom leaned in close and lowered her voice. "When will you realize you're a very pretty young lady? And that dress that matches your eyes ..."

Her dad apparently overheard part of the conversation. "Will you excuse me, ladies?" he said to them. "I need to go find a stick."

"Excuse me, Karia," Karia heard a boy say behind her.

Her dad leaned in toward them and said more quietly, "A very, very big stick."

Her mom looked past her to the boy and said, "Just a moment, Rekon." *Rekon*, Karia thought. *I thought he was courting that blond girl ... oh gosh, the one with the ... well, the figure.* She blushed.

Lowering her voice again, Karia's mom said, "And don't you think for a moment that this is just because you're the only one here who's just turned fifteen. There are a lot of available young ladies here, and none of them got the attention you're getting."

Karia blushed again. She was wondering if her face would get stuck that way. She hoped not. But most of all, she still felt confused. Her picture of herself was a tall, pale, skinny stick, and not, as her mom had said, "a pretty young lady."

"Just be nice, and if you're not interested, be polite but honest. Don't let this go to your head, but you must let this change your own picture of who you are."

Karia nodded, not sure how she was supposed to do that, especially when she was sure her picture was accurate. Even if it didn't square with what was happening.

"I'm sorry we kept you waiting, Rekon," her mom said, and she gently turned Karia in his direction.

"Hi," she said, looking up at him. Rekon was the oldest in his family, and his dad was the miller, so that meant he would inherit the mill. Karia knew that's why several of the girls had their eyes on him. She wasn't so sure about him, however. His hair had always seemed rather too blond to her. *Well, now*, she thought, looking up at him, *it doesn't seem all that odd*. Maybe it even looked nice.

"Hi," he said back, and she noticed he had green eyes. She liked green eyes. "Your dress matches your eyes."

"I know." *Oh, no, stupid stupid stupid.* "Do you like it?"

"I like it very much. But it probably wouldn't fit me."

"Huh?"

"I was joking, Karia," he said.

"Oh. Ha-ha." *Oh, he'll never know that was fake. Stupid stupid stupid.*

"I hope that you'll be at the dance tonight," he said.

"Oh, no, I was planning to go see the magician." *Oh golly, did I just say that?* She wanted to run and hide.

"Well, I guess, then, I could see you some other time," Rekon said.

"OK," she said, turning abruptly away. *He thinks I'm brain-addled and don't like him. And the slow, drooling boys think I like them. Great start!* She chucked the melons into the wagon. One of them split. She felt bad wasting food, but it felt good to break something.

Karia saw that her mom had two cots out next to the wagon, and went to help her. Each of them were about to take an end of one, when an enormous boy walked up and took one in each hand.

"Permit me, ladies," he said. "Karia, would you be so kind as to show me where these go?"

She was stunned, and mute, and just pointed to the tent.

"Karia will take you to the tent and show you, won't you, dear?"

"Um ... uh-huh, I mean, yes." She started toward the tent. She recognized the boy. No, she recognized the man. He was Gerik, the only son of the village smith, and he was not only a smith but a creative and skilled worker of precious metals. She had heard that his work was known as far as Talitakaya.

He was nineteen, and had declined to court any of the ladies of the town. That started rumors about him, but she had heard he told one girl he was waiting. She never heard what he was waiting for.

He certainly wasn't waiting to grow. He stood at least six feet tall, and Karia thought his shoulders must be about that broad as well. He had thick black hair, and had already grown a mustache. As he put the cots where she directed, she wondered why he was out among the farm-folk instead of in town.

He turned to her and held out what looked like a misshapen bundle of tiny *vitiri* fruit. At least, that's what Karia's family called them. She didn't remember the Teneka name.

"I'd be honored if you'd wear this," he said.

Wear it? That's a relief. I thought I was supposed to eat it. But how am I supposed to wear it?

She started to reach out her hand to take it when suddenly her mom stepped in and reached her hand right between Karia's and the wreath.

"Oh, Gerik, excuse me, I'm sorry for butting in, but is that a *tsikatrila?*" She sounded nervous, perhaps upset.

"Excuse me, Ma'am, I don't know that word," Gerik replied. Karia didn't either, but she tried to work it out. *Tsika, that I know. Promise. Trila ... Trila ... Tri, la ... oh, no, there's no Tri. Could that be short for Turi? If so, let's see, Turi, la ... life, long ... Oh!* She gasped.

"Gerik, perhaps I'm misunderstanding," her mom continued. "You have to understand, we're Teneka Sil, and even though we've been here for years we still don't fully understand your ways here – or sometimes your words," she said, smiling pleasantly. *I'm not ready for life, Mom! Tell him that!*

135

"I understand, Ma'am," Gerik said. "I didn't intend to do anything to offend you, or Karia." *I'm not offended – I'm terrified!*

"I appreciate that Gerik. It's just that, among my people, when a boy gives a girl a hair garland of *vitiri*, it's a sign of betrothal."

Now Gerik gasped. "I'm sorry, Ma'am. I'm sorry, Karia. I would never think of doing anything like that without giving you the opportunity to get to know me, and talking to your parents first." He turned again to Karia's mom. "Though I have no shame in saying to you, in front of Karia, that that is ultimately my intention."

Karia felt a rush of emotion inside her – shock and fear and excitement all rolled into one. She blushed and looked down, and her stomach rolled. *Oh, gosh, don't throw up! Not now!* Into her mind came memories of seeing Gerik at so many of the Gatherings when the townsfolk attended. She remembered a couple of times when she saw him looking at her, and he'd smile at her, or smile and tip his cap, and turn away. She remembered thinking he was a very nice looking young man. She never remembered seeing him dance with any of the girls. *He was waiting … for me?* Her head spun and her stomach heaved again. *Oh please don't throw up!*

"We call this a daypledge, Ma'am," Gerik continued. "It just means we'll spend the day together." Karia was not at all sure she was ready for that either. "It also means that all the boys will leave her alone." That part sounded very good to Karia, and she noticed that he made the word "boys" sound like an insult.

"Well, I suppose then that it's completely up to Karia whether she accepts your daypledge, Gerik," her mom said. "Just let me make sure my husband understands that's all it is, or he's likely to come after you with a big stick."

"Ma'am?"

"It's OK, Gerik. I'll leave you two alone." Her mom turned away. *Oh, no, please don't leave I don't know what to do I don't know what to say I don't want to mess this up …*

"Will you wear it, Karia?"

"Yes," she squeaked. *Now what do I do?*

Gerik solved the problem. He stepped behind her and put the garland on her head, then tenderly used his big hands to gather her hair and tie the garland under it. She felt her legs weaken as he ran his hands through her hair.

"You have beautiful hair, Karia," he said.

"Thank you," she squeaked. *I sound like a mouse.*

"You're nervous, but you don't need to be. I only want to spend time with you. I want you to have the opportunity to get to know me, and I'd like to get to know you. Shall we go see if your family needs more help setting up camp?"

"OK," she squeaked.

Ian Fallis

CHAPTER FORTY-TWO

"Maybe you should hold my hand so we don't get separated in this crowd," Gerik said. There were more people packed into the village lawn than Karia had ever seen in her whole life.

"I, I …" Karia looked down. She didn't want to say yes, but she didn't want to say no to him.

"You're not ready for that, are you?" he said. She looked up, and saw him smiling at her. *He has tender eyes.*

"No. I'm sorry."

"You don't need to apologize."

"What if I just walk behind you? You probably don't have any problem getting through the crowd."

"How will I know you're behind me?"

"I'll keep my hand on your back."

"Is that all that different from holding my hand?" he asked. She blushed and looked down. "I'm sorry, you already said no. But how will you see where we're going?"

"I guess I'll just have to trust you," she said, smiling and looking into his eyes. "Can I trust you?"

"You know you have the most-blue eyes I have ever seen?"

"Thank you," she said. He just stood there looking into her eyes. She blushed and looked away. "You didn't answer my question."

"What question?"

"Can I trust you?"

"Yes."

"OK, then – lead on." He started into the crowd and she put her hand on his back and followed him. "Just one thing," she added.

"Yes?" he said, glancing over his shoulder.

"I really want to see the magic show."

"OK."

"And I really want to get there early to be near the front."

"OK."

"Maybe even at the very front."

"Right. We can do that."

He led her on through the crowd and stopped. "Do you like apples?" he asked.

"Yes." *Oh I hope they're the big red juicy ones!*

"Two please," he said, handing the man two small copper coins and getting two apples in return. He turned around and handed her one. It was large and a deep red, just as she remembered from so long ago. She smiled, and he smiled back at her, and she blushed.

"Let's go over there." He motioned to a few benches on the edge of the crowd, near the apothecary. She followed him over and they sat. They each took bites of their apples, Karia feeling embarrassed that she took a bigger bite than he had. He finished his bite first.

"Karia," he said. "Is that an Inamali name?"

Karia choked on her apple. Gerik gave her a rap on the back that nearly knocked her off the bench and sent bits of apple flying from her mouth. She saw one piece hit the shoe of a man in the crowd, who walked on without seeming to notice. She hoped he wouldn't figure out where it came from.

"I'm sorry!" Gerik said. "Are you OK?"

"Yes," she choked out, and laughed. "Please don't break me."

"I'll try not to. But your name – is it Inamali? I just thought, since you're Teneka Sil …"

Actually, I'm Inamali. But Karia had never actually thought about it. It sounded like an Inamali name, and it certainly looked right in Inamali. "I don't know. But my dad gave me an Inamali …" She stopped just short of telling him her nickname. She remembered that she shouldn't be spreading that around.

"An Inamali what?" he asked.

"Nothing. I'm sorry, I shouldn't talk about that."

"OK," he said, and they ate the rest of their apples without speaking. *Great. I killed the conversation.*

"How about we go play tug-of-war now?"

Karia hesitated. She hated tug-of-war. She was strong, but she was so thin and light that she always seemed to be on the losing team. Then she looked Gerik up and down.

"Would we be on the same team?"

"Of course."

"Then lead on!"

They walked along the edge of the lawn toward the field where ropes were already out for the tug-of-war. Their course took them through a crowd waiting for the storyteller. This was one of the early shows, for the children, and Karia could not help but smile as she saw all the little ones bouncing impatiently as they awaited the show.

"Karia! Karia!" she heard from the left, and she turned to see Sikarra running her way. Shijih, her mom, followed behind, an embarrassed smile on her face. Sikarra grabbed Karia's hand. "Come and see the storyteller with me! Come and see! They're going to tell the Making of Man!" She tugged at Karia's hand.

Shijih caught up. "Karia, I'm sorry. Sikarra, Karia was on her way somewhere with her young man, dear." Karia blushed. *My young man? Gosh, my face is going to stick this way!* "Let her be, and you and I will go listen."

Karia looked down at Sikarra, and the little girl looked up at her, tears welling in her eyes. "Please, cousin? Please?"

Karia couldn't bear to say no to her. She turned to Gerik. "Gerik, would you mind if I stayed and spent a little time with Sikarra? I'm not that good at tug-of-war anyway, and I'll come find you there when we're done. Would that be OK?"

He smiled and said, "Sure. I'm glad you like children." He turned and started walking toward the tug-of-war field, and Karia turned to go with Sikarra and her mom back to where they were sitting. Karia had gone a couple of steps before what Gerik said registered and she stopped. *Oh, hey, hold on there, I don't want any children for a long time!*

Sikarra tugged on her hand, pulling her toward her blanket. Karia walked with her and sat next to Shijih. The moment she sat on the blanket, Sikarra climbed into her lap. "Sikarra!" her mom gently scolded.

"It's OK," Karia said, and wrapped her arms around the little girl. Sikarra snuggled back and rested her head on Karia's shoulder. That pulled on Karia's hair, so she moved her hair out from behind the little girl's head, and looked down at it cascading over Sikarra's. *Almost the exact same shade,* she thought. *I wonder if my kids ... oh, gosh, what am I thinking?*

A man came out onto the stage dressed as Gnome, with brown clothes and a floppy brown hat, his face smeared with mud. The children hooted and cheered. Though there had been no storytellers since before any of them were born, their parents had kept the old stories alive. Everyone knew Gnome, and knew that with his appearance the story had begun.

Sikarra leaned forward as he began reciting what all knew as Gnome's Proposal. Karia thought she heard her whispering the lines along with him.

"The world in perfect balance lies,
Blue still water 'neath starry skies,
Earth of brown and fire's bright light.

"And yet ... and yet it bores us all,

141

In kelpy glen, in rocky hall,
In fiery lab'rinth and glitt'ry thrall.

"I know! We must a creature make,
A balanced one this pall to break,
Each take a part – his clay I'll bake.

"I'll summon Nymph, and Sylph I'll call,
And Dragon from her fiery hall,
And we shall make him one and all."

Gnome exited to the wild cheers of the children – and their parents. Sikarra turned and looked at Karia, her eyes wide with delight. "Oh, it was just like I knew it would be!" she said.

Now a clay man was propped up on the stage, and Sikarra and the other children cheered as they recognized the other characters of the Making of Man. Nymph wore a blue, flowing costume that resembled her watery home. Sylph was in a white outfit that sparkled like the Sylph were said to sparkle in the air. Dragon appeared to be three men in a bright red, undulating, scaly costume. Yes, it must have been three men, the one in the middle moving something inside to make the wings beat.

Dragon looked at the clay man and turned to Gnome, and her voice rang out loud and, incongruously, deep as smoke rose from her mouth.

"I see that you have chos'n the form,
Yet why not wave or star or worm?
Why should the Gnome be our new norm?"

Nymph recited,

"He should upon the water dwell,
Not in some dry and dreary dell,
But riding on the ocean's swell."

Sylph said,

"I would he stay in this, his shape,
With clay that forms his earthly cape,
Not 'mongst the stars, lest he escape."

Gnome replied,

"Why, thank you Sylph, and would you please,
Now give him breath, his life to seize,
And we alone are his trustees."

Dragon roared,

"No not so fast, my counterpart,
I'll put the fire within his heart,
Lest all your balance fall apart."

Nymph said,

"I'll make within him rivers and streams,
His life to carry to all four beams,
And thus fulfill our fullest dreams."

All four of them touched the clay form, and a man broke out of the clay, and raised his hands above his head. The storytellers bowed as the children and their parents cheered.

As they left the stage, Sikarra turned and looked up at Karia. "They're not done, are they?"

"I'm afraid that's the end of the story," Karia said.

"No it's not!" Sikarra said.

"Sikarra, I don't think Karia knows the third part," Shijih said. She looked up at Karia. "A lot of people don't. And it probably would have been too sad for children. But I've told it to Sikarra. We have to keep the old stories alive."

"You should come over to our farm and I'll tell you sometime," Sikarra said. "I can even storytell it. I could do all five storytellers!"

"I think you could!" Karia said with a laugh.

"Tomorrow?" Sikarra said.

"Sikarra, I think Miss Karia needs to go now. Tell her thank you, then run along and play," Shijih said. *Miss Karia. I really don't like the sound of that.*

Sikarra's face fell. "Thank you, cousin," she said. "Bye."

"Bye, Sikarra," Karia said, tousling her hair and leaning to give her a kiss on the forehead. She helped the little girl up, and Sikarra ran toward three other girls who were playing with dolls. Karia stood up to head toward the field to find Gerik, bothered that she never realized there was more to the Making of Man. *Of course there's another part. All the old stories have three parts. And some of the really old ones have four.*

Before she got far at all, she felt a little hand take hers, and saw that Sikarra had come running to her.

"Karia, you should marry my brother," she said. "He talks about you all the time. Then we would be sisters!"

"Sikarra, stop that!" her mom commanded. Shijih had apparently chased after her little girl. "Off with you, you bundle of mischief!" Shijih swatted Sikarra playfully as she turned to run back to the other girls, then turned to Karia, who was blushing again and had no idea what to say.

"I'm so sorry, Karia," Shijih said. "My boy Drical is a nice boy, but he's still a boy. Oh, well, at least he's aiming high."

"It's OK," Karia said, but she wasn't sure what Shijih meant by "aiming high." She didn't have time to think about it, though, before Shijih leaned in closer and spoke more quietly.

"I'm sorry I've never told you how grateful my family is to you, Karia."

"Grateful?" Karia asked.

"For what you did for Sikarra," Shijih said.

"What I did?" Karia asked. *Is this the day for everyone to go mad?*

"When Sikarra was so ill last year," Shijih said.

OK, Karia thought, *that I remember.* At the Harvest Gathering the previous spring, Karia got so caught up in serving that she missed dancing with Sikarra. She promised Sikarra that she would dance with her when the summer Gathering came around. But when the time came, Sikarra was very ill. There was even talk that she would not recover. Instead of going to the Gathering, Karia asked her mom take her to Sikarra's house. She held the little girl in her arms and danced. At first Sikarra did seem very ill, but seemed to be doing better before Karia left, and recovered fully in a couple of days.

"I just kept my promise to dance with her," Karia said.

"Sure," Shijih said. *Why doesn't she look like she really means that?* "Maybe that's all it was. Having you visit encouraged her." She paused. *Why is she looking at me like that?* "Were you, um, wearing perfume that night, dear?" Shijih asked.

Karia laughed. "Ma'am, I'm a farm girl! I'm just glad I don't always smell like manure."

Shijih laughed with her, then said, "I'm sorry, dear. I was just sure I smelled, you know," she leaned in even closer and whispered, "akinasta."

"I don't know what that is, Ma'am," Karia said.

"Alright, dear," Shijih said. "I'm sorry I brought it up. I won't mention it to anyone at all. You run along and find your man now."

"Yes, Ma'am," Karia said. *What was that all about? Oh, gosh, wait a minute!* She turned around. "Ma'am, just a moment, please," Karia said.

"Yes?" Shijih said.

"I don't smell like manure, do I?"

Shijih laughed. "No, dear. Now go. Don't keep that man waiting. There aren't many like him."

"Yes, Ma'am," Karia said before she hurried off.

CHAPTER FORTY-THREE

Karia thought she and Gerik were arriving at the magician's stage early enough to be near the front, but there were already quite a few people waiting when they got there. Gerik worked his way through the crowd, explaining, "The young lady can't see," with Karia following close behind. She was a little embarrassed, but when he got them right to the front she forgot all about her embarrassment.

A raised wooden stage had been built, about six feet up and twenty feet wide. The backdrop was painted with pictures of all kinds of magical tricks, and there in the center was a depiction of a magician creating fire. Fascinated, she studied every detail of every picture on the backdrop, as Gerik stood silently and patiently just behind her left shoulder. She did not realize how long she had been studying the backdrop – and ignoring Gerik – until the magician came out onto the stage through a gap in the backdrop, and she glanced up and saw how large a crowd had gathered.

She was going to apologize to him, but the magician began to speak and she was completely absorbed. He was quite a showman, but she was disappointed to see that most of his act was sleight-of-hand – *not really magic at all*, she thought. Nobody else seemed disappointed, however, and she had to admit that some of his illusions were really quite clever and she could not figure them out. In fact, as he went on, she wondered if one or two were perhaps real magic, real illusions. *No, he would never do real magic, even if he could. It's too dangerous.*

Yet it was real magic she had hoped to see. She was about to suggest to Gerik that they go to the dance when the magician shouted.

"But enough of the trickery!" he said. He walked to the gap in the backdrop where a man handed him a candle, and he walked back to the front of the stage.

"Ladies and gentlemen, this simple candle contains the most dangerous substance in all of magic: Fire. Why, anyone with even the slightest bit of true magical ability at all can take fire in!" He lowered his voice and leaned conspiratorially toward the crowd. "But only a few trained, experienced magicians – after years of practice and training – can send it out!"

And, apparently, one fifteen-year-old stick-girl.

"Tonight, as the grand finale of my show, I will take fire in, and I will send it out. But – more! I will make fire – I will show you mastery of fire such as has not been seen in public in more than a decade! And then – after all that – I have an even greater surprise for you!"

He put his right hand in the candle's flame. Several in the audience gasped. Then he put down the candle and held up his hand, fingers splayed, and showed them it was not burned. People started to applaud and he gestured for them to stop with his left hand. Then a tiny flame appeared and grew at the end of his thumb, just like a candle being lit.

He really can master fire. And he really is doing it, right out here in public.

Then his index finger kindled like a candle, and on and on, until his right hand looked like a candle stand. He flourished with his left hand, and the crowd erupted in applause. Karia clapped enthusiastically. Gerik leaned forward and said in her ear, "He's good." His warm breath in her ear sent a pleasant shiver up her spine. She nodded.

Now the magician picked up the candle and blew it out, and then blew out his fingers one by one as if they were candles. The audience applauded again, many laughing as well.

Two men walked out on stage carrying a large, shallow iron pail on legs, with a large log on it. The magician walked to the pail, and the men walked backstage and then back on the stage with pitchers of water, which the magician took and poured onto the wood. One, two, three, four pitchers of water he poured on the log. The log was soaked, and the water formed a pool in which the log sat and even dripped onto the stage.

Then he stepped back to the other side of the stage. "I need complete silence," he said, and even the murmuring in the audience ceased.

He held his left hand aloft and extended his right hand toward the log. He appeared to be concentrating very hard. After a second or two, there was a sound from his hand like, well, it reminded Karia of someone passing gas. She thought she saw a tiny flame dart across the stage. A miniscule puff of steam came up from the log with a brief *pfft*.

Karia laughed out loud, then realized no one else was laughing and several people were looking at her. Including the magician. For a split-second, he had an odd look on his face, then he turned back to the crowd.

"Ladies and gentlemen, this is an extremely difficult feat of magic – even conjuring up a tiny tongue of flame. So please permit me to try again. Complete silence, please!"

He went back to his pose, closed his eyes and looked as if he was concentrating hard, furrowing his brow. This time there was a soft *whump* as a jet of flame shot from his hand to the log. It kindled instantly. The audience went wild. Karia clapped, but not terribly enthusiastically. *I wonder why he didn't just reduce it to ashes.* It didn't occur to her that perhaps he couldn't.

"And now, ladies and gentlemen, I have a surprise. Tonight, on this very stage, one of **you** will perform this most difficult and dangerous of magical feats." One of the men walked out on stage and poured a pitcher of water on the flames, dousing them. The other one brought a small ladder to the edge of the stage. The magician stepped to the ladder, and turning from the right to the left, sweeping his hand across the audience, drawing his words out, said, "Yes, one of you!"

As he turned toward Karia, however, something unexpected happened. Their eyes met, his expression changed for a split-second, and she clearly heard the word, "Don't!" in her head, though his lips did not move. It was so clear that at first she thought everyone had heard it, and she glanced around. No one else reacted. He continued his sweep of the crowd.

The magician walked to the log to be sure it was wet, then walked again to the edge of the stage and began looking throughout the crowd. "Who is brave enough to try? Who thinks they can master fire?!" Again he fixed his eyes briefly on Karia, and again she heard, "Don't!" Again his lips did not move, but his voice was clear, the message plain.

This was a real magician, and he was talking inside her head. She would have been rather frightened at that point if something else had not stolen all of her attention. Someone was moving through the crowd toward the stage. He – or she – was apparently rather short, because Karia could not see them. Then they began mounting the ladder.

She first realized it was a young man. Then she recognized him.

Narek!

Ian Fallis

CHAPTER FORTY-FOUR

Narek climbed the ladder to the stage. The magician held out his hand and welcomed Narek to the stage, then turned and put his hand on Narek's shoulder, turning him so they were facing the audience side-by-side.

"Tell everyone your name, young man."

Narek turned to face him and spoke. "My name is Narek."

"Narek, welcome," the magician said, turning Narek so he was facing the crowd again. "Now, Narek, I have to ask you, why have you come onto the stage this evening?"

"I'm going to show you that I can master fire."

"Well well," the magician said, chuckling. "I'm intrigued. I studied for more years than you've been alive in order to master fire. And you think you can just shoot fire out your butt?"

The audience roared in laughter, almost drowning out Narek, who had turned again to the magician and shouted, "No, out of my eyes!"

The magician quieted the audience again, turned Narek back to face the audience and then said to him, "Very well, young man, let's see what you can do."

Narek turned to face the log, his arms at his side, and craned his neck toward it.

"Are you feeling ill, boy?" the magician asked.

Again the audience laughed.

"That's not how it's done. Didn't you watch me? All you have to do is stand the right way!" The audience roared with laughter as the magician posed Narek.

Karia could see that he was embarrassed. No, it was worse. He looked humiliated. The magician was making a laughingstock of him. She couldn't let this happen to him. Without thinking, she focused her mind on sending fire out of Narek's hand. Nothing was happening, and the audience was howling with laughter. Karia pushed harder – and flames erupted from Narek's hand with a sound like a clap of thunder. Narek and the magician

149

both fell backward. The flames rushed across the stage, obliterating the log and partially melting the large iron pot it was in. The entire audience went silent, all eyes on Narek.

All eyes except the magician's. He was staring at Karia, wide-eyed, his mouth hanging open.

CHAPTER FORTY-FIVE

"Seize him!"

The silence was broken by a hooded man who stepped out from the audience to Karia's right, near the stage. He threw the hood back and everyone stepped away. He was only about ten feet from Karia, and she could clearly see his bald head, his shiny yellowish skin and his red eyes. She could see that under the drab tunic he wore a crimson robe fastened at the neck with a small white crescent, perhaps made of bone or ivory.

Karia wanted to look and see what was happening with Narck. But she was struggling to stay upright, to not give in to dizziness and fatigue, and she could not take her eyes off the Dr'Zhak ... who had now turned from the stage and was looking straight at her. Without taking his eyes off her, he said loudly, "And tell me, Seeker, what is special about this one?"

Karia didn't know what to say. *Seeker? Is he talking to me?* The magician rushed to the ladder and was now running toward them. The Dr'Zhak walked toward Karia. Everyone around her stepped back, but she stood as if in a spell.

"Nothing," the magician said. Karia thought he was trying to sound cheery, but actually sounded very nervous. "Nothing at all."

"Why do you stare at this one?" the Dr'Zhak said.

"Oh, forgive me," he said nervously and quickly, looking at the Dr'Zhak. He turned to Karia. "Forgive me young lady, but you have to admit," he said, turning back to the Dr'Zhak, "sir, she's very attractive, and she caught my eye. That's all. Forgive me, young lady," he said, turning to Karia again.

Does he know I did that? She did not have time to think it through. She felt exhausted, and the Dr'Zhak, who had continued to close on her, now stood in front of her. Still he did not stop. He moved within inches of her face, and she realized he was about an inch shorter than her.

"This stick?" he said, and she felt his words on her face, and deep inside her. But in her head she heard the magician say, "Stay calm."

"So pale." She wanted to push him away. She heard in her head, "No!"

"Ugly little spots on her face." She wanted to push him harder than she had pushed Timbal. That desire was building in her. *Burn,* she even thought. In her head she heard, "Don't!"

"And where she should have spots ..." She was stunned to realize his hand was grasping the top of her bodice, his fingers inside her dress and touching her. She was too surprised to move. She heard a ripping sound and could not believe what was happening. She felt compelled to push him away, hard, as "Don't! Don't! Don't!" echoed in her head. She slammed her eyes closed.

Suddenly she heard, just in front of her face, a sound she recognized instantly. It was one of those sounds that made even the farm girl flinch whenever they were butchering hogs: the sound of bone crunching and muscles ripping. She heard more tearing, and felt something warm splash across her face and neck and chest. She opened her eyes in time to see the Dr'Zhak flying backward. She saw him slam to the ground, and watched his head snap back and hit the ground. He was still. The right side of his face was shattered. Orange blood trickled from his mouth and ear.

Soldiers were running toward her. *I've killed him! I've killed him!*

She felt her legs buckle and she fell to her knees. She tried to focus on the grass, but it was moving. *It's dancing,* she thought. She felt her eyes starting to close. It was getting dark.

CHAPTER FORTY-SIX

The feeling of a hand on her chest snapped her eyes wide open again, and before she could react a plump hand came into her view and slapped the hand on her chest – hard.

"Ow! Oh, my, no, I wasn't, I mean, I was …" It was a man's voice. It sounded familiar, but she couldn't place it.

Her dress started to fall open again – she realized it was torn – and she felt a shawl thrown over her shoulders as the plump hand gingerly lifted her dress back up and held it.

"Shoo! Away!" she heard a woman say. Then, close to her right ear, "You'll be fine, dearie." This voice, too, sounded familiar. She knew she had heard it before, but did not know where. She fought off the urge to throw up.

The man leaned close to her ear and said, "I think I can help the big one, but there's nothing I can do for your brother." The man's voice now registered with her. It was the magician, but what was he talking about? Now he stood and was talking with someone else, and she could hear the words but her mind wasn't processing them.

The woman spoke again. "Do you think you can stand?" she asked. Karia nodded, but it was more of a reflex than an answer. She felt the woman begin to lift her to her feet, but let her down again as soon as she realized Karia was not helping. "You've got to try to stand, dearie," the woman said. Then, away from Karia's ear, she heard the woman say, "Hestra, give us a hand." More softly, still directed away from Karia, "We need to get her out of this place of death. No place for a pretty young thing."

She called me pretty. In somewhat of a daze, she remembered that the magician had called her "very attractive." *Why?* Those thoughts were overshadowed by the memory of the Dr'Zhak calling her a pale stick with ugly little spots on her face. She felt dizzy and sick to her stomach, and so very tired.

She slumped away from the woman, and someone came along her right side and put an arm around her. As they lifted her, Karia saw long brown hair and smelled flowers and decided it was another woman. They turned her around and Karia saw the magician talking to another man, two men holding Narek – he was limp and bleeding but his eyes were open – and two other men, nervous looking small men, holding Gerik.

"See here!" a man said behind her. "You're not taking that girl anywhere until I get this all sorted out."

The plump woman simply called over her shoulder, "If you need her she'll be at the smith's," and kept going. *Gerik's mom*, Karia realized. *This is Gerik's mom, and she's helping me while soldiers are holding her son.* Then, *Oh, my, boys come with mothers ...*

"Karia?" came a weak, strained voice behind her. It was barely recognizable as Narek's. Then louder, "Karia! Karia! Help me!" It tore at her heart. Then he began again. "Karia, you did this! Tell them you did this! She can make ..." A sudden sound like a wet mop hitting the floor cut off his words, and Karia realized someone had hit him. Things started spinning again and her knees felt weak.

"Oh, Hestra, hold on! There she goes again!" Gerik's mom said.

CHAPTER FORTY-SEVEN

Words drifted into Karia's blackness.

"Blood."

"Scared."

"Young."

She recognized her mother's presence before she recognized her voice. There was a second voice as well. The words began to form phrases, and the phrases, sentences.

"Such pretty eyes."

"Hands just like yours."

"Horrible thing to have to see."

"More excited to see Karia than the carnival."

She stirred at the sound of her name.

"I think she's coming around." Karia recognized the voice of Gerik's mom, and opening her eyes, saw her mom on one side of the bed and Gerik's mom on the other. It was morning – or at least day. If Karia had known which way the room was oriented, she might have been able tell the approximate time from the shadows cast from the window. As it was, she could only tell it was neither early nor late.

Karia looked over at Gerik's mom. She'd seen her before, but hadn't paid much attention to her. Then, she was the blacksmith's wife. Now she was Gerik's mom.

Ample, Karia thought. That was the word her dad would have used. Light-skinned and dark-haired, like her son, and ample. Not ample like Aunt Heather, however. Aunt Heather was ample like a draft horse, she thought. *Sorry, Aunt Heather.* But Gerik's mom was ... soft. *Overfed*, Karia thought. *Oh, gosh, stop that and be nice, young lady!*

"You're getting too big to keep fainting and needing to be carried around, dear," her mom said with a smile. But she looked concerned.

Karia was still trying to sort through what had happened and how she ended up here. She vaguely remembered the magic show, and the Dr'Zhak revealing himself, but almost everything else was a blank.

"What happened?" Karia asked.

"Don't you remember, dear?" her mom asked.

Karia thought a moment. "No."

"Then let's take that as a blessing for now and not talk about it," her mom replied.

Gerik's mom stood and reached into a washbasin on top of the dresser. She took out a washcloth, squeezed it out and leaned over Karia, reaching toward her forehead. "One more little spot, dearie." She scrubbed gently, then stood back up. She quickly moved the cloth away from Karia and dropped it in the washbasin. "All taken care of now."

But she was not so quick that Karia did not see that it was smeared with something orange. *Blood*, she thought. *Dr'Zhak blood.*

Suddenly into Karia's mind jumped the memory of that horrible sound, and something splashing across her face – *blood*, she realized – and the Dr'Zhak flying backward and to the ground. She sat up abruptly and hugged her mom.

"I killed him," she said.

She felt a hand on her shoulder. "No, no, dear, no you didn't," Gerik's mom said. "That boy chose to go up on the stage all by himself, chose to make fire in front of all those people. He can't blame you for that. He was making no sense at all."

What boy? Karia thought. *Narek!* Now she remembered him being led off in chains, shouting at her. *He blamed me … why did he blame me? I did something … what did I do?*

Then she remembered Gerik being held as well, and let go of her mom and turned to ask Gerik's mom, "Is Gerik OK?"

That's when she saw the large mirror at the foot of the bed. She was surprised at how large it was. She didn't know mirrors came that big. She noticed the girl in the mirror wasn't wearing anything but a locket around her neck, and she felt embarrassed for her. She was mortified when she recognized the locket, and realized the girl in the mirror was her. She immediately lay back down and pulled the covers up to her chin, turning bright red.

"Oh, he's fine, dear," she said. "He's downstairs, quite worried about you. He was mostly worried he had hit you too, but I assured him there wasn't a mark on you."

Karia was very confused now. *Hit me too?* "The Dr'Zhak … is he … ?"

"Yes, dear, I'm sorry, but he's dead," her mom said.

"Well, I'm certainly not sorry," Gerik's mom said. "I'm very proud of my boy for decking him, after what he did to Karia."

Her boy … decking him … did to Karia … Gerik hit him? What did the Dr'Zhak do to me?

Her mom's words intruded on her thoughts. "I am very thankful that Gerik was there, and thankful for his concern for Karia, but I mourn the passing of any man."

"That wasn't a man, it was a Dr'Zhak," Gerik's mom said.

"They're different, Elestra," Karia's mom said, "but they are people too, men and women." She reached out and put her hand on the other woman's hand. "Let's not argue about this right now, OK?"

Gerik's mom nodded. They both looked back at Karia.

"Wait," Karia said. "Gerik hit the Dr'Zhak?"

"Why of course, dear. What did you think happened?" Gerik's mom asked.

"I … I just didn't remember," Karia said.

"Poor thing," Gerik's mom said. "You've been through so much. It's probably too much for a … I mean, too much for any girl."

You don't know the half of it. "But they let Gerik go?"

"Yes, dear. That magician is a very smooth talker. Convinced the soldiers to let Gerik go. I heard that it helped that he got the crowd kind of excited about arresting my boy when all he did was protect your honor." Her smile slipped as she said, "Awful big chance to take for," but then she suddenly stopped and smiled again. Karia, lost in thought, barely noticed.

Protect my honor? Fire and ashes, what am I not remembering? "Wait, Narek he went up on stage …," Karia said. She remembered helping make fire, and the shout, and him being led away … *I made the fire. It **is** my fault.*

"They've arrested him and taken him back to their camp," her mom said. "Opa and your dad went to talk with them, and the soldiers refused to release him. They intend to take him back to Talitakaya to face charges of sorcery."

"I'm afraid this could mean trouble for the rest of us, too," she added.

"No good ever comes of magic, I say," Gerik's mom said. She looked displeased, perhaps even angry. *I wonder how she'd like a witch for a daughter-in-law,* Karia thought, and then, *Daughter-in-law?! Where are these thoughts coming from?*

Seeing Karia was still cowering under the covers, Gerik's mom asked, "Would you like some clothes, dearie?"

Karia nodded. "Silla volunteered to take care of your clothes," Gerik's mom said. *Silla … right, the village seamstress. Mean woman. Always calling my stiches uneven and awkward.* "She said that mending your chemise would leave an ugly mark that would remind you of … you know … every time you wore it."

No, I don't know, but I'm not sure I want to know.

"But she said that pretty dress of yours tore along a seam and mended just fine, and she's pretty sure she can get all the blood … I mean, that she can get it clean."

"She thought you made the dress," her mom whispered to her. "She was quite impressed. I didn't tell her otherwise."

Karia smiled. *Thanks, Mom.*

Gerik's mom got up and walked toward the foot of the bed as she talked. "Luckily for you, I still have some of Failean's things." She opened a drawer and reached in.

Wait, why does she have my mom's things … oh, right. She had a daughter named Failean too. Karia remembered her as a little older than she was, but younger than Gerik. *It would have been, I think, about two years each way. And she died about two years ago. Drowned, I think. Gosh, that would mean she was about fifteen then, like I am now.*

"This was hers," Gerik's mom said, holding up a beautiful chemise. It was white – clean, pure white, not the grayish tan of Karia's farm-girl chemises – and had decorative white stitching around the neckline, shoulders and cuffs. It was gathered at the top and at the waist, and it was fine – so fine that she could see Gerik's mom's hand through both layers as she displayed it for Karia. It wasn't as luxurious as the silky chemise at the house in the Old Wood, but it also looked better suited for someone with, well, with less ample curves. *OK,* she thought, *with a distinct lack of curves.* And it would certainly be one of the nicest chemises on any of the girls for miles around, if not the nicest.

"It'd be good for this to get some use, instead of sitting in a drawer," Gerik's mom said.

"It's beautiful," Karia said. "Thank you."

"Well, here you go dear," she said, holding it out to her. *Does she expect me to just climb out of bed and put it on? In front of her and my mom? Wait, does she really think I'm going to let her see me in that – just that?!*

Karia's mom must have seen the fear in her eyes, and said, "Why don't we step outside while she puts it on?"

Karia was very relieved when they stepped outside and closed the door. She thought she heard Gerik's mom say, "self-conscious after what happened." *What happened?*

She started to sit up, but that big mirror at the foot of the bed made it feel like someone was watching her. Finally she steeled herself, hopped out of bed and reached for the chemise – and felt very dizzy and nauseated. First she had to fight back the urge to throw up. Then she had to stop and lean on the bed for a couple of seconds, growing more embarrassed by the moment.

Finally, after what seemed to her like a very long time, she grabbed the chemise and pulled it quickly over her head. But she got stuck with it around her shoulders and still covering her head. The gathered waist and top befuddled her, after all these years of wearing chemises that were like sacks with arms and a hole for her head. She was mortified by the thought of someone coming into the room with her still flailing to try to get this thing on, and worried that she might have to call her mom for help.

"Karia, is everything OK?" her mom called through the door.

Oh please don't come in! "Yes, Mom," she called back. *Please don't come in!* She pulled the chemise back off and tried again, more slowly. This time it didn't bunch, and when she got her arms and head through, she saw that it fit quite well.

In fact, catching her image in the mirror, she was surprised at how well it fit. She was surprised this was her reflection. Because the chemise came in at the waist, she could see curves in her body that she had not noticed before. No one would call her curvy; "stick" or tsilinki was still a pretty good description, she thought. But now she realized that she had curves. Small curves, but curves nonetheless.

Oh, gosh, I'm staring at myself, she thought, and blushed. She climbed back into bed and pulled the covers up to her chin again.

"Mom?" she called.

"Yes dear."

"You can come in now."

Her mom came into the room. Gerik's mom was not with her. She closed the door behind herself.

"Not going to let me see you in that lovely chemise?" her mom asked.

"No! Not until I have a dress over it."

Her mom laughed. "Well, maybe now you won't forget to put a dress on in the morning."

Karia blushed. "I hope not!" she said.

"Gerik would like to see you," her mom said. Karia pulled the covers up over her nose. "Will you let him talk with you?"

"No," she squeaked.

"Young lady, that young man risked his life for you." Her mom took the covers. "Put your arms up," she commanded. Karia lifted her arms, and her mom tucked the blankets in at her sides, under her armpits. "There, put your arms down now. You're perfectly decent."

"He can see my shoulders."

"Yes, dear, but that's not what boys want to see, so it's not a problem." Karia blushed again. "Oh, roses!"

"Huh?" Karia said.

"The stitching along the top of the chemise," she said. "It's little roses. How pretty. Now, I'm going to go and tell Gerik he can come and talk with you, and I'll be right here the whole time. OK?"

"No."

"Karia," her mom said sternly but not harshly.

"OK."

Her mom fixed Karia's hair a minute, smiled at her, and went out of the room.

Karia looked down, and had to lift the edge of the chemise up to see the stitching. It formed little flowers alright, but they looked more like daisies. Certainly not roses. She smiled. Her mom may not know flowers, but Karia loved her anyway, just the way she was.

CHAPTER FORTY-EIGHT

Her mom and then Gerik came back into the room. Her mom went to her left side, and Gerik to her right. He was looking down.

"Karia, I am very sorry."

Karia was completely unprepared for that. She had expected him to say something like, "Hi, how are you, can I call at your house next week?" She gave her mom a panicked look. Her mom mouthed something, but Karia couldn't tell what. Time was passing, and Gerik was standing there, and she didn't know what to say.

"I had a good time, Gerik." *Oh, great. Yes, it was a great time, before whatever it is that I can't remember happened, and you killed that man and his blood splattered all over me. Right, then, that's what I should have said. Oh, I'm so stupid!*

"Neither Karia nor I blame you for what happened, Gerik," her mom said.

Still he looked straight down. "That's very kind of you, Ma'am."

Karia's mom gestured to Karia. *What? What am I supposed to say?* Her mom apparently figured out what she was thinking from the confused look on Karia's face, and mouthed something again. This time Karia got it.

"I don't blame you, Gerik."

"Thank you, Karia."

He just stood there, silent. Her mom motioned with her hand, and mouthed, "Take his hand."

She shot her mom a confused look. *Mom! Hold his hand, right in front of you?!*

Again her mom gestured, more vigorously, and emphatically mouthed, "Take his hand."

Karia reluctantly reached over to put her hand in his. She was fascinated that while his hand was much thicker and wider than hers, they were very nearly the same length. But what truly fascinated her was how it felt to hold his hand. It made her insides feel warm.

161

He looked at her and smiled, and suddenly words just spilled rapidly from her mouth: "Gerik, I don't remember everything that happened last night. But I'm very glad you were with me, and I really did enjoy our time together before what happened happened, and I don't want to talk about how last night ended any more, OK?"

"OK," he said, and he squeezed her hand. Karia thought something snapped out loud, but perhaps she only felt it and did not hear it. Gerik certainly didn't seem to hear anything. She knew he was trying to be affectionate, but she was very glad when he released his grip, and she hoped she hadn't winced from the pain. She didn't think any bones were broken. *Golly, he **is** going to break me one of these days.*

"Alright, Gerik," Karia's mom said. "I think she needs to rest some more."

"Yes, Ma'am." He let go of Karia's hand and looked at her, and stood there a moment. He looked like he was getting up the courage to say something. "May I call on you at your home later this week?"

"Yes," she squeaked.

"I'll come by in three days, a little after noon, if that's OK," he said.

"Yes," she squeaked.

"Um, no, please," Karia's mom interjected. "Best give her another day, Gerik. She's just gotten over Ylintera fever, and the shock of this on top of that, well, I just think it's best she have another day to get better."

"Um, OK," he said. "If that's OK with you, Karia. I don't ever want to rush you."

"Yes," she squeaked.

Gerik walked out of the room. Karia mouthed, "Ouch!" to her mom and rubbed her hand. *OK, no, nothing seems to be broken.* Her mom went to the door and closed it, and came back and sat on the bed, a broad smile across her face.

"It took your dad a while to figure out how to squeeze my hand without crushing it," she said, adding, "'I had a good time'?"

Karia blushed, put her arms under the covers, and pulled them back up over her nose. "Stop it, Mom. I didn't know what to say."

"I'm just kidding you, dear. You had a rocky start, but then you did just fine."

"Because you told me what to say and do."

"No, dear. When you spoke from your heart, you said exactly the right thing. Remember that."

"I rambled," she said.

"But you said the right thing," her mom countered. "Just try to slow down next time. You did fine."

Karia sat up and gave her mom a hug.

"Not embarrassed?" her mom asked.

"Not until you asked that," she said. They both laughed.

Karia lay back down and pulled the covers up – but not to her chin. "Why am I so tired, Mom?"

"You made the fire that looked like it was coming from Narek, didn't you?"

"Yes." *I made it look like he was a sorcerer, and now he's going to die because of me.*

"Karia ... I don't think ... it's just ..." She stopped and took a breath. "If I didn't know that's the only way it could have happened, I would have said it was impossible."

"Then how ..."

"I think you're the only one who can answer that one, Karia. Maybe someday you'll be able to. But I think that's why you're so tired. Mastering fire is hard work; making it look like someone else mastered it must be even harder."

"Mom, it's my fault Narek was arrested," Karia said.

"Then why did you do it?"

Karia was crushed. *Does she blame me too?* She realized she was hoping her mom would say it wasn't her fault.

"Why, Karia?" her mom asked again.

"Because he was up on that stage, and everyone was making fun of him, and laughing at him, and I didn't want him to be humiliated."

"I knew you did it for a good reason. Yet it came out badly. Right?"

"Right."

"Sometimes, dear, even when you do things for the right reasons, things don't turn out for the best. Sometimes that means there was a bigger picture you didn't pay attention to, and sometimes it's out of your control and just works out poorly. So always think carefully before you act, but never second-guess something you thought out and acted on with the best intentions."

Thought out ... "Mom, I didn't really think this out."

"I know, dear. Sometimes we hurt others as we're learning and growing. It can't be helped. I don't know any other way to grow up."

"That stinks," Karia said.

Her mom brushed back an unruly strand of Karia's hair. "That it does." Her mom looked at the shadows cast from the window, apparently checking the time. "Karia, Silla said she thought your dress would be ready about now. If it is, do you feel up to the trip home?"

"I think so, Mom."

"I wouldn't ask that of you if I didn't think it was important. I think you probably should spend another night resting here, but I ..."

It dawned on Karia that she'd spent the night at Gerik's house. "Mom! I spent last night here! People are going to talk!"

"People who would talk like that aren't worth listening to, young lady. Gossip tears us all down. Now listen to me, I think we all need to get back to the farm. So I'm going to go check on your dress. Unless you want to just go home like this."

Karia blushed, pulled the covers back up over her nose, and squeaked "No."

CHAPTER FORTY-NINE

Hinar was pacing. This was not the assignment he had in mind when he joined the cavalry. He had never even expected to be a sergeant, in charge of a troop.

The Seeker stepped in front of him, pointing to the body of the Dr'Zhak, wrapped in a sheet and lying on the ground. He said, "I think you need to do something about that."

The sergeant looked at the body, then back at the Seeker. "We're taking him back to Talitakaya," he said.

"Oh, no, Sergeant, bad idea, very bad idea," the Seeker said. "The Dr'Zhak believe that if you don't bury a body within a day, the soul will be trapped in the grave forever. You need to get him buried."

"How do you know so much about this?" the sergeant asked.

"Oh, I was part of the force that took Talitakaya, Sergeant. Fought right alongside the Dr'Zhak. Saw a lot of death. Why, sometimes they would stop in the middle of a battle to bury their dead, they were so worried about their souls getting trapped."

"You were in the force that took Talitakaya?" he asked.

"Oh yes, I was a scout. Thought helping them would keep me safe. You know, always looking out for myself. Lot of good it did me."

"A day, huh?"

"Oh yes, Sergeant. If you take that body back to Talitakaya, they're likely to kill you. In fact, if they find out you waited this long, they might kill you."

The sergeant stared at him.

"Besides," the Seeker added, "you need to bury the evidence of your incompetence."

"What?!"

"Well, you let him get killed, and then you failed to arrest the person who did it."

"That was your doing," the sergeant said angrily.

"Yes, probably so. But it was still your responsibility. Now see here, if you go back to Talitakaya with a Dr'Zhak prophet with his head bashed in, it doesn't matter what you say, and it doesn't matter if I'm telling you the truth or not, because you let him get killed and you didn't bring back his killer.

"And you don't really want to go back and arrest that boy, because you also felt like the Dr'Zhak had it coming after exposing that poor girl. Right?"

The sergeant paused before answering, and even then answered reluctantly. "Yes."

"But if you bury him, and, I don't know, say the sorcerer burned him to ashes, or say he fell off a cliff or something, they'll just be happy you brought back the prisoner. Right?"

The sergeant looked the Seeker in the eyes. He felt like he was being manipulated, but he couldn't see any flaw in the Seeker's logic. "Yes," he said.

"There you have it, then. Brilliant, Sergeant! Form a burial detail and your problems are solved."

The sergeant stared him down a while longer. Then he ordered, "Ligit, round up three more men. Dig a grave and put this in it."

"Yes sir!" Ligit said.

"And Ligit!"

"Yes, sir."

"Don't do it halfway. Six feet deep, and cover it with rocks. And no marker, got it?"

"Yes, sir."

"Well done, Sergeant. Now that I've helped you, I suppose I'll be on my way." He turned and started to take one step, and the sergeant grabbed his shoulder and stopped him.

"No. You're coming back with me," the sergeant said.

The Seeker turned back around. "Well, I suppose if you're still looking for a way to get yourself killed, certainly."

"What are you talking about?"

"Think about it. The Dr'Zhak was going to kill me after he captured the sorcerer we were seeking. Sentence has already been passed on me. My life is forfeit. So if you take me back, you've failed to carry out your duty, and then we both get killed. Not a great plan, that."

The sergeant put his hand on the hilt of his sword. "I can solve that problem."

"Oh, Sergeant, you've such a wonderful sense of humor – that's quite rich!" The Seeker laughed.

"Why shouldn't I kill you? I'm sure you have a great answer for that, too. You have an answer for everything, don't you? And somehow it always works out in your favor, doesn't it?"

"Oh, Sergeant, your words cut me! I'm simply trying to help you out of your predicament. Think about this: You go back to Talitakaya, and you say the Dr'Zhak is dead, and you tell them you killed me, and you bring them the sorcerer, and they think you've done your job and everything is fine."

"Right," the sergeant said, beginning to draw his sword.

The Seeker laughed nervously and stepped back. "But – and just hold on a minute, hear me out – the first time you don't do your job, you're on your own, aren't you?"

"Right."

"But only if you kill me. If you let me live, and you need my help, I will use my powers to help you. Dead, I can't help you. But alive, I might be able to return the favor and save your life!"

"Sure, and how exactly am I supposed to get you to help me when I need you?" The sergeant drew his sword.

"Oh, but I have just the thing!" The Seeker went to the table and rummaged in his bag. He drew out a small velvet sack, and from that he extracted a ring, intricately worked in silver and gold to look like a series of knots. "This ring – uh, this ring, I mean, these knots, they bind me to this ring, yes, and to the person who owns it. In your time of need, all you need to do is put it on and think of me, and I'll hear you and help you."

"And let me guess," the sergeant said, pointing his sword menacingly toward the Seeker, "it only works in my time of need, so there's no way to test it, right?"

"No, Sergeant, there's no way to test it. I stand before you holding out this promise and asking you to trust me, just as I am trusting you right now not to run me through with your sword."

The sergeant sheathed his sword and grabbed the ring. "I suppose the safest thing to do is let you go before you talk me into letting you go and giving you 500 gold pieces and a horse."

"Oh, Sergeant, 500 gold pieces, no, I would never ask that of you," the Seeker said. "But now that you mention it, I should point out that it would seem quite odd if you returned with an empty saddle."

"Well, if I get in trouble, I can always call on you, now, can't I?"

"Oh, Sergeant," the Seeker said, laughing. "You don't want to waste my help on something you can fix right here and now. So it's best if you simply give me a horse."

"Oh, you perverter of words, you warper of minds! You want a horse, and you don't have a good reason, so you're bluffing in hopes of not having to walk to town, or wherever it is you want to go. Off with you!" he shouted.

"A good reason? Well of course I have a good reason, Sergeant. I simply didn't mention it because I thought it would be obvious. I should be quite surprised if I have overestimated you."

"Blast it all, man!" the sergeant shouted. "Hirket, saddle a horse and give it to this charlatan. And you," he said, turning to the Seeker, "shut up. I don't want to hear even one more honeyed word from your forked tongue. Take your bag, take the horse, and get out of here!"

The Seeker smiled and bowed, picked up his bag and mounted the horse. He rode carefully down the hill from the camp, and onto the road to town.

Riding slowly, he softly said to himself, "It's a good thing the person who makes those exquisite rings now owes me a favor. After I take care of some unfinished business, I may have to get another."

CHAPTER FIFTY

Karia thought her mom was taking a long time coming back, and she was feeling nervous about being in Gerik's house when her mom was not there. She lay in bed with the covers drawn up to her chin – shoulders covered, no matter what her mom said – and waited.

She had plenty of time to think. She realized that before Narek told her about the carnival, all she wanted to do was see Timbal. Now here she was a day later, and Timbal seemed like a boy, and Gerik – *Gosh, did he really say he intended to ask permission to court me?* She felt guilty, but she also knew she couldn't undo how she felt now. And she did not want to. Of all the things that had happened to her recently, this seemed like the only good one – and it was very good.

But she also wondered why her mom seemed to be encouraging her relationship with Gerik. *Relationship. Now there's a word.* She thought her mom had been dead-set against Timbal because he wasn't Inamali. So did that mean Gerik was Inamali? *Is that why he asked me if Karia was an Inamali name – because he wanted to reveal to me that he was Inamali?* Karia didn't think someone, well, someone that broad could be an Inamali. She thought they were all slender and tall.

Right, twelve feet tall. And don't forget the flaming hair.

She remembered that she actually had no clue what an Inamali looked like.

But if Gerik's mom was so against magic, she couldn't be Inamali. So maybe Gerik was adopted like she was. *What if we're both adopted and we're actually related?*

She stopped working herself up and took a deep breath.

Wait, she thought. *I'm adopted.* Yet she thought that when she was waking up, she heard Gerik's mom say she had hands just like her mom. Other people had said that too. Some had also mentioned their noses. Her mom was also thin and rather delicate, just like her. *Maybe those are just*

Inamali things, she thought. Again, she remembered with disappointment, she had no idea how to tell an Inamali from a Teneka.

At least she would know a Dr'Zhak if she saw another one. She shuddered. Now she remembered what had happened. She remembered the Dr'Zhak's hand at her chest, her dress tearing, the hand on her chest … she began to cry softly, and between her tears and her exhaustion, she fell asleep.

CHAPTER FIFTY-ONE

Karia began to wake up, feeling her mom's presence. It relaxed her and calmed her, and she was allowing herself to drift back toward sleep when she heard another woman speak.

"You haven't lost her, Failean," she said. "Treasure the time you have."

Right, Gerik's mom.

Karia opened her eyes to see Gerik's mom leaving the room, and her mom trying to keep from crying.

"Mom?" Karia said.

Her mom sat on the edge of the bed, wiped the tears away from Karia's eyes, and leaned in and hugged her, just as she had when Karia was a little girl who had a bad dream.

But then her mom started crying.

"What is it, Mom?" Karia asked.

Her mom shook her head and wiped away her own tears. "We need to go, dear," she said. "Your dress is hanging by the mirror. Please put it on quickly and come down. The wagon is out front." Then she left the room, closing the door behind her.

Karia got up. She paused because she felt dizzy, then felt something like a rumble deep inside herself – she never could say where – and a spasm passed from her head to her feet, almost knocking her down. She took a couple of deep breaths, steadied herself and went to the mirror. She wasn't quite as scandalized by the mirror or the chemise anymore, and noted that she hadn't just dreamed the curves. Then, scolding herself for acting so vain, she quickly put the dress on. She rushed downstairs. Somehow she misjudged one of the steps, almost stumbled, and went awkwardly and too quickly down the last few steps. She stopped and leaned on the wall, swaying slightly.

She immediately felt an arm around her waist. "Oh, Dearie, are you sure you should be traveling right now?" Gerik's mom asked.

She was out of breath, and all she could say was, "Uh-huh." She had heard urgency in her mom's voice, and though she did not understand it, she knew there really were life-and-death matters in her world now. She took a few tentative steps and swayed again, and Gerik's mom grasped her tightly around the waist and put Karia's arm over her shoulders. She helped her across the parlor to the front door.

She let Karia lean on the wall next to the door while she opened the door. Karia felt she had been rude at the stairs, while Gerik's mom had been so nice to her, so she took a deep breath and said, "Ma'am, I am greatly indebted to you for your gracious hospitality." *That sounded strange.* Gerik's mom gasped and stepped back. *It didn't sound that strange.*

Karia's mom hastened to the door. "I'm sorry, Elestra," she said with a quick laugh – a laugh Karia could tell was strained. "But you know we're Teneka Sil, and when we want to be especially polite – such as Karia in this case wanting to thank you for your gracious hospitality – our people say it in Inamali."

I said that in Inamali?

Gerik's mom seemed convinced, and smiled at Karia. "You're very welcome, dearie. I hope it's OK if I respond in Teneka!"

Karia opened her mouth to speak but her mom cut her off. "It's perfectly fine," her mom said, and she stepped in and wrapped her arm around Karia's waist and started helping her to the wagon.

"Mother, I'd like to express my gratitude to the young man also," Karia said. *What? And why is Mom looking at me like that now?*

Under her breath, her mom said, "Karia, stop speaking Inamali!"

Softly, Karia said, "I'm not trying to," but she heard herself say, *"Tulititsinaliti tli."*

"Shh. Don't speak." Her mom helped her down the porch steps. Karia was concentrating so hard that she heard Gerik's mom say something but it didn't register. Her mom supported her all the way to the back of the wagon, and her dad gave her a hand up. They'd prepared a place for her to lie down, and they got her situated.

"There's Gerik. Just sit up and wave. Don't say anything."

Karia did as she was told, smiling – *like a fool* – and waving. He waved back, and she felt like a complete idiot. Quickly her mom had her lie back down, and put a blanket over her. Then her mom and dad hurried to the front of the wagon, and they began rolling – rather fast, Karia thought. She heard only the one wagon, and had seen only her parents. She wondered where Opa and Nana and Aunt Heather and the other wagon were.

That's when it hit her that she wasn't just speaking Inamali. She was thinking Inamali.

Worse, she realized what Gerik's mom had said when she was going down the porch steps: "Such a frail little thing."

Frail little thing? Frail?!

CHAPTER FIFTY-TWO

No matter how much padding there is, it's not possible to sleep in the back of a moving wagon. And Karia's parents did not have a lot of padding. It didn't take Karia long to realize that she was lying on the tent, and that was either a pole or a stake digging into her thigh with each bump.

"I can't wait until we get to the rise near Milliken's farm," she said to herself, thinking about the rocks ahead. But again it came out in Inamali. She was frustrated. Frustrated with looking frail and feeling dizzy. Frustrated with this whole not a girl, not a woman thing. Frustrated with what she didn't know. And now, frustrated that she couldn't talk without it coming out in another language.

She decided not to talk again until this was fixed, and to sit up and see if she could shift before whatever it was in the tent left a big nasty bruise. *Maybe a bigger, nastier bruise by now.*

As she sat up, she caught a glimpse of something behind them. It looked like a rider. But her vision was hazy, the wagon was jolting, and there was so much dust billowing behind them, that she could not be sure she had seen anything. She tried looking a while longer, straining to focus, but it only made her feel weaker and dizzier, so she closed her eyes.

The wagon jolted again – *ouch! OK, that's definitely a stake* – and she opened her eyes and sat up again. Again she caught a momentary glimpse of something, but once more she lost sight of it almost as fast. Now the sunlight was fading, and she thought her eyes were playing tricks on her.

Two weeks ago, she realized, she never would have worried that someone might be following them. If she had seen a rider, she probably would have hoped they would catch up and share some news. But now? Now it could mean they were in danger. Nothing was right anymore. Her frustration built. She lay back down.

Soon she could see the tops of trees and feel the wagon turning right, and she knew they had reached the wooded bend just before the rise, where the road turned back toward the north after skirting the southern edge of the rocky hills. She was glad her dad was slowing down. The wagon rumbled over the rocks, slowing still more as it ascended. She wondered if her dad was thinking about her or giving the horse a breather. He was going slower and slower, and at the top of the rise he came to a stop.

Karia looked toward the front of the wagon and saw her dad hand the reins to her mom and set the brake. He stepped down and stood in the road next to the wagon, looking back at the bend.

He knows someone is following us, she thought. She wondered why her dad had stopped here, since they wouldn't be able to see the person following them until he came around the bend. Then she realized that the person following them could not see them either. The rider would have to show himself, and then decide what to do. *My daddy's smart.*

She had barely finished thinking through that when she heard hoofbeats from the roadway behind, and then a horse and rider appeared at a gallop around the curve. The rider slowed. *He gave himself away,* Karia thought.

He brought his horse up the rise at a walk. He came alongside the wagon and stopped. Karia thought he looked familiar, then realized it was the magician.

"Good evening, kind sir!" the magician said. "It appears you are having some trouble – else why would you stop at such an inopportune location – and it is very fortunate that I am here to render you aid."

He alighted gracefully from his horse, and stepped toward Karia's dad, who simply stood still and watched him approach. "How may I …"

That was the instant the magician stepped into her dad's reach. Reva swept his right arm from his side and, in a movement Karia thought was almost as graceful as the magician's dismount, grabbed the magician's collar, lifted him off the ground and pinned him against the side of the wagon.

"Not another word," her dad said.

"Oh, of cour …"

Her dad released his grip a little and let the man down, but it was only to readjust. Now he grasped the man around the throat, just below his chin, and said again, slowly, "Not. Another. Word."

He looked into the man's eyes, and then squeezed his throat harder. The man let out a gurgling noise; Karia was afraid her dad was going to kill the man. "Not that way either," her dad said. Then he let go entirely, and the man's legs went out from under him and he slumped to the ground.

"I know exactly what you are, sorcerer. And while I can't do magic, I can crumple your body into a little ball and leave it in the ditch by the road here. So I want you to use just your mouth, and as few words as possible, to tell me exactly why you're following us."

176

"I wasn't ..." the man started to say, so her dad picked him up by the collar again.

"Try again," he said, letting the man go and making a show of straightening his shirt.

"Her," the magician said, gesturing to Karia. "I've come to swear my allegiance and fealty ... oh!" Her dad had slapped him.

"As few words as possible," her dad repeated forcefully.

"I've come to serve her."

Her dad looked at her. "You want this in your service?"

Karia shook her head no.

"The lady does not require your services. Go away. Far away."

"May I speak, please?"

Her dad put his face within an inch of the magician's. Then, softly, he simply said, "No. Go."

The man walked back to his horse and mounted. He looked into Karia's eyes and in her head she heard, "I can help you."

Her dad, watching the whole thing, said, "Don't listen to him, Karia. This kind always lies."

The magician rode back down the road and around the corner. Her dad stood by the wagon until the hoofbeats of the magician's horse had trailed off into the distance.

Karia crawled to the front of wagon, then, with her mom's assistance, climbed unsteadily over the back of the bench and sat down, cuddling against her mom. Her mom wrapped her arms around Karia, and handed the reins back to her dad as he clambered back up. They had not even reached the bottom of the rise before Karia fell asleep.

Ian Fallis

CHAPTER FIFTY-THREE

Karia awoke in her own bed, a comforting, familiar feeling washing over her. But before she even opened her eyes she could tell it was already light. Out of habit, she scolded herself for oversleeping and leapt from her bed, only to feel herself sit back down feeling dizzy and weak.

She noticed she wasn't wearing her dress. She vaguely remembered being half-awake as her mom and dad helped her get down from the wagon and walk inside, then her mom helping her get out of the dress. *She saw me in just this.* She blushed.

My blue dress, she thought. She looked and saw it hanging on her wall, draped over her ratty farm dress. She wanted to walk over and put it on. She tried to will her head to clear, but it did not. She was not tired, just weak, so she simply sat there on her bed.

My blue dress. My blue dress. She said it over and over in her head, wishing she could tell whether she was thinking in Inamali or Teneka. She remembered how frustrated she was the night before, and it all came flooding back.

Her door opened and she looked up to see her mom standing in the doorway. She stopped and looked at Karia. Karia thought about lying down and covering herself, but she was so frustrated she didn't care. She just put her head down.

Her mom picked up the brush from the rickety old table that was the only other furniture in Karia's room, sat down next to her on the bed and started brushing her hair.

"How are you this morning, dear?" she asked.

Karia just turned to her and made an angry face, then put her head down again.

"That good, huh?"

Karia nodded.

"Why don't you try saying something, dear."

Karia shook her head no.

179

"Eventually you're going to have to say something."

Karia again shook her head no.

"So you're still speaking Inamali?"

Karia shrugged her shoulders.

"Why don't you say something and we'll find out."

Karia shook her head no.

Her mom stopped brushing her hair. "Karia, enough. Say something."

"I hate this," she said.

"Well, that sounds better," her mom said.

"Do you mean my Inamali is better or I'm speaking normal again?"

"Normally, dear."

"Are you correcting me or answering me?"

"Both, dear."

"OK. Then I don't hate everything quite as much."

Her mom put her arms around Karia and laughed. Karia felt a small smile creep up at the edges of her lips. Her mom said softly in her ear, "I don't think I've told you this enough, but I love you, and I will always love you."

Karia returned the hug. "I love you, too, Mom."

"Karia, I need you to do something today, if you think you're up to it, dear."

"I'm gonna mess it up."

"I don't think so, dear. I just need you to take Grandpa's diary to your house in the Old Wood."

Karia looked at her mom. "Why?"

"Your dad and I, and the other adults, have talked, and we think it's likely our homes will be searched, if not this week, then next week. It won't be good if they find anything written in Inamali."

"Mom, I'm sorry, but I couldn't even get up to get my dress on."

"Then rest today, dear. We have a few days." She let go of Karia, stood and adjusted the blankets.

"I'm not tired, Mom. I'm just feeling dizzy and weak."

"Sure, dear, but I think you'll feel better lying down, and perhaps you'll be able to get some sleep and start to feel better," her mom said.

"I don't want to lie down. I want to get up and help you and … oh, I know, Mom, can you bring the mending in here? I can do that while I sit on the bed."

"Are you sure, dear?" her mom asked. "You slept all day yesterday."

"I slept … here, you mean?" Karia asked.

"Yes, dear," her mom replied. "We brought you home the night before last, and you've been sleeping since then."

"Well, then, gosh, yes, please bring the mending in," she said, feeling guilty. "I need to do something besides just lie around. It's all I've been doing lately."

"Alright, then. I'm sure Timbal will be happy to hear that. His mom brought his new pants over to be let out a bit."

Karia blushed. "That wasn't on purpose," she said.

Her mom stood up and started toward the door. "Really, dear? You sound like you feel guilty about it."

"Yes, really, Mom. Before I decided to be nice to him, I thought a pin would make my point better."

Her mom laughed, and went to get the mending and Karia's sewing kit from the parlor.

Ian Fallis

CHAPTER FIFTY-FOUR

By the time her dad came home for dinner, Karia had gotten through a lot of the mending, taken a little nap, and even got up, dressed and helped her mom in the kitchen.

As the three of them sat at the table, her mom said, "Karia, dear, your dad has something to talk with you about."

She saw her dad give her mom a look. Karia figured he wanted her mom to say it, but he was stuck with it now. He put his spoon and bread down, squared his shoulders and took a deep breath. "The adults talked last night. We think it would be OK for you to go and see Timbal," he said. "He'd like that."

Karia smiled. She was afraid he would never want to see her ever again.

"But we all decided there would be two conditions," her dad said.

Karia's smile faded, and she nodded and focused on her dad.

He cleared his throat, took a drink, then put the cup down.

"First is, you need to promise your mom and I, so we can assure everyone else, that you no longer harbor romantic intentions toward him."

As soon as Karia sorted out what "harbor romantic intentions" meant, she nodded.

He looked at her a moment. "Are you certain, Karia?"

"Dear," her mom said, "I think she has her eyes on someone else."

Karia blushed and looked down.

"Ah, right," her dad said. "OK, second, you need to apologize to your Uncle Avar, your Aunt Heather, and Timbal," he said.

She nodded again, looking up and smiling now. She was glad to apologize. She truly was sorry for what she had done.

"Now, the question is, do you think you're up to going over there tonight?" her dad asked.

"I'd like to try," Karia said. "Would you come along to steady me, Daddy?"

"Your mom and I were planning to come along anyway," he said.

They went back to their meal, and Karia finished quickly. She wanted to brush her hair and make sure she hadn't spilled food or left crumbs on her dress. She stood to put her dishes on the sideboard, swayed, then walked slowly over to it. She put her dishes down and just stood there for a short time, leaning on the sideboard.

Her mom stood up and stepped to her. "Need a hand, dear?"

"Thanks, Mom. Sorry to interrupt your meal."

"You've been doing it for fifteen years, dear," she said with a laugh. "Don't let it stop you now." Her mom surprised Karia by leading her daughter toward her own room. She had seldom been in her mom's and dad's room, but her mom steered her to the bed and sat her down facing the dressing table mirror. She left and came back with Karia's brush.

"Thanks, Mom."

But she didn't hand the brush to Karia. She sat down next to her and began brushing her hair for her. "Tonight," she said, looking into her daughter's eyes in the reflection in the mirror, "you need to remember that you are a young woman. Look your Uncle Avar and your Aunt Heather in the eyes, and be sincere but firm. You're fifteen, and you're apologizing as an adult for a mistake you made, not like a child for being naughty. Do you understand?"

"I think so," Karia said.

"The same applies with Timbal. But remember as you look at him that he is a boy who is a friend of yours, and there is a man who has every intention of asking permission to court you, and who is doing you the courtesy of waiting until you are ready for that. Do you have that?"

"I think so."

"OK, then, the next thing," she said, taking a deep breath. "Your Uncle Avar, your Aunt Heather and especially Timbal haven't seen what this fitted chemise, along with this pretty blue dress, does for your figure. It's like you've grown up overnight." Karia blushed.

Leaning close to Karia's ear, she said more quietly, "Here's what you need to understand: People want to agree with a pleasant, pretty young lady. And that depends on you, dear. First, you need to smile, a lot. Not at inappropriate times, of course, but even when you don't feel like smiling. Second, you must offer them something pleasant to agree with. Harmony would be a nice choice in this case. Does that make sense, dear?"

"Yes," Karia said.

"Good. Third, you must believe in yourself. Sit up straight. Look in the mirror and you tell me what you see."

Tentatively, Karia said, "Me?"

"Pretend the girl in the mirror isn't you. Tell me what you see."

I'm not sure, Karia thought. She wasn't sure she recognized herself. Her long auburn hair cascaded over her shoulders. Her blue eyes were almost piercing, and thanks to the dress, very striking. Her small nose and the freckles still made her look girlish, maybe playful. But there was something else. Something she had seen in the house in the Old Wood, but hadn't thought much about because she wasn't sure how to put it into words. It was like she didn't see a girl anymore, but she wasn't sure she saw a woman yet. Thinking about that put a very serious expression on her face.

"Smile," her mom said. She smiled, and her eyes lifted and her whole face lit up. A little embarrassed, she lowered her gaze. That made her notice curves, and now she was more than a little bit embarrassed, and she blushed.

"What do you see, dear?"

Breasts, she thought. *I see breasts. I'm not saying that!*

"Karia, it might help if you look a little higher, dear."

Karia looked up.

"For goodness sake, young lady," her mom said. "Sit up straight, smile, and look in the mirror. Tell me what you see."

"Am I pretty, Mom?"

"You tell me, Karia."

"I think maybe I am?"

"That's not very convincing," her mom said. "Remember, pretend the girl in the mirror isn't you. What do you see?"

Karia took a deep breath and turned red again. She crossed her arms over her chest. Her mom pulled them back to her sides. "Focus, Karia, and tell me what you see."

"This is hard, Mom."

"No, it isn't. Just be honest with me. If you saw a new girl in the village or at one of the big Gatherings, you'd be able to tell me in an instant if she was pretty. Oh, do sit up straight, dear, and smile! Look at that girl" – she pointed to the mirror – "and tell me, is she pretty?"

"Yes?" Karia said softly.

"What?"

"Yes," she said a little louder.

"Was that so hard?"

"Yes."

"OK, dear, let's go over it again."

CHAPTER FIFTY-FIVE

Karia and her mom and dad walked to Uncle Avar's house. Karia's dad held her around the waist, and Karia had her arm over her dad's shoulder.

When they got to the porch, her mom stopped them. Helping to support Karia, she had her husband hold out his arm as if he was escorting Karia, and steadied her as she shifted her weight and leaned on his arm. Karia struggled a little with the porch steps, but she pushed through it, understanding what her mom was trying to do. *She wants me to look like a lady, and I'm going to do my best.* But she felt like she was pretending to be a grown-up.

"Smile," her mom said. *Right.*

Uncle Avar opened the door, and while he wasn't scowling at Karia, his expression wasn't exactly kind. But as she stepped into the light of the parlor, she looked him right in the eyes and smiled, and his face softened. *It works. Wow.* As she came into the room, she saw Timbal's eyes go wide. She looked away to keep from blushing.

Her dad helped her to the big blue chair near the door – the chair that, when they were all there, Nana sat in. She had never sat there before. *It's a grown-up chair,* she thought. *I guess I am growing up.* But she still felt sort of like she was pretending as her dad helped her sit down, and then stood to one side of her. Uncle Avar took a seat across from Karia and next to his wife. Timbal sat on the other side of his mom. He hadn't gotten up when she came in, but she decided that was because it must hurt to move when you're recovering from broken ribs. Karia's mom walked across to stand on Karia's other side, and as Karia said nothing, her mom discretely poked her.

Karia's smile slipped, but she quickly recovered. She sat up straight, looked serious, and began, her voice trembling only a little.

"Uncle Avar, Aunt Heather, I need to apologize for what I did to Timbal. He was trying to help, and I hurt him. I was wrong, and I'm sorry." Smiling now, she said, "Can we please not let my mistake ruin the harmony of our families?"

"Oh, certainly dear," Aunt Heather said. Karia smiled at Uncle Avar – and it was easy because of what Aunt Heather had said – and he actually almost smiled at her and said, "Sure, dear."

She looked over at Timbal, and slightly flushed as she realized he had been staring at her. Again she recovered nicely. "Timbal, I apologize for hurting you. For as long as I can remember, you've been my friend. Please accept my apology and let's be friends again."

Timbal smiled and said, "Sure." *But that's not a real smile, and he sounds disappointed.* She felt sort of bad for him, but not bad about what she had chosen. She remembered what Shijih said about her son Drical: *'He's a nice boy, but he's still a boy.'* She thought that applied to Timbal too. But Gerik … well, Gerik was a man. And he was very serious about her.

She realized she had drifted off to another place, and everyone was sitting there, looking at her not saying anything. *Oh, gosh, what now?* Her smile slipped.

She was relieved when her mom spoke. "Avar, Heather, Timbal, thank you. Now if you'll excuse us, Karia is not well herself, so we'll be going."

Karia's dad extended his hand and Karia used it to help her stand. He led her toward the door, which Uncle Avar held for her. Her dad went through the doorway, and Karia followed. But she caught her foot on the sill, and her hand slipped off her dad's arm. She grabbed toward him with her left hand but just grazed the leg of his pants. She caught the doorknob with her right hand, but she could not grip it. She saw the porch coming toward her, and realized two things at the same time. The porch wasn't the one moving, and she could do nothing. She hit the porch, flat on her face.

Karia heard a commotion of movement and voices, but the only thought going through her mind was, *Fire and ashes, that hurt!* Her dad helped her up, and her mom steadied her with one hand and began brushing the dust off with the other. Aunt Heather brought her a damp cloth and put it under her nose. It was then that she realized she had a bloody nose.

Walking home, her dad held her waist again, and Karia held the rag against her nose and tried to hold her head back and not trip again.

"You did so well, Karia," her mom said.

"Oh, yes," Karia said, her words muffled because of the cloth on her nose. "I'm just a picture of ladylike grace."

CHAPTER FIFTY-SIX

In the morning, she woke up at the right time, meaning it was actually before dawn. She was able to get up and dress before she felt at all dizzy. Hurrying out her bedroom door, she found her mom preparing a lot more than they needed.

"Oh, good!" her mom said. "You feel up to helping, dear? Uncle Avar and his family are coming over."

"Sure, Mom," Karia said, stopping to steady herself on the sideboard. *Maybe I hurried too much.* "What about Opa and Nana?"

"Oh, dear, you didn't hear, did you? They came back while you were still at the smith's, packed up some things and went to Talitakaya to see if they could do anything for Narek."

"Oh," Karia said.

She helped her mom with bread and eggs, then needed to sit down. After breakfast she felt well enough to help clean up. But throughout that time she was feeling bad about what happened to Narek – *what I did to Narek* – and what that meant for Opa and Nana.

"You seem to be feeling better," her mom said as Karia put the plates away.

"I am, Mom. I think if I can catch my breath a while, I can take care of the book today."

"That would be quite a relief for all of us, if you could do that, dear. But … are you just tiring quickly, or is something else bothering you?"

"I just … I wish there was something I could do for Narek," she said.

"I know, dear. I know. But there's really nothing you can do."

This witch has done enough harm already, Karia thought.

Ian Fallis

CHAPTER FIFTY-SEVEN

The day was bright and sunny, and even though it was late morning it was still cool. Karia's gloom began to fade almost as soon as she stepped down the front porch steps and was greeted by the familiar sight of the three houses surrounded by fields where tsilinki was growing, the smell of Nana's flowers in bloom, and the feeling of sun and a mild breeze on her face. She felt refreshed, and no longer dizzy or tired.

She picked her way between two fields that had been planted recently. She remembered how, a little later in the year when the tsilinki was about her height and the fields were flooded to irrigate them, she would play peek-a-boo with her own reflection. She laughed at the memory, and even thought to herself, *I should remember to play later in the fall. There's plenty of time before I have to be a serious grown-up.* She paused a moment. *I hope I never get so serious I can't play now and then.*

From the ground rose the smell of the wet, rich soil here, another of those scents that just said "home" to her. The feel and the sound of her boots in the soft ground were pleasant to her.

Past the damp fields came a pair of drier fields, and some movement in the distance to her right caught her eye. She stopped and gazed, and saw Timbal out helping his dad and her dad, and she allowed herself to feel like things were getting back to normal.

All she had to do was put this book where it wouldn't be found, and they'd all be safe. She even allowed herself to hope that the Dr'Zhak would realize Narek had no magical powers, and any day now, she'd see Narek and Opa and Nana arriving back at the farm. She would apologize to them just as she had to Timbal and her family, and everything would be fine.

She nearly skipped up the little rise between the fields and the forest, and took pleasure in the chill and dampness that surrounded her as she disappeared into the shade of the big oaks at the edge of the woods. Following a path she knew by heart, she felt completely at home. *Normal. Safe.* That thought made her smile as she passed the Liliki tree.

191

A ways further in and slightly higher up the wood had more pines and the soil became more sandy. The smell of the pines took her back to all those times she and Timbal and Narek laughed and played here. She deliberately walked to the right of the trail, pushing into the branches to let the pine needles brush across her face, savoring the aroma and enjoying the feeling.

She was shocked as a black bird flew right in front of her. She assumed it had been in one of the branches she had disturbed. She waved her arms and it flitted only a short distance away and returned almost immediately. *The rumply bird,* she thought. She shooed it away again and hurried toward the hedge, the feeling of magic growing stronger as she briskly walked.

If I could do anything to just get rid of magic once and for all, I would, she thought.

She felt a broad smile spread across her face as she walked down the lane. The sun broke through the trees here, and it was pleasantly warm. But … something was not right. She slowed. Everything seemed so perfect, and she could not identify one single leaf out of place. She thought perhaps she was just too worried after all that had happened recently, and resumed her pace.

Then a shape on the ground coalesced in her mind into a horse's hoofprint. She realized she'd been seeing them all along the lane, and now her eyes followed them to …

"Any word on your brother?" the magician said. She was angry, and apparently her face gave it away, because he added, "I wouldn't …"

She pushed him just as she had pushed Timbal, and suddenly she felt as if she herself had been pushed, hard. She flew backward, hit the hedge and fell to the ground.

The magician walked toward her, speaking calmly. "I was going to say, I wouldn't do that if I were you, for two reasons.

"First, I am not quite stupid enough to come up against a sorceress of your power without taking precautions. And second …"

Karia thought, *Fire,* and lifted her hand out toward him.

"Are you so very sure that won't bounce back on you also, Sprout?"

She put her hand down.

"Now, as I was saying, the second reason you shouldn't work magic is because it's like lighting a huge bonfire for everyone to see. You are so undisciplined, so inexperienced, that every time you work magic the energy goes flying all over the place for anyone like me to see."

His tone grew increasingly angry. "I saw you all the way from Talitakaya. So stop doing magic before someone far worse than me comes for you and your family, little girl!"

Karia pushed herself up on her hands. "I am not a little girl!" she shouted.

He began speaking, his tone menacing, and as he spoke, it grew darker and darker. "Oh, so you must be all of fifteen now. I saw you wearing the daypledge, so that must have been your all-grown-up young man with you at the show. So big, eh? All grown up now, you think?"

Karia felt like she was getting smaller, and he was growing. He leaned over her. "You're a long way from being anything other than a little girl!" He was so large now, and she was so small, that he cupped his hands around her, and his mouth filled the hole at the top of his hands, and he shouted, "You're nothing but a scared little girl!"

As he spoke, Karia fell again and curled into a ball on the ground, crying.

"Oh, stop that," he said. She opened her eyes and it was light again. He was normal size, and so was she. "That was an illusion. I didn't mean to make you cry. You should have seen right through it." He offered her his hand, and helped her up. Kindly, he said, "I just want you to know how much you still have to learn, and I'm here to teach you."

The moment Karia got to her feet, she felt something like a little rumble deep inside. She could not say exactly where it came from, but she sensed rather than felt that a door had opened. She saw her hand wrench out of his and slap him, and heard herself say, "You will never raise your voice to me. You will teach me because it is your duty to serve me." *Oh, no, I'm speaking Inamali again!*

The magician just stood there, looking down at this little girl, stunned.

Karia heard herself speak Inamali again. "Cast your eyes down, and kneel before me."

He complied.

And then she heard herself say nothing. She just stood there, with this man kneeling in front of her. She looked down at him, and he looked down at the ground.

"Forgive me," he said.

"Um, OK," she said. *Oh, good, I'm speaking normal ... normally.* "You can probably get up."

He looked up. "Probably?"

"Yes, probably. I'm not sure what just happened, so I can't guarantee it's not going to happen again."

"Fair enough," he said, and got up, dusting off his knees. "I guess you just needed to set some boundaries."

"That wasn't me," Karia said.

The magician laughed. "Oh, but it was, Sprout."

"Don't call me that," Karia said.

"What should I call you, then? Karia? That's not who you are."

"Yes it is."

"No, dear, that's the name people have given you. But it's not what you are. Do you want to know what you really are?"

"My name is Karia, and I'm Tsilinakaya," she said.

"Yes, precisely. So you're deluded but not completely ignorant … I mean, you know that much, good. That was Tsilinakaya speaking – and that's you. That's more proof of just how much you need my help … sorry, just how much I am bound to serve you," he said.

"I don't trust you," Karia said. *'Don't listen to him, Karia,'* she remembered her dad saying. *'This kind always lies.'*

"Good," he said. "You shouldn't. Don't trust anyone. Remember everything anyone ever does to you, and settle every account. Expect the worst from everyone, and prepare for it."

Karia digested that for a moment, then said, "What a horrible way to live."

"It is," the magician acknowledged. "But the option is not living."

CHAPTER FIFTY-EIGHT

Karia dusted off her dress, and remembered that the haversack had fallen from her shoulder when she pushed, well, herself. She bent and picked it up, dusting it off and putting it over her shoulder.

"What's in the bag?" the magician asked.

Karia had been raised to be polite and to answer her elders, and she almost told him. Then she realized it was an impolite question. What a woman has in her bag is her business and hers alone. Especially when it's illegal. "It's none of your concern," she said.

"Well, actually, I'm quite concerned about everything having to do with you, and I can't help if you're keeping secrets from me," he said.

"Then you might as well be on your way."

The magician looked hard at her. "You really do have a great deal of potential."

"Fine. Now go. I need to … do something." She looked toward the hedge.

"You mean pee?" he asked.

Karia blushed, and lifted her hand to slap him. This time it was her lifting her own hand.

He stepped back. "Well, I suppose you could have all the privacy you want if you just crawl under this hedge."

Karia glared at him.

"Have you ever seen a slug?" he asked.

Karia was taken aback by the question, and replied warily, "Yes."

"And you can see where it's been, right?"

"Yes."

"Good. Now, how do bees find flowers?"

Karia had no idea where this was going. "By smelling them, I guess."

"So how did I find this place, and why didn't you know I was here?"

Karia could not keep up with him. "I … I don't know."

"Well, Sprout – sorry, but I still don't know what else to call you – if you'll forgive the analogies, this place is sort of like a flower and I probably could have sniffed it out. It has great magic, but you can only, let's say, smell it up close. And that, if you will, masked my scent. Convenient, I'd say.

"And you, Sprout, are like the slug. As I said, excuse the analogy, but your magic is so sloppy you leave a trail for a while afterward. And this is where it led."

She looked at him, not knowing what to say.

"So I asked what is in the bag in hope that it would give me a clue what's on the other side of the hedge, so I didn't have to admit I don't know," he said.

"You didn't go in?" she asked.

"Oh, believe me, I tried. Ended up crawling into a thorn bush before I realized I'd lost your trail. Whatever it is, it's yours and yours alone. And since you didn't know that, I must be correct that you didn't make it."

Karia was upset to understand that just asking him questions was giving him information, so she was very much on guard when he asked, "So what is behind the hedge?"

"I'm not sure the person who made it wanted you to know," she replied.

"Oh, you can be sure on that point. The person who made it worked very hard to conceal it from other sorcerers. The only reason I found it was because of you, and I still can't tell what it is."

"Good," Karia said, walking toward the gap under the hedge.

"I'll wait right here then," the magician said.

Karia got onto her hands and knees. "Good," she said again, and crawled into the darkness under the hedge.

CHAPTER FIFTY-NINE

Karia stood up in the study. She halfway expected the magician to come through any second now. She watched and waited, but eventually was satisfied that he had been telling the truth. Only she could come into her house in the Old Wood.

She walked over to the bookcase. She took the diary out of her haversack and scanned the shelves, and decided it belonged in the middle. *Well, it's more like literature than magic or farming. Poetry even. 'An ode to beard trimming.'*

She carried the haversack to the bedroom – and stopped. There was a bedroom door again. It looked new, and was wide open. She walked in and glanced at the bed, and it was covered with the bedspread. There was no sign of splinters.

"Thank you," she said

She jumped when she heard, "You're welcome." The haversack again fell off her shoulder.

She looked around the room, her heart racing, and saw no one. Cautiously, she peaked behind the door, then in the wardrobes. She saw no one else, and heard nothing else.

"What are you doing?" she heard from above her, and she looked up while backing away, slamming her back into a wardrobe.

"Please don't break anything else," she heard. Following the source of the sound, she looked up, and saw a tiny figure on top of the canopy bed, peering over the edge at her.

Stunned, Karia just nodded. She gasped when he jumped from the edge of the canopy and began plunging toward the floor, but then tiny wings began beating and he flew up – fast – right in front of her face, stopping just as she winced, thinking he would collide with her nose.

"What's wrong with you?" he asked.

"You … you're … you're a faerie!" Karia said.

The tiny man threw his hands over his eyes and began flying in a little circle. "Oh, no, please, no! How can that be! I thought I was a butterfly!"

Karia just stared at him. He stopped and put his hands on his ample hips, and looked disappointed. "That was funny," he said.

Karia just nodded, staring wide-eyed at him. "You're a very fat faerie," she said. He crossed his arms, and he looked rather angry. "Oh, I'm so sorry!" Karia said. "That was so rude!"

"This is your fault," he said.

"What?"

"All that magic flying out of you, leaking all over the place."

"What?"

"Don't you know? Look, try to control yourself a little bit, please. Faeries are like magic sponges. We just soak it all up. That's why most of us are so small. There's actually not a whole lot of magic out there. We usually have to eat nuts to survive, like we did before magic returned. But around you, well, it's like somebody's rolling wheels of cheese down my throat all the time."

Karia just stared at him. "You're a faerie," Karia said.

"You said that."

"Faeries aren't real," she said.

"Right, and little girls can't do magic," he said.

"I'm not a little girl," Karia snapped.

"Oh, the fat little faerie is so sorry for talking truth."

"I'm fifteen," Karia said.

"I'm 978. Or is it 979? Golly, it could even be 989. Tough to tell time in a place where time doesn't move, you know. And you're fifteen? You're a little girl."

Karia tried to push him away with her mind. He puffed up a little.

"Oh, thank you! Thank you so much. More of that I'll have to walk everywhere."

CHAPTER SIXTY

The faerie flew over, picked up Karia's haversack and flew into the wardrobe with it.

"Oh, I'm sorry," Karia said.

He poked his head past the wardrobe door. "Sorry?"

"For dropping the haversack," she said. He stared at her. "For making you pick up after me."

"You're a sorceress, right?"

"I guess."

"Good golly, I've had about enough of this." He flew out of the wardrobe and flitted right and left just in front of her face. She had to resist the impulse to swat him away like you'd swat a fly or a gnat. "Listen," he said. "You're a sorceress, and I'm a faerie. A very powerful sorcerer offered me the opportunity to take this position, and I'm glad to have it. I take care of the place – sorry about the mess when you showed up the first time, but I wasn't getting much to eat – anyway, I take care of this place, and ..."

"That happened to you since I got here?" she said, pointing at his large belly.

"Yes, yes, I'm fat, OK? But look, here's the thing. Instead of living in the forest and being hungry all the time, I get to live under a roof and get fed. In return, I do the cleaning and the picking up, and I do things like replace doors when you make them explode."

"I didn't know how to get in," Karia said.

"Oh, silly me, I thought you sneezed."

"You're a sarcastic little faerie," she said.

"No, I'm a wisecracking big fat faerie, thanks to you."

"Wait," Karia said, blushing, "you've been here the whole time?"

"Yep." He winked. Karia turned red. He laughed, and fluttered in a quick circle. "I'm sorry, that was mean. Look, please don't take this personally, but it really doesn't make any difference to me whether you're wearing clothes or not. You're a completely different type of creature, and

I'm not interested. Look at me, and tell me – you aren't at all interested in me, are you?"

"No. Sorry."

"Don't apologize. I mean, I could be flying around naked, and it wouldn't mean anything to you, right?"

Karia didn't want that picture in her head. She must have frowned.

"OK, bad illustration," he said. "Try this. Have you ever seen a horse?"

"Yes."

"Have you ever seen a horse with clothes on?"

"No."

"Did it really matter to you that the horse didn't have clothes on?"

"No."

"Well, that's kind of how I see you. When I see you." Karia blushed again. "If I see you," he added quickly. "I hope you won't be offended, but to me, horses are more attractive than you, so it's not like I'm trying to see you. This is your place, and you can wear, or not wear, what you want, and I'll just stay out of the way unless you speak to me or call me."

"Wait, what do I call you?"

"Generality."

"Generality?"

"Yes. I like that word. It has a nice ring to it. You couldn't pronounce my name, so you can call me Generality. It's better than 'very fat faerie.'"

"I said I was sorry."

"Faeries don't forget."

CHAPTER SIXTY-ONE

Generality had flown back to the top of the canopy, so Karia assumed he lived there. She went back to the study and got out the farming book again, and carried it to the kitchen table. She went back a second time for the ornate book with her Inamali name on the spine.

She started to sit down, then stood back up and walked into the bedroom. She sat on the bed and looked around. She didn't see Generality anywhere. She took off her shoes and put them in the closet, catching a glimpse of the embroidered slippers as she did. She started to go back to the kitchen, then turned around and went back to the wardrobe. She picked up the slippers, sat down and put them on. She smiled. They were so pretty, and so comfortable. She padded back to the kitchen in the slippers and sat down.

Opening the farming book to about the middle, she was a little surprised to realize that she could now read it almost as well as she could read Teneka.

She moved it aside and opened the ornate book to the first page. Now she was surprised again, for this was still quite a struggle. She thought she could sort out some of the root words inside the constructed words on the page, but there were so many things added at the front, the back and even the middle that she was getting very confused. And the first paragraph still seemed backwards to her. It seemed as if the first sentence said something like, "What you have read here is true."

If she was reading the tense correctly. And that character in that place meant "here." And she was right that those three words could be translated as "what" in this context. And the long subject was some formal way of writing "you." And all those characters whose function she didn't understand weren't important. And she had the words in the right order.

"Aaaaaargh!" she said, and slammed the book.

She pushed that book to one side, and padded to the study. She took a moment to stop and admire the slippers – and smile – again.

She scanned the bookshelves. More of the titles made sense to her now.

She pulled another volume out of the middle shelves – she deliberately chose one that looked far less ornate – and opened it on the desk. The pages looked fresher – newer – than the pages of the ornate book, so she took it to the kitchen and opened the two books side-by-side.

She looked at the paper in the simpler book, and the paper in the ornate book. She ran her hands over each. Looking carefully, and feeling the pages of the ornate book, she thought, *This book is ancient.*

With them side-by-side, she also noticed that the words in the simpler book were shorter. She opened the farming book, and saw that the words were of similar length. The paper looked similar too. *And I can read this*, she thought. But at this point she was just scanning for words she recognized, and not trying to read the simpler book.

She looked again at the ornate book, and looked closely at the characters. Now she ran to the study and got her syllable sheets. She compared them to the ornate book. Surprised, she began comparing the characters of the ornate book to those in the simpler book. *They're different,* she thought. At first, they had looked the same. And a few were. Many appeared to be just fancy variations of the characters on Karia's syllable charts. But studying the first page of the ornate book, she found two characters she had not seen before, not in any form.

She now knew why she had been unable to read the ornate book. It was not just that the subject matter and therefore the words used were different. It was a different form of Inamali – apparently an ancient form. The words and the characters used to form them had apparently grown simpler.

I can't learn two more languages! One is hard enough.

She walked back to the library to see if she could find another old book. Along the top shelf she spotted a spine that looked somewhat like the one on the ornate book. It looked like leather, and seemed to be gilded and embossed, with the letters finely carved. She got it down, brought it to the kitchen and set it on the bench a moment. Then she moved the simpler book aside, and put this older book on the table next to the ornate book and opened it. It seemed that from use, it opened to a page rather near the front.

She looked at it, blushed and slammed the book shut again. On one side had been a drawing of a naked man. On the other side was a drawing of a naked woman. *What kind of book is this?*

She opened it again, slowly, as if she feared the drawings would do something lewd. She noticed there were tiny, fine lines all over the drawings, with arrowheads at one end and words at the other end. She turned to the next page and saw an unfamiliar word at the top, and matched it to a word on the drawings.

Oh, she thought with relief, *this is a Healer's book*.

She scanned the page, looking at the writing and the paper, and the size of the words, and decided this also was in old Inamali, as she was calling it. She had a thought, but decided to put this book back first. She didn't want anyone to get the wrong idea about the kind of books she was looking at.

Returning to the kitchen table, she called, "Generality!"

She jumped when she almost immediately heard, directly in her ear, "Yes?"

"Don't do that!" she said.

"But you called me."

"No, I mean, when I call you, please don't zip up and suddenly talk right into my ear. Come up in front of me, please."

"Yes, Ma'am."

"I'm not a ma'am."

"Yes, Mistress."

"OK, I guess that'll work. What do you know about these books?"

He scanned the books from over her shoulder. He flew in closer, carefully moving down a page of the farming book. Then he flew to the ornate book and scanned down one of its pages. He landed on the edge of the table, putting one hand on his hip and the other on his chin. His brow furrowed; he raised an eyebrow.

He looked up at Karia. "They're big," he said.

"That's it? They're big?"

"Well, I can't read, but they seem rather pretty, too."

She sighed. "Thank you. That's all." He dashed away faster than she thought possible.

Now she closed the ornate book and put it away. She would have to try to read it another time. She sat down at the table and began to read the simpler book.

It turned out that the simpler book wasn't simple at all. It was filled with words that were apparently a wide variety of plants and animals she had never heard of, and worded in a way that baffled her. She wondered if it was some kind of poetry, and the plants and animals were symbols. Yet as difficult as it was, it was somehow fascinating, and attractive. When she realized she was on the last page, she suddenly felt hungry, and her rear felt sore.

She stood and stretched.

Ian Fallis

CHAPTER SIXTY-TWO

After a lunch of cheese and onion, she ground some more anarka flour and prepared some bread. She mixed in the leftover cheese and onion for some variety.

Then she sat down and began leafing through the book of poetry again. She had decided it most definitely was poetry. She could understand bits and pieces, and sometimes entire stanzas. At least, she could read the words and fit the sentences together. But what they meant? That was another matter. It was as if the Inamali looked at the world differently, and until she understood how they saw things, their poetry would not make sense to her.

She wondered how much bearing that would have on other subjects.

She put the poetry book back on the shelf, then read through the rest of the farming book. She was glad she did. She understood it well, and it helped her to remember that in the last several days here, and with her mom's help at home, she had learned a lot of Inamali.

She gathered her syllable sheets and took them back to the desk, then put the farming book back on the shelves. After a meal of bread and wine, she went to the bedroom and looked to see if Generality was looking. She couldn't see him.

She went to the waterfall room and closed the door. Then she checked the door, just to make sure it was closed. She undressed, took off her locket and stepped into the waterfall. Again she found the waterfall soothing and refreshing, and she stepped out and toweled off.

She put on her locket, then wrapped the robe around herself again, tied it, and made sure it was secure before she opened the door. She took her clothes to their respective wardrobes and put them away. She ran her hand over the silky chemise again, then picked up the farm-girl chemise and took it into the waterfall room.

Again checking the door twice, she took off the robe and hung it up, then put on the chemise. She looked in the mirror. It was not as flattering as the white one, but it was comfortable. It not only felt good, but she felt good in it, and it wasn't revealing. She didn't care what the faerie said, she didn't like the idea of him seeing her. She didn't think that was an issue in this chemise.

Walking back into the bedroom, she sat down at the dressing table and picked up the hairbrush. A thought occurred to her.

"Generality?"

She saw something flash past the left side of her face, turn sharply at the mirror and come directly – fast – straight at her face. Karia was terrified that he was going to slam right into her nose, but she had no time to react. He stopped fractions of an inch from her. "Is that better?" he said.

After she managed to catch her breath she said, "A little slower next time, OK?"

"Sure," he said.

"The man who gave you this position – you met him?"

"Yes."

Karia looked in the mirror and began to brush her hair, which was odd with a faerie hovering just in front of her nose. "What was he like?"

"Ugly." Karia focused on the faerie. "I mean, by faerie standards. Little shoulders. Hardly big enough for wings, and of course no wings."

"Can you describe him?"

"I just did. Sorry, shoulders and wings are mostly what matters to faeries."

"Did he look like me?"

The faerie backed up, then said, "Yes, little shoulders, not big enough for wings, and of course no wings. Sorry, you're just not very attractive either, by faerie standards."

"No, I mean, his face. Do you remember that? Did his face look like mine?"

Generality came in close to her left eye, so close that Karia started blinking. Then he went over to her right eye, and down her nose. "Hmmm," he said. He went down to her mouth and seemed to trace the edges of it. Abruptly, he darted to one ear, circling it, and he dashed to the other one. The breeze from his wings tickled. "Hmmm," he said again. Then he darted back to her nose.

"His nose was more masculine, but somewhat like yours. And the shape of the eyes, for sure. Not the color, but the shape. He had earlobes like yours too."

"Earlobes?" she asked.

"Yes. You have beautiful earlobes. Very aerodynamic. And I guess he was tall and thin, and had long fingers like you too, come to think of it."

"Was he nice?"

"What do you mean?"

"Was he nice to you?"

"Well, I suppose so, in a powerful sorcerer sort of way. He didn't burn me to a cinder and he gave me a place to live and fed me."

"What was his smile like?"

"I only saw him smile once, when he talked about his children. But it was something like your smile. Then again, all humans look pretty much alike to me."

"Wait," Karia said. "He talked about his children?"

"Only once."

"He said children?"

"That's what I said."

"As in more than one?" Karia asked.

Generality stared at her for a moment. "Look, Teneka may not be my first language, but I know the difference between singular and plural nouns."

"Fine," Karia said, frustrated. "What did he say?"

"Hmmm. I don't really remember."

"Wait – you said faeries don't forget!"

"Did I? Really?"

"Generality, please, think. You have to remember what he said."

"I remember part of it. He said he was making this place for his younger daughter, who was going to be a great sorceress."

"He said his younger daughter?" Karia asked.

"Yes. Most definitely. Younger daughter. Said she'd be a great sorceress. Failed to mention her lack of magic control that'd make me swell up like a dead horse just before it pops."

Karia had not been listening to him. She was thinking, *I have a sister. A sister!* But she halfway caught the end of his words, and said, "Huh?" Then it dawned on her what he had said. "Ew! That's disgusting!"

"That's right, ew. Disgusting, that's what I am, a disgusting fat faerie."

"Please, you must try to remember everything he said about his children."

"Sorry, that's all I remember."

"Generality, you must promise me something."

"I'm pledged to your service, Mistress."

"You need to promise me that you'll try to remember."

"I will."

Ian Fallis

CHAPTER SIXTY-THREE

Karia slept well in the big canopy bed – so much larger than her bed, with sheets so soft and elegant. As on every morning here – if they could be called mornings – she awoke refreshed, her thoughts clear.

She felt she needed to get more confidence in Inamali with books she could read before she dared open any of the magic books, so she went to the study and got Jiki's diary. She briefly considered saving it until she got insomnia, but she never had a problem sleeping here. She walked into the parlor, thinking that since she was just reading, it might be nice to sit in a padded chair. But she just couldn't stand to sit in those horrid orange chairs, to rest her back against the ugly spots.

She walked to the bedroom instead and pulled out the chair at the dressing table, and began reading where she had left off. Somewhere between the description of peeling potatoes and the account of his battle with a field mouse, Karia felt it was time for lunch, so she put the book down and headed to the kitchen.

Her hunger satisfied, she returned to the book, glad to read that Jiki proved victorious over the mouse. In a few more pages she came to the disturbingly detailed account of the birth of Jiki's son, and decided she didn't actually want to have children after all. Ever.

She read that he named his son Lukaliva, which Karia thought was a very nice name – strong and beautiful at the same time.

Karia tried to read more of Jiki's diary, but it seemed she had had just about enough of it for today. She put the diary back in the bookcase. She stared at the rows of books. She wished there was a diary here from her grandfather.

Her eyes kept gravitating to the top shelf, and to the one large volume on the left she had used to make fire. She tried to look at the books at the bottom shelf, because she knew they'd be good practice. And because she didn't want anything more to do with magic.

209

But they all looked boring, and without thinking she looked back to the top shelf. Back to the large volume. She forced herself to look to the middle shelf, but she was afraid she wouldn't understand anything. Her eyes went back to the top shelf. Back to the large volume.

She forced herself to at least look to the right, and that's when she noticed the tiny book wedged into the shadows between two large books. She reached in, pulled it out and opened it on the desk. Inside the cover, she discovered, were not pages, but one large piece of paper, folded over and over. She unfolded it, and it began to tear at some of the folds. The paper was brittle and old. She went about unfolding it much more carefully, then gently smoothed it out. Not gently enough, apparently. It tore a little more. She stepped back, and found herself looking at a map. It was a map of the area where she lived, though at first she did not recognize it.

The first thing she noticed was that what they had always called the Old Wood – what everyone around called the Old Wood – was not even on the map. In its place was drawn what looked like an estate house. Something was written next to the house, and at first she took it for Inamali. Looking closer, she thought perhaps it was Old Inamali, as it contained one of the characters she had not yet deciphered.

She realized that the road was about where the lane ran past the hedge in the Old Wood.

She traced that road west, and saw that it petered out at the one section of the Wrecked Coast that was not strewn with rocks and wreckage, the place that the old stories said the Inamali and Teneka had come ashore. She remembered the small stone obelisk she and her dad had found on its side there, and thought that perhaps it had once marked the end of the road. He had told her then about the obelisks that used to mark the road to town and on to the Dentanal Mountains. Most of them were now fallen or knocked over, or part of a farmer's stone wall.

Next she followed the road east, to the large stone bridge, which was sketched with its tower and gate and had what she assumed was a name next to it, also apparently in Old Inamali. A few figures that appeared to depict small thatched huts were drawn here as well, on either side of the river. She saw the river road running south from here, and was surprised to see a bay depicted on the map. The road led to a town along that bay.

Her family had taken the road south before, and it had indeed continued much farther than they expected. But it led to muddy flats from which she and her dad fished. She laughed. *He's not much of a fisherman.* She remembered that they had taken little food, caught far less than they had hoped, and were hungry for much of that trip. She looked at the map again. It clearly showed a town with a bay, and even ships in the bay. *There's nothing like that there now.*

She went back to the stone bridge, and ran her finger along the road to the rise near Milliken's Farm, south of the rocky hills. There was drawn the tower as it must have looked when it stood intact. Either the map exaggerated, or the tower was actually quite a bit taller than she had pictured it. Following the road farther, she saw a crossroads and a small fort where the town was today, and the road trailed off the edge of the map headed toward the pass in the Dentanal Mountains, just as it did today. A small arrow pointed in that direction. There was an Old Inamali word next to it, and though she did not know all the characters, she tried to sound it out. It seemed similar to the word they used today, Dentanal.

She took her attention back to the crossroads. A road led west from the town, through a passage she had not known existed in the rocky hills, to the ford on the Heldasfar. *If this map is accurate, that's a shorter way from our farm to town.* But she did not know whether the route was still there, and did not know of anyone who had ever successfully crossed those hills. The stories said compasses did not work there, and even the sun and the moon changed positions.

There at the Heldasfar was a junction, and another tower was depicted there. Karia had never seen even the ruins of a tower near the ford. And on the map, the road along the river did not falter just past the large stone bridge. It continued to the ford, and even went north from there.

For now she followed the road to the west, and saw that instead of being the trail that today bent south toward their farm, the road bent north and west, to what appeared to be a large castle wedged between the coast and the mountains, and she saw – quite unexpectedly – that the road continued on there over the mountains. *I don't think anyone knows there's a pass there, let alone an old road.*

She went back to the ford and traced the river road north. There, instead of the vast marsh, was a lake with a town on its south shore, with yet another name written in Old Inamali.

Karia stepped back to take it all in. Where today there were scattered small farms with one small village, there had apparently been at least three towns, some settlements and a few forts. She took in a few more details. Ships in the bay. Huts around the castles and the fort and the towers. Lines in the fields. All the fields. She already knew that today, her family tended only a fraction of the fields this farm once had, but she had not thought much about it, or about how far north those fields went. Now she saw they went almost all the way to the mountains, and there were several other fallow fields in the area.

That many fields means a lot of farmers, and other people too. Had they been Inamali? Is this actually where her people came from?

211

No, that can't be. The stories said the Inamali couldn't go home, but if they came ashore here, they were already home. Who were these people? And where did they go?

"Why did they need castles and towers?" she asked aloud. She thought of the skull she and Timbal and Narek had found in the ruins of the bridge tower. She remembered the jagged hole in the forehead, and realized now that was probably a result of battle. *Who were they fighting?*

She turned and leaned against the desk, her arms folded. She looked up at the bookshelves. She had thought they would be full of answers. She was wrong. They were full of questions.

CHAPTER SIXTY-FOUR

Karia fixed herself some dinner and sat to eat as she looked at a slim volume from the middle shelf. She didn't try to read it, or even sound out the words. She simply ran her eyes over the characters on the page. She expected to get a feeling from it, as she had so many times with Jiki's diary. But something quite unexpected happened.

Pictures began forming in her mind. She saw some kind of large black-and-white speckled cat running swiftly and gracefully through long yellow grass. A sleek golden-tan animal with long legs and thin, curving horns bent its long neck to drink at a waterhole. Flocks of blue-gray birds with pointy beaks and short legs with knobby knees alighted from a reedy marsh into a cloudless blue sky. Many other animals walked and trotted through her thoughts, ate and drank, bellowed and roared and snorted. It was a large, lush land, with grasslands and marshes, forests and jungles. Karia felt like she was there, and was there for a long time, drinking it all in. It was beautiful, and she smiled.

Then the earth began to shake. A mountain in the background began to tremble, and from it fire shot into the sky and poured from it like rivers, across the forests and marshes and plains. The grass burned and all was black. The animals ran, but there was nowhere to go. They ran until they fell. Their bodies lay on the ground. The air and the sky were filled with smoke, and a gentle rain of ash settled over everything. Darkness became complete.

She blinked and realized she had come to the end of the book. Her dinner, half-eaten, was stone-cold. She stepped to the fireplace, and where there had been a fire on which she had cooked her dinner there was now only ash. She touched it. *Cold ash.*

She looked again at the book, and she could not read the words. But ... had that been a dream, or had she seen what was in the book? How could a book do that? *Or did I do that?*

She took her plate and cup to the sideboard and took the book back to the shelves. She was very tired.

She walked to the bedroom and pulled back the covers. They felt so soft, so welcoming. She had a thought.

"Generality?" she called.

Nothing happened. Concerned, she called him again. "Generality?"

He zipped from the top of the canopy, coming straight at her face at high speed until he was about a foot away. Then he abruptly slowed and came toward her at a glacial pace.

She chose not to wait for him to arrive. "Is everything OK?" she asked.

"Yes, Mistress," he said.

"You just took longer than I expected."

"Oh, sorry, I was bowling."

She stared at him a moment. She thought perhaps he was being sarcastic, but she wasn't sure.

"What, do you think I'm too fat to bowl?" he said.

"No, no, it's just that ..." she looked toward the top of the canopy, "... bowling?"

"Yes. It's just a single lane, and I have to play alone and keep score and reset the pins myself, but it's entertaining."

Karia still wasn't sure he wasn't being sarcastic. She looked toward the top of the canopy again. *What else does he have up there?*

"Did you want something?" Generality asked.

"Oh, yes, right. I wanted to ask you," she said. She blushed and paused. "I wanted to ask you, if I put my chemise on the floor next to the bed, if you would leave it there, please."

"Why?"

"Well, because I was thinking of sleeping," again she blushed, "without it, but I want to be able to reach it in the morning without getting out of bed."

"Why?"

"Because ... well, I don't want to have to walk across the room, you know, and get it out of the wardrobe."

"Why not?"

"Are you always like this?" she asked.

"Like what?"

"Do you always have so many questions?"

"How many?"

"I don't know!" she said, growing exasperated. "Look, I just want you to leave my chemise on the floor, OK?"

"OK." He hovered there, looking at her.

"You can go now."

"OK." He continued to hover.

"I meant, go."

"May I ask you a question first?"

"You have more questions?" she said, getting more than a little frustrated with him.

"Yes." He just hovered.

"OK, fine, what?"

"Have I failed you?" He seemed genuinely hurt.

Karia felt bad. As odd and sarcastic as Generality was, she liked him. *Why do I keep hurting people?* "Why would you think you've failed me?"

"My job is to serve you and make sure you are comfortable. I tried to explain to you that I don't watch you, and that you don't need to worry about me seeing you, and you still seem to be afraid of me looking at you. It seems that I've done something to make you uncomfortable in your house. So I want to know how I've failed you, and I want to assure you that I will do everything in my power to correct it."

She smiled at him. "No, you've misunderstood. It's just that it's important to me to be modest – and before you ask, I really can't explain it, but I don't want to put myself in a position to be seen by anyone, even someone who assures me they find horses more appealing than me."

"So as long as I am in this house you will not feel as comfortable as you did before you knew I was here?"

"Well, no, I guess not."

"Do you want me to leave?"

"No! This is your house, too, and you're serving me well. I don't want you to leave."

"Thank you, but you've misunderstood my role. This is your house. I'm in your service. If you want to dismiss me at any time, for any reason, you can."

"Well, I don't want to dismiss you. And I want to keep thinking of this as your house too. And since I'm in charge, that's the way it's going to be."

"OK," he said.

"All right, then, good night," Karia said.

"Could I ask one more question?"

"Generality, if you ask me one more question, I am going to push magic into you again. Is your question worth that?"

"No, I suppose not." He flew away to the canopy.

Karia decided to climb under the covers before undressing.

Ian Fallis

CHAPTER SIXTY-FIVE

She awoke and one clear thought was on her mind: She wanted to ask her mom about her sister.

She climbed out of bed and – glancing up at the canopy first – walked over to the wardrobe and put on her nice white chemise and, this time, the green dress. She could tell that Generality had cleaned the chemise. It was bright white and fresh. She put away the farm-girl chemise that Generality had, as instructed, left on the floor.

She sat down to brush her hair, and a thought occurred to her.

"Generality," she called, wincing for fear of what he was going to do this time.

Again she felt him zip past her ear, saw him streak toward the mirror before turning at the last minute, and head for her face. But about two feet away, he slowed to an agonizingly slow pace, and again came to rest not more than a freckle's width off her nose.

"Yes, mistress."

"Did my father tell you the names of any of his children?"

Generality put his hand on his chin and looked down, as if he was thinking about it, then looked up and answered, "No, I'm afraid he didn't."

"OK," Karia said, and she stretched.

Suddenly Generality was darting around her chest and shouting, "Oh! Oh! Oh!"

Karia clasped her arms around her chest and shouted at him. "Hey! What are you doing! Stop that!"

"I remembered!"

"Remembered what?"

"What he said. I remembered because of your teats."

Breasts, she thought, but she wasn't going to say it.

"Faerie women have six teats, so they can nurse their litters," Generality said. "But you only have two." He fluttered about, chest-high, and looked up at her face. "Why do you cover them, by the way?"

"What?"

"Why do you cover your teats?"

"Look, I'm not going to have this conversation with you hovering around … there. Come up here."

Generality flew back up right in front of her face, and asked, "Well, why?"

"What?"

"Why do you cover your teats?"

"Well, it's just, well, I'm not going to go around with them uncovered!"

"Why not?"

"It wouldn't be decent!"

"Why not?"

"Because, well, it wouldn't."

"Faerie women don't cover their teats. They need to be able to nurse their litters. Doesn't the covering get in the way of nursing your babies?"

"I don't have babies!"

"Yes, but if you had babies, wouldn't it get in the way?"

"I am not having babies."

"Oh, you probably just don't know how yet. It probably works the same for you as for faeries. Let me explain …"

"No! No, thank you, I'm fine. Look, what does all this have to do with what you remembered?"

"Remembered? Oh, right. Your mom only had two teats."

"All women only have two breasts," Karia said.

"No, faerie women have six, and Dr'Zhak women …"

"All Teneka women and all …" She stopped. She realized she couldn't say that all Inamali women only have two breasts. She wasn't sure. *Oh, gosh, please just two!*

"What did you call them?"

Keeping up with him in a conversation was like trying to watch him fly. "What did I call what?" she asked.

"Your teats," he said. Karia blushed. "And why do you keep turning red whenever …"

"Stop!" she said. "What's the big deal about my mom only having two … you know?"

"Oh, right, you see, I thought that was unfair, because what was the third one supposed to do?"

"The third … what? You said she had two!" Karia said. *He is so frustrating!*

"That's not what you called them a minute ago."

"What are you talking about?"

"Your teats."

"Can we please stop talking about my, fine, breasts, we call them breasts," she said, blushing again. "And can you please tell me what you're talking about. It was unfair to the third one – the third what?"

"The third baby."

"What third baby?" Karia asked.

"He said you were the oldest of triplets."

Ian Fallis

CHAPTER SIXTY-SIX

After a long, awkward silence, Karia had dismissed him. *I have a sister, a big sister. And I'm the oldest of triplets.* She thought she knew what that meant, but she didn't want to think about that. She did want to think about her sister. She finished brushing her hair, and decided to talk to her mom about it.

She had to stop and think about what time and day it was back home. It was the third day since she came back from town, so Gerik would be coming the next day. Sitting before the mirror, and thinking about Gerik looking at her, she noticed that while the blue dress had brought out her eyes, the green dress seemed to make her hair shine. And it was no less flattering. She blushed and again felt like she was being vain. She saw the young woman in the mirror, and she was pretty, but she couldn't quite believe that was her. It didn't reconcile with her picture of herself as a pale, skinny stick-girl.

She decided not to eat anything here, since it would be about lunchtime when she got home. She remembered to take the chemise back off the hanger so she could take it along.

As she stepped through the house's out door, she was thinking about hanging her chemise in her room when she got home, and stepped out into her room. She stopped. *This isn't random. This could be very useful.*

She hung up her chemise and stepped out of her room. Her mom, who was in the kitchen, jumped.

"Karia, I didn't see you come home."

"I came into my bedroom," Karia said.

"What do you mean?"

"I walked out of my house and right into my bedroom."

"How did you do that?"

"I just thought about it as I left the house," Karia said, excited. "I guess that's the way the door works. I wanted to be safe the first time I left the house, and I came out at the Liliki tree. The second time I wanted to be home, and I came out in the kitchen. Now I was thinking about my room, and here I am."

Her mom looked sad. "I guess that's good. I just am not terribly fond of all the magic," she said.

"Neither am I, Mom. I want to be like you, and put all the magic behind me and live a normal life," Karia said.

"I've found that magic keeps intruding, and I think you'll find that even more true, my dear. Now, help me with lunch, please."

Karia got busy, distracted by the talk about the door and the magic. It wasn't until after the family ate lunch, and she had gotten changed and was doing some mending, that she remembered what she wanted to talk with her mom about.

She put her needle in the pincushion and set the mending aside, and went to the kitchen where her mom was kneading bread for dinner.

"Mom, what do you know about my sister?" Karia asked.

Her mom stopped kneading. "Why do you think you have a sister?" she said.

"Generality told me." She explained to her mom about the faerie, and what he had said.

Her mom listened, resuming her kneading. When Karia was done, she did not answer, but continued to knead.

"Mom? Do you know anything about my sister?"

"Karia," she said, still looking down and kneading. "Magic keeps intruding into my life and tearing it apart. It's done the same in yours, dear. It tore your family apart, and ripped your sister from your family. But I suppose it also brought you and me together. You lost a sister and gained a mom." She stopped kneading and looked up, smiling. It seemed rather sad for a smile, but she added, "I'm happy with that. Can you be, dear?"

Karia put her arms around her mom. "I love you, Mom."

"I love you too, dear, but I'm not going to hug you because I don't want to get flour all over you. Now, let me finish this bread, and you get back to the sewing, OK?"

"Yes, Ma'am."

CHAPTER SIXTY-SEVEN

Karia awoke the next morning from a pleasant dream, a smile on her face. This was going to be a wonderful day. This was the day Gerik was coming to call.

As she sat up, the faintest whisper of her dream played across her memory, and she stopped. It wasn't a sound or a sight she remembered, but a fragrance. A light, sweet fragrance. For the first time she remembered why the smell of the waterfall room and the stronger aroma of the blue ointment seemed so familiar. *My secret dream.*

She didn't remember having the dream for ages. The second time it came to her, as a child of perhaps eight, she told her mom about it. Her mom told her that when people have recurring dreams that have to do with who they are, those dreams are special. *'We shouldn't tell anyone about such dreams,'* she remembered her mom saying. *'Those are our secret dreams.'*

Who I am? she thought. Besides the fragrance, all she could remember now was what she recalled from the dream in the past. She remembered being in a forest, following that fragrance. It led her to a clearing, where she danced with the stars.

So, I'm a girl who follows pretty smells through the forest to dance with stars?

She laughed, dismissing the dream as a little girl's fantasies and deciding she'd focus on how good it made her feel. She threw the covers back and danced to her door and out to the empty kitchen. She glanced at the shadows and did some quick calculations, and realized she had probably just beaten her mom and dad by a few minutes. She was about to start breakfast, but she realized she didn't know if they were serving breakfast to everyone, or going to Uncle Avar's, or eating alone. She hoped Uncle Avar and his family would be coming over, since she wanted to cook. She wanted things to get back to normal.

Oh my, either way, I had better get a dress on! She hurried back to her room and started to put the green dress on over her linen chemise, then remembered that she would want the other chemise on when Gerik came over. *Having more than one dress and chemise is so confusing!*

She closed her door and changed. She brushed her hair. When she stepped out again, her mom was just coming out of her bedroom headed for the kitchen, and her dad stepped out to go to the fields.

"Good morning, farm girl!" her dad said.

"That's farm woman, sir," her mom corrected with a laugh.

Her dad stopped and smiled at her. "That it is, Failean." Turning to Karia, he said, "Please forgive an old farmer, young lady."

Now Karia laughed, stepped over to give him a hug – *still can't quite reach all the way around* – and went to the kitchen as he left for the fields.

"Are we having breakfast with Uncle Avar and his family today?" Karia asked her mom.

"Yes, dear. They're coming over here. So I'm glad you're up early to help. Let's get busy."

They prepared a rather elaborate breakfast by the family's standards, using up the last of the cheese Karia had brought from her house in the Old Wood, and breaking out some bacon. As they all sat around the table later, Karia felt like it was almost a celebration of things returning to normal.

Well, almost returning to normal. She noticed that Timbal was looking at her – a lot. But he was more like a brother to her now, a playmate she had grown up with. And while Gerik was a man, Timbal still seemed like a boy to her. *Just a boy,* she thought, making it sound in her head like an insult, the way Gerik had said it.

Karia and her mom cleaned up after breakfast, and Karia was able to finish her mending that morning in time to help her mom with lunch. They ate, and her dad returned to the fields, and time just seemed to drag. Karia was getting very nervous. She brushed her hair again, and checked to be sure her dress was clean.

It was barely past one when she asked her mom, "Do you think he's not coming?"

Her mom laughed and told Karia to sweep the house. She had almost finished sweeping the kitchen when she heard hoofbeats outside. She started to rush to the door, and her mom issued a sharp but hushed, "Karia!"

"You don't want to appear over-eager, Karia. Just wait for him to knock, and let me get the door and take care of this, OK? And you probably ought to put the broom away."

Karia looked down at the broom in her hand. *Right,* she thought, scurrying to the corner of the kitchen to put the broom away. *But, wait, and let her get the door? That is most certainly not OK.* Karia was practically crawling out of her skin, and now her mom wanted her to stand still and wait?

It seemed to her that it took Gerik forever to get off his horse, come up the steps and to the front door, and knock. And when he did, Karia jumped and had to hold back a little squeal.

What is mom waiting for? She was standing right by the door, but she didn't answer it. *Open the door!*

After what again seemed like forever, her mom opened the door. "Gerik! What a pleasure!"

Oh, no, I can't even see him! I should have been in the parlor!

"Why don't you take a seat on the porch? I'll send Karia right out." *She's closing the door? Why are you closing the door?*

Her mom turned to Karia and softly said, "Just wait." *Wait? Wait? He's right out there and we're making him wait?*

Her mom stepped to the cool door in the pantry, and drew out a small bottle. Karia recognized it as the ale that her dad made and shared. Her mom then got down a large cup, uncorked the ale, and poured it slowly into the cup. *Just dump it in already! He's waiting!*

Then, after agonizing seconds, she held the cup out to Karia. "Take this out to him, dear." Karia grabbed the mug and was about to turn and practically run to the door, but her mom caught her shoulder.

"Slow down, dear," she said, smiling. "You shouldn't rush." She reached up and brushed back that one unruly sprig of auburn hair. "This is something to savor." Karia thought she was talking about the ale, and looked down at the mug. She felt her mom's hand on her chin, urging her head up. "No, not the ale. The time. Slow down. Take a deep breath, then walk to the porch. Walk."

Karia took a deep breath and went out on the porch.

Ian Fallis

CHAPTER SIXTY-EIGHT

Gerik stood and smiled at her somewhat awkwardly as she stepped out onto the porch. She barely noticed how awkward his smile seemed. She was just happy to see him. She handed him the ale and they both sat down. He tasted it and said, "That's very good. Thank you."

"My dad makes it."

"I'll bet he used mostly tsilinki, and only the best. Makes a good hearty ale."

Karia had no idea what to say about ale, and they sat in silence for a short time. He took another sip of the ale, then set it down on the porch and turned to face her.

"Karia, I appreciate you seeing me."

"I appreciate you calling, Gerik."

After a moment of awkward silence, he said, "This is a lovely farm."

Karia started to laugh, but caught herself. "It's just a farm," she said.

"I suppose," he replied. "I'm not exactly an expert on farms."

She thought she may have made him feel bad, and didn't know what to say. He picked up the ale and took another drink.

"So what do you like to do?" he asked.

The first thing that came to Karia's mind was playing hide-and-seek in the forest with Timbal and Narck. *Oh, gosh, I can't say that! He'd think I'm a silly little girl, and what will he think about how close I am to Timbal?* She blushed, and then became very nervous as she realized she was blushing and taking a long time to answer a very simple question.

"Sew," she blurted out. "I like to sew. I mean, sewing. I like it." *Oh, gosh. Stupid stupid stupid.*

"Really?" he asked.

"No," she said. "I mean, sort of no. If I didn't have to do the sewing, and I was good at it, I'd like it. So, yes, sort of."

Gerik smiled at her. She thought he was trying to keep from laughing. "But ... I mean, you're responsible for the sewing for your family, right?" he asked.

"Yes," she said, feeling as if he had caught her in a lie. She didn't really like sewing for those very reasons – she had to do it, and she wasn't very good at it.

"So how can you say you'd like it if you were good at it?" he asked. "I think you're being too modest."

Now Karia was seriously confused, and when she realized it must have shown on her face, she smiled to cover it. *Oh, I'm sure that fooled him. Stupid stupid stupid.*

"You made that dress, right?" he asked.

She had to look down to remember that she was wearing the green dress. "No," she said.

"No?" he asked. He looked as if he didn't believe her. "Then who made it?"

Oh gosh, I don't even know! I think my father who isn't my dad but was a great sorcerer made it with magic and put it in the magical house in the Old Wood for me. I can't say that!

"OK, right, I made this," she said.

"Then you are quite good at sewing, and I heard even Silla thinks so," he said. "Don't be so modest. It's good to be good at something you like doing."

This was followed by another awkward silence. Karia had no idea what to say, and almost sighed with relief when Gerik spoke again.

"I'm making you nervous, aren't I?" he asked.

"Yes," she squeaked, looking away from him. "Or, really, no. It's not you ... it's ... I just don't know what to say."

"Are you afraid of saying the wrong thing?" he asked.

She hesitated, then looked at him sheepishly. "Yes," she said. *He sees right through me. I am such an idiot.*

"Do you know how I know that?" he asked.

Because I'm as transparent as this chemise, she thought, though she sure wasn't going to tell him how she felt, and then she blushed because she was thinking about undergarments. Realizing she was blushing and again taking forever to answer made her even more nervous.

"I know that because I feel that way too," he said.

She looked at him, incredulous. To her thinking, she was an ugly, pale little stick-girl. The young woman she was becoming was still just someone she noticed in a mirror now and then. She didn't really think that was her.

Gerik, on the other hand, was a man. A strong man, a big man, a manly man. There was no reason for him to be nervous.

228

"You don't believe me?" he asked.

"I'm sorry," she said, looking away. "It's just that I'm, you know, and you're, like, you, and you know?"

He laughed, and she hurt. Now she understood. He was playing with her. Toying with her feelings. *I don't cry!*

"That's exactly how I feel!" he said. "You are so beautiful, and I'm this big clumsy oaf who doesn't know how to make you like him."

She turned and stared at him. *How can he do this? How can he be so mean?* She felt tears forming in her eyes, and she wasn't going to give him the satisfaction of knowing he had made her cry. She abruptly turned away and stood. She took one step toward the door and stopped. There was something about the way he had looked at her.

"Karia, I'm sorry," he pleaded. "I don't know what I did, but please, forgive me!"

She turned and saw that he was near tears. "You really mean that?" she asked.

"Yes, yes, I mean it," he said softly. "I'm sorry."

"Not that," she said, sitting down again, looking at him expectantly. "The part about ... pretty."

"I said beautiful," he said.

She looked away. She knew that. She just couldn't bring herself to say it.

"Yes, that part," she said almost in a whisper as she looked at the porch boards. "Do you mean it?"

She felt his hand on her arm. "Yes," he said.

"You're not a clumsy oaf," she said, again almost whispering.

"Maybe," he said. "But sitting here with you, not knowing what to say or do — hurting your feelings without even knowing what I did wrong – I feel like one."

"I thought," she said, hesitating. "I thought you were mocking me." She looked up at him. Now he looked incredulous. "I feel like a silly little girl, and you're a man." She reached over and took his hand.

"I guess we should start over," he said.

Karia heard footsteps crunching on the graveled walkway. She abruptly let go of Gerik's hand, scooted away from him and sat up straighter. She blushed as she saw Aunt Heather walking past. Aunt Heather smiled broadly, shook her head and kept walking.

Karia and Gerik sat in another brief, awkward silence after that, at either end of the porch bench.

"So what do you like to do?" Karia asked.

"Well, I'm a pretty good smith, and my mom says there's nothing that pays the bills consistently like being a smith," he replied. He sounded as if he was trying to sound manly, and she smiled, thinking that maybe he was trying to prove himself to her.

"I could provide well for you," he added, confirming her suspicions.

"But you didn't answer the question," Karia said. "What do you like to do?" she asked.

He looked away. "I really like," he began, and stopped.

"What?" she asked.

"It's foolish," he said. "You might even think it's not manly."

"Gerik, I don't think I could ever think of you as not manly," she said, laughing. "Tell me."

"I want to be an artist," he said. "I want to work in metals to make, well," he paused and looked at her, "jewelry." He seemed to be afraid to hear her response.

"That doesn't sound foolish to me," Karia said.

"But I'd give that up to provide for you," he said quickly.

"Now that sounds foolish," she said.

He looked surprised.

"Why wouldn't I want you to do what you want to do?" she said. "I've heard you're quite good with metals. I've never seen any of your work, but I'd like to."

"You've heard that I'm good?" he asked.

"Yes," she said. "Didn't you know that everyone knows that?"

"No. Really?" he said. "My mom says it's silly."

"Well, she's wrong," Karia said. She could tell from his expression she had said something she shouldn't have, and it took her only a moment to figure out what that was. "Oh, my, I didn't mean to say that!"

"Well, you just did," Gerik said.

"I know," she replied. She studied his face, and couldn't tell how he felt about what she had said. "Are you upset with me?"

"Not really," he said. "But I have a lot of respect for my mom, and I don't think you should tell her she's wrong to her face."

"I wouldn't," Karia assured him. "Will you forgive me?"

"Sure," he said. "As long as you tell me what you really like to do."

"Oh," she said. "Now we're talking about foolish."

"Tell me," he said.

"I like to play in the forest," she said, adding quickly. "You must think I'm childish."

"No," he said. "I hope you never stop playing. Some people get so serious they forget to have fun."

"You mean, like people who give up their dreams to make a good living?" she asked.

He stared at her a moment. He looked surprised. "I guess so," he said. He kept staring at her, and just about the time Karia was thinking that perhaps she should not have said that, he smiled.

She blushed and had to look away. "What?" she asked.

"I'm so glad I came to spend time with you, Karia," he said.

"So am I," she replied. She felt warm inside, but also suspected he was getting ready to leave. She glanced up at the sky and was surprised to see the sun had made a great deal of progress toward the horizon. It was a little past mid-afternoon.

"I need to leave soon to make it back to town before dark," he said, standing. Karia stood up as well. "May I call on you again, say, the day after tomorrow?"

"Yes," she said, smiling up at him. "I'd like that."

She was staring so intently into his eyes that she was surprised to feel him taking her hand and lifting it. He bent forward slightly and kissed her hand. A warm shiver radiated all the way from the back of her hand down her back.

"Farewell, my …" he said, and stopped. He looked perplexed.

Karia was so nervous she giggled. "Karia," she offered. "Karia will do. For now."

"Karia," he repeated, and stepped down the porch to his horse. He mounted and rode away. Even after he was out of sight, she stood leaning on the porch post and watching after him.

She felt her mom's presence close behind her, surprising her. She had not heard the front door open or close. She turned to her mom, still smiling.

"I take it that went well," her mom said, smiling too.

"Yes," Karia said, "once we got past me lying to him, calling him a liar and telling him his mom was wrong."

Ian Fallis

CHAPTER SIXTY-NINE

The rest of that afternoon passed in a pleasant blur for Karia. She remembered her mom passing her bits of advice like, "Don't be disrespectful of his mom," and she almost grimaced when she thought about some of the awkward moments they shared.

But she didn't actually grimace. She couldn't stop smiling. She couldn't stop remembering that he called her pretty, and he made clear that he really meant it. Sure, he had actually said beautiful, but that was still too much of a reach for her. And yes, she still thought of herself as a pale stick-girl — perhaps not ugly, but certainly not attractive.

But Gerik told her she was pretty, and she replayed that moment again and again and again in her head.

"Karia," she heard.

She looked up at her mom, smiling.

"Dear," her mom said, "you can stop kneading the bread when you feel the texture change."

Karia looked down at the dough. It was definitely pliable and elastic, as it should be. She had no idea how long she had been kneading it. "But you said it doesn't hurt to knead it longer," Karia replied.

"Sure," her mom said, smiling broadly. "But eventually we need to let it rise so we can bake it and eat it."

Karia looked down at the dough again. "I've been doing this for a long time, haven't I?" she said.

Her mom laughed. "Your hands have been. Your head's been somewhere else, and I think I know where."

Karia blushed.

At dinner she was glad her mom let her simply describe Gerik's visit to her dad as "pleasant." She could tell from his expression that he wanted to know more, but could also tell that he could read a lot more than that from her non-stop smile.

He asked only one question: "Was he a gentleman?"

233

"Yes," Karia replied, but she blushed. It was perhaps somewhat forward of her to take his hand, and rushing things a bit for him to kiss her hand. It was still all very gentlemanly, however. "Yes," she repeated.

Her dad looked at her skeptically. "Karia, I know you've been brought up properly, and I know you are a young lady," he said. Karia blushed again. "And I've known Gerik since he was a boy, and I know his dad, so I don't expect any trouble from him."

He hesitated. He looked concerned.

"But those city boys can view things differently," he said. "Hikila found that out the hard way."

"Reva!" her mom exclaimed.

Karia was not sure what her dad was talking about, or why her mom had objected. She could not place the name, until her mom continued, wagging her finger at her dad – something Karia could not remember her doing before.

"Gerik is not Rekon, and our Karia is most certainly not Hikila," she said. "I'll not have any more talk like that in this house." She rose abruptly and began clearing the table.

That precluded Karia from asking what they were talking about, but now she knew enough. Hikila, she remembered, was the blond girl from the farm on the road to the Central Valley. She was the girl whom Rekon, the miller's son, had been courting. Karia had not seen Hikila for a few months.

At a recent farm get-together, Litara had tried to tell her something about Hikila being with child, but Karia had dismissed that as gossip. The older a maid Litara became, the more bitter she was, and the more she developed a reputation as a gossip and a busybody, out to undermine and ruin relationships.

While Karia now wondered if there was truth behind the rumor, she also knew there would be no answers to that in her house. Her mom was steadfast against gossip. "It tears us all down, Karia," she said. She had gone so far as to tell Litara she was no longer welcome on their farm.

Karia knew that was wise and right. She understood that just the rumor had already colored the way she thought of Rekon and Hikila, even though she had no clue whether it was true.

She knew that it could also impact her relationship with Gerik. She may react inappropriately to perfectly proper statements, or something as simple and appropriate as him taking her hand.

Gossip tears us all down, Karia thought.

CHAPTER SEVENTY

The following day she was up before dawn like any good farm woman. She did not complain when her dad asked her to help out with farm chores. She knew they were shorthanded with Opa and Narek away, and Karia actually liked feeling useful again. She fetched oil, a few rags and a whetstone from the shed.

Then she went to the barn. In the empty stall next to the Great Smelly Beast all the implements were gathered – from knives through machetes and scythes all the way to the ploughs. They needed to be sharpened and oiled before they were stored for the winter, or they would rust and be useless.

She sighed as she saw the magnitude of the work, and for a moment questioned whether she wanted to be quite this useful. But a memory made her smile.

She was twelve and her dad had her standing calf-deep in a pond, scooping out soft mud to deepen it. She and her dad were working while Timbal and Narek were in town with Uncle Avar. When they got back, she expected her dad to let her go play, or thought he should tell them to pitch in.

"It's not right that I have to work all day while they get to play," she grumped, standing up and planting her shovel. When she saw his expression change, she quickly added, "Well, that's just how I feel."

"This isn't what you want to be doing, is it?" her dad asked, hardly slowing the swings of his shovel.

"No," she replied, thinking he was going to let her go play.

Her dad planted his shovel and smiled. In fact, it looked like he was going to laugh, and that made Karia cross. "Right and wrong have nothing to do with what you want or what you feel, Tsil," he said. "Nor do they have a lot to do with what others are or are not doing."

"Well, what do they have to do with then?" she demanded angrily.

"Right and wrong have a lot to do with our responsibilities to others," he said evenly. Then he raised his eyebrows. "And with respect for others, especially our elders."

Karia felt her anger melting into shame. "I'm sorry, Daddy," she said.

He put his big muddy hand on her shoulder. "It's OK, Tsil," he said. "Now let's get back to work."

Karia looked around the barn stall at the implements again and knew she wasn't going to disappoint her dad. She decided to start with the knives. She first took down one of the leather aprons hanging in the stall and put it on over her ratty old farm dress. Then she got a milking stool, plopped it down in the middle of the stall and sat down. She picked up a knife. It was rusty already. She looked around, and several of the implements were. She sighed again and went back to the shed for a hunk of steel wool to polish them.

Returning to the barn, she was surprised to see Timbal standing by the stall, apparently waiting for her. She knew her dad and Uncle Avar were pulling weeds from among the growing tsilinki, a backbreaking, painstaking task, and wondered why he was here instead.

"I needed a spade," he said, apparently in response to her quizzical look.

"OK," she said. She sat down, oiled a knife, pulled off a piece of steel wool and began polishing the rust off, but he did not leave.

"I don't like him," Timbal said.

"Who?" Karia asked, though she suspected she knew.

"Gerik," he said. "He's just courting you because he has to."

Karia looked up, not sure whether to laugh or scold him. "Why on earth would he have to court me?" she said.

"Because otherwise everyone would know he doesn't really like girls," Timbal said.

"That is gossip, and I'll hear no more of it," she said, leaning back over the knife and polishing. She was also wishing Timbal would just go away, and thinking, *Does he not realize I'm holding a knife?*

"He hasn't courted anyone else," Timbal said.

Karia dropped the knife and steel wool, stood up and stepped directly in front of Timbal. She glared down at him. "I said, that is gossip and I'll hear no more of it," she said. At the same time, it stung her inside. She still had doubts about what someone like Gerik would see in her, and Timbal was stirring them. That was making her angry.

Timbal stepped back. "I just don't want you to get hurt," he said.

"You're just jealous and selfish," she replied. "Get back to your work and let me get to mine." She sat down and picked up the knife and steel wool, which had dirt sticking to them because of the oil. She tossed the bit of steel wool aside, wiped the knife with a rag, broke off another piece of steel wool and began polishing some more. She looked up as she put some more oil on the knife, and was glad to see that Timbal had gone.

She looked around at all the implements again, and calculated that this was going to take precisely a very long time. "And there's one more spade to boot," she said aloud. She took a deep breath, tried to ignore what Timbal had said and decided to remember what her dad had said.

But she found she was no longer smiling. She kept wondering if Gerik had been waiting for her, or if there was a darker reason he had not courted other girls.

Gosh, I hate gossip, she thought, and attacked the rust with vigor. '*Gossip tears us all down.*'

Ian Fallis

CHAPTER SEVENTY-ONE

All that day she polished, sharpened and oiled mattocks and hoes and knives and machetes and more. Her hands were stiff and sore by evening, and worse the next morning, but that was part of life on the farm. There was work to do, and it wouldn't get done by itself.

All morning long she worked, and was surprised when her mom came and told her it was time for lunch.

"And you'll probably want to get cleaned up," her mom said.

She looked at her hands, covered with oil and rust and dirt, laughed and said, "Yes, I don't think I want to eat anything like this."

"Karia, have you forgotten?" her mom asked.

"Forgotten what?" she asked, but she remembered before the words were out of her mouth. "Oh my gosh, Gerik is coming calling!" She looked down at the leather apron and her ratty old farm dress, which regardless of the apron was also spotted with oil, rust and dirt. She felt a wave of panic and began to look around quickly.

"Take a breath, dear," her mom said.

Karia did, and she looked at the huge stack of farm implements, waiting to be readied for winter or lost to rust. She looked down at her hands and her dress again, and she remembered all the times she had seen Gerik busy at the smithy, covered in soot. She wiped her hands on her dress and looked at her mom.

"I've got too much work to do to just sit around and wait for him to come calling," she said. "But I don't want him to think he's not important to me. What should I do?"

"Let's go discuss this with your dad over lunch, shall we?" her mom said.

They walked into the house. Her dad was already seated at the table, which was set and ready for lunch. Her mom sat down, and Karia quickly washed her hands in a basin by the sideboard, then joined them.

As they ate, her mom looked at her dad and said, "Your daughter is a hard-working young lady."

He looked up at Karia and smiled. "That she is," he said.

"Do you think a young man like Gerik would appreciate that in her?" her mom asked.

"He sure had better," her dad said.

"Well, he's supposed to come calling this afternoon, and she still has a lot of work to do," her mom said. "It wouldn't be like Karia to sit around waiting for him to come calling when there's work to do. How do you think he'd react to finding her at work instead of waiting for him to call?"

Her dad looked like he was thinking for a moment or two before he spoke. "I'm not sure he'd really think about whether she'd be working or waiting," he said. He turned to Karia. "You'd be taking more of a risk by having him come see you working and dirty, that's for sure. But I think it will give him a better idea of the kind of young woman you are. And I think a man like Gerik would appreciate it."

Karia smiled, stood up to give her dad a kiss on the cheek and sat back down. "Thank you, Daddy," she said.

CHAPTER SEVENTY-TWO

A couple of hours later, Gerik looked befuddled as Karia's mom led him to the stall in the barn. Karia looked up from the machete she was oiling, after she had sharpened it to a fine edge.

"Hi!" she said, standing and putting the machete on the stool.

"Hi," he said. He looked her up and down, and then looked around the stall.

Oh, gosh, this was a mistake, she thought.

"Gerik, I'm sorry, I just had a lot of work to do, and I didn't think you'd mind, and it's not that I didn't think seeing you was important, but this is a farm and I can't really sit around and wait." She realized she was rambling because she was nervous and made herself stop talking.

"No," he said. "This is fine. I understand."

Karia was having a hard time reading his expression. Perhaps he was simply thrown off balance by seeing her filthy and hard at work. But she sensed he was uneasy, and she did not think hard work would make someone like Gerik uneasy.

"I think," he said, "this shows me you're a strong, mature young woman."

She smiled, blushed and turned away.

"That will make this easier," he said.

She looked back at him. "Make what easier?"

"I think you'll understand what I need to say."

What?

"Karia, you are a beautiful young woman, and I allowed myself to be drawn in by that, and neglected to consider the difficulties that would be posed by the differences in our age and social standing."

I'm not good enough for you?!

"I trust that you will appreciate that this is still very difficult for me to say, and also appreciate that it is good that we have come to this realization so early. I will be unable to court you."

We came to this realization? You'll be **unable** *to court me?* She wanted to scream at him, or hit him, or any of another dozen violent things. When her thoughts drifted to the razor-sharp machete right behind her, she willed herself to take a deep breath. She noticed that he noticed, and blushed. But she also realized, *I've still got his attention. Think.* She allowed herself to not speak as she tried to gather her thoughts.

"Karia?" he asked.

"Gerik," she said firmly. She deliberately paused to make sure of what she wanted to say. Then she looked him in the eyes. "The only difficulties are in your mind." She paused. *That was good. Don't get angry. Stay calm. Breathe. Think.* "This is a choice you made." She felt like running on and starting to yell at him. She stopped herself and took another breath. *What's that word? I need that word Mom uses on me. Oh, right. Gosh, how could I forget?* "You disappoint me, sir. Not just because you stir my heart" – *Oh golly it's true but did I really say that?* – "but because I thought you were a better man than that." She saw pain in his eyes, and she had to look away. She decided she had said enough. "Excuse me, sir. I have work to do."

She turned around quickly, hoping he didn't see the tears in her eyes. She was also hoping to feel his hand on her shoulder, to hear him say he was wrong. Instead she heard him walking out of the barn, and then listened as he rode away.

She could feel tears rolling down her cheeks, but inside she just felt numb. She didn't know how long she stood there before she felt her mom's presence in the barn.

"Karia?" she said.

Karia turned around to face her mom. She knew there were tears on her cheeks, but anger was building inside her.

"I'm not good enough for him!" she shouted. "Me! I'm not good enough for a man who toils in soot and smoke! Well, fine! Just … fine!"

"Oh, Karia," her mom said. "I'm sorry, dear."

Karia turned and picked up the machete. "I'll be fine, Mom," she said. She felt tears welling up inside her, and just got more angry. *I don't cry.* "Now if you'll excuse me, Mom, I'm going to hack the Great Smelly Beast into little bitty bits."

"I'm not sure your dad would approve, dear, and the horse hasn't done anything to you."

Karia tossed the machete in the dirt and the tears started rolling down her face. She felt her mom's arms around her, and she just let go and sobbed.

CHAPTER SEVENTY-THREE

Karia went to her room and – pausing just long enough to tear off the oily, dirty, ratty farm dress that she partially blamed – threw herself face-down on her bed. Fragments of thoughts collided in her head.

Everything was getting back to normal at home, and she was going to marry Gerik and – *OK, that's right*, not *have kids* – and she'd be happy. And now he had told her she wasn't good enough for him.

She couldn't understand it. He called her pretty. And she believed him. Then he used that as an excuse to call it all off.

At first she blamed her dad and mom for making her work, but she couldn't stay angry at them. Working had been her choice. And she knew Gerik had breaking up in mind even before he called on her. She now knew that was why he had that expression on his face that she could not read.

Magic, she thought. Magic made her look like a fool as she left Gerik's house. That had to be the reason he called it off. *He saw the stupid, frail little farm girl in the back of her mommy's wagon.* She felt sorry for herself, then got angry. *I am not stupid*, she thought, *and I am not frail.* She sat up. *And I am most certainly not a little girl!* She slammed her fist against the wall. *Oh gosh that hurts!*

But her anger couldn't overcome the fact that she also hurt down deep inside. She lay back down and, try as she might not to, she cried herself to sleep. Her mom let her sleep through dinner.

The house was dark when Karia awoke. She didn't feel tired, but from the shadows it seemed it was about midnight, so she tried to go back to sleep. And tried. And tried. She could not. It was as if a jumble of thoughts were elbowing each other out of the way in her head, and keeping her awake.

She got up from her bed and walked quietly to the porch. She looked up at the almost-full moon, and could tell that she had been right – it was about midnight. As she stood at the porch rail, a cool, soft breeze carried the scent of moist dirt and growing tsilinki from the fields. It was a sweet smell to Karia, a familiar smell, one that said "home," and she drank it in and treasured it.

It relaxed her, and seemed to clear her thoughts and clarify her feelings. She was not angry with Gerik, nor was she sad. She felt, truly, disappointment. As she thought about it, she realized that what disappointed her most was what he let get in the way.

I'm Inamali! I'm his superior in every way! she thought. Stunned, she stepped back from the rail. Her mom and dad had not simply raised her as Teneka; they had instilled in her respect for all other people. After her experience at the carnival, she was certain, she would have a difficult time respecting a Dr'Zhak. And Inamali had always seemed, well, somehow not like people. But she could not recall ever feeling superior to anyone before, and she was ashamed of herself.

It's the magic. Magic can only kill and burn and tear. Magic separated Gerik and me. Magic is changing who I am. She was again startled by her own thoughts. *Magic separated Gerik and me ... deliberately? Does magic ... think? Plan?* She began to feel as if she had a disease, a malevolent disease, a disease that chose her and was consuming her in order to use her for its own ends. *No, that's crazy. The Inamali rule magic, not the other way around.* She didn't convince herself.

She felt the presence of her mom – could place exactly where she was, even though she had not heard her come out onto the porch – and turned and threw her arms around her.

"Oh, you're freezing," her mom said, feeling her shiver. "You really shouldn't stand out on the porch half-dressed." But Karia said nothing, and she knew her mom would realize soon that she was warm enough. "You're not cold, are you?"

"No," Karia said softly but clearly.

"And you're not crying. You're scared, aren't you?"

Karia nodded her head, still holding her mom tightly.

"Come with me, dear."

She led Karia down off the porch and along the hard-beaten path to Opa and Nana's house, and up onto the porch. The fragrance of flowers mixed with the aroma of warm soil and growing tsilinki here. To Karia, it smelled like Nana. It had been a long time since she had wondered about her real grandmother; after the wars, many people had been displaced or otherwise lost track of their families, so she wasn't alone in not having a grandmother around. But Nana was like a grandmother to her. *I miss Nana.*

"We can talk here without disturbing anyone," Karia's mom said. Then she added, as she tenderly pushed Karia's hair back, "And without anyone disturbing us."

She waited a moment, looking into her daughter's striking oh-so-blue eyes, then said, "What is it, dear?"

"Magic," she said simply.

Her mom sighed, and drew her daughter close again. "I thought maybe you were still dwelling on what happened with Gerik."

"I am, sort of, Mom," Karia said. "Do you think magic did that, deliberately?"

"Did what, dear?"

"Broke us up," Karia said.

"What are you talking about?" her mom said, looking confused.

"Mom, I feel like, I don't have magic. Magic has me. And it's doing things to me, and to my life, so it can use me for what it wants to do."

Her mom was silent. She hugged Karia. After a time she said, "I suppose that's one way of looking at it, dear. Our people used to call it the gift of magic. Many these days call it the curse of magic."

The two sat silently for a while, holding each other in the soft, cool breeze and the gentle moonlight. For Karia, it was almost like those times she was sick as a little girl. She even leaned back and reached over to spin her mom's ring a couple of times – until she remembered the odd sensation she got when she picked it up, like it was somehow alive too, and sticking itself to her. She fell back into her mom's arms. She remembered all those times in the past when she'd just let her mom hold her, and everything was all better. Only she wasn't so sure her mom could make her better this time. She thought about magic – almost as if it were a person – and she grew angry with it.

"Mom," Karia said, "I wish I could just take a knife and kill magic. Stab it in the heart and make it go away forever. And then every year we could all hold a big party – everyone, Inamali and Teneka and Dr'Zhak – and celebrate the Day Magic Died."

Her mom was silent for a moment. When she spoke, Karia realized her mom was trying to keep from crying. "I think you'll find, dear ... that even if it's that simple ... it's still terribly difficult. Maybe the most difficult choice you've ever faced."

Karia didn't know what to say. She held her mom, felt her mom's tears drip into her own hair, felt her trembling now, as she had been. "What's wrong, Mom?"

Her mom let go of Karia and used her sleeve to wipe away her tears. "There's just so much I need to tell you, and I don't know where to start."

"Can you tell me about my sister?" Karia asked.

"Yes, dear. Yes. Now that you know Reva and I are not the parents who gave birth to you, you should know about your family. But I'm afraid that to do that properly, I'll have to start a lot further back," her mom said.

Oh no, Karia thought. *My mom's going to try to tell a story.*

CHAPTER SEVENTY-FOUR

"Have you kept reading Jiki's diary?" her mom asked.

"Yes," Karia said.

"But you haven't reached the end yet, have you?"

"No, Mom."

"Well, you need to. I'll tell you a little bit about it tonight, but you need to go and read it in his words later. How far have you gotten?"

"I read about the birth of his son, Lukaliva," Karia said, pausing. "I think if I have kids, I'm going to have to adopt them like you did. I'm not going through that."

Her mom laughed. "Alright, dear. Well, if you've gotten that far, I'd say you can jump to the end and read it. It's not far off from what you're feeling toward magic.

"You see, dear, Jiki's mom was the last Tsilinakaya, Irina. He saw the death and destruction magic wrought in his life, in his family, and through his family, and he wanted nothing to do with it. He and his wife withdrew to a distant Teneka village, and raised their son as a Teneka. They tried to simply be Teneka again. And in the end, it didn't work."

"Wait, what do you mean, 'be Teneka again,' Mom?"

"Oh, yes. I'm not a great storyteller, dear. I forget what you know and what you don't know. The first Tsilinakaya was a Teneka farm girl, who was given the gift of magic. That's where the Inamali came from. From that one girl, who brought magic to us."

"So we're really … Teneka?"

"In a way, dear, yes. But along with magic – or maybe as part of magic – came a new language, and new ways of looking at things, and we became a different people. We called ourselves the Inamali. You don't know what that means, do you, dear?"

"No," Karia replied.

"It doesn't translate directly to Teneka; there's no word that means the same thing. But it's something like a combination of 'better' and 'proud,' but the kind of proud that's justified by being better. If that makes sense."

Karia felt that she knew that word now. That's what had stirred in her heart, and surprised her, as she stood at the porch railing earlier.

"Wait, Mom, how did she get the gift?"

"I don't know, dear. That part of the story – and, oh, so much of the story – I don't know. I think your father knew. He collected all the books he could, and read them and re-read them and figured a lot of it out. But that was after … oh, sorry, I'm getting off track again."

"So maybe the answer is in all those books in the house?"

"Perhaps, dear, but why?"

"Because if it was a gift, maybe we could find a way to give it back."

Her mom's expression looked like a smile and a frown combined, and Karia wasn't sure what to make of it. "Again, dear, it sounds so simple, doesn't it? Let me get back to the story and tell you about Lukaliva, and perhaps you'll understand better."

"OK," Karia said. "But, Mom, what's this have to do with my sister?"

"Just listen, dear. It will all make sense.

"As a young man, Lukaliva shared his dad's views, and tried to live as a Teneka. He married a Teneka girl. Her name was Jherah." Her mom's eyes teared up, and then she managed to take control again. "She was my mother. But there I go getting off track again."

"Lukaliva and Jherah lived together on a farm. They lived as Teneka, and I'm not sure my mom even knew he was Inamali. I was just a little girl when everything changed. I don't know why. Maybe Lukaliva was tired of the hard life of a farmer; maybe he wanted better for his child. It could be that he saw how his dad felt after all those years of trying to be Teneka. Perhaps the magic seduced him. I've thought about it so many times over the years, and I've reached the conclusion it was probably a combination of several of those things.

"And what scares me most about it is exactly what was scaring you this morning, Karia. Magic had to seduce him for its plan to be carried out."

"What do you mean?"

"Patience, dear. I'm telling you about your sister, remember?"

"Sure, Mom, but what's your family have to do with my sister?"

Her mom tousled her hair and smiled at her. "Didn't I just ask you to be patient?"

"Sorry, Mom."

"Lukaliva left my mom, and went off to study magic. My mom always made it sound like she threw him out because she wanted nothing to do with magic. I suppose that was part of the problem, but I think it was more my dad's doing.

"My mom couldn't tend the farm by herself, and we moved into town. She was cheated out of the farm, and we had nothing. We found a place to live at the tavern. She took a job there. It was the only work she could get." Her mom's eyes teared up again, and then she lifted her eyes and looked directly into Karia's.

"And I don't mean she was serving food and ale, dear," she said, her tone stern. "She did what she had to so she and I would have food and a place to live. Do you understand me, Karia?"

Karia was dumbfounded, and could only nod. *Magic only destroys.*

"Don't you dare, not even for a moment, look down on my mother," she said, sounding as if she was scolding Karia. Then her tone softened. "She loved me, and took care of me. I had no idea how she was able to take care of me. Not for many years." A tear rolled down her mom's cheek, and Karia hugged her again.

"I can tell she loved you a lot," Karia said. "Because that's how you've loved me."

That did it. Her mom began to weep, and Karia held her and gently ran her fingers through her mom's hair, as her mom had done so many times for her.

CHAPTER SEVENTY-FIVE

Her mom sat up and wiped her eyes on her chemise again. "I'm sorry, dear."

"Mom!" Karia gently scolded. "It's OK."

Her mom took a deep breath.

"Mom," Karia said, "About my sister …?"

"I'm sorry dear, for such a long story. I needed to make sure you understood some things before we got there. Let's see … ah, right …

"Lukaliva became very powerful, and because of his lineage – remember, his grandmother was Irina – he was highly respected among the Inamali. And he married again. An Inamali woman. Her name was Tirisa, and she was about my age. I knew none of this until years later; I was not part of his life. He told me later that the marriage to my mom wasn't valid because she was, in his words, 'only a Teneka.'

"He and Tirisa had triplets," her mom said. She stopped and looked at Karia a moment. "Do you know anything about Inamali triplets, dear?"

"No," she said. *I've not even really heard of Inamali having triplets, or Teneka. Except for what Generality said …*

"It's extremely rare. It runs in my family, Karia. And as far as I know, in my family alone."

Wait a minute …

Her mom apparently could see Karia's mind was working. "Just stay with me, dear. I don't know what you're thinking, but listen to me and this will all make sense. I'm going to just barrel through this, dear. I don't know how else to do it.

"When triplets are born in my family, it's always a girl first, and then two boys. It heralds the arrival of the next Tsilinakaya. So Lukaliva tried to keep it quiet, because that put his wife and children in danger. That's when he came to me, when he came back into my life. I was married to Reva. Avar and Heather were our neighbors and friends, as were Opa and Nana. He

251

asked us to each take in one of the triplets and raise them as our own. And to be safe, he said, we should move to this distant place and run a farm."

"So … you're … my sister?" Karia asked, even though she already knew the answer.

"Yes, dear. Please don't be upset with me. I did it to protect you, and I've loved you like a daughter and a sister."

Karia was silent for a while. Again thoughts were colliding in her head. She remembered what her mom had told her when she asked about her sister earlier: *'You lost a sister and gained a mom.'* She fixed her very blue eyes on her mom's eyes.

"Mom, you were wrong. I didn't lose a sister and gain a mom. I have both." She hugged her mom, and they cried together. *I only cry when I'm happy.*

CHAPTER SEVENTY-SIX

After a while Karia and her mom separated, and each wiped her tears.

"Karia, there's more you need to know about your father, and about triplets.

"I did not know until years later, but your father – our father – told Tirisa he was sending her to a safe place. He kidnapped three Teneka babies and sent them along with her. He told her that this was to protect their children – to protect Tsilinakaya especially, in case they were found.

"Only he did not send her to a safe place. He sent her to a place that he knew their enemies would find her. He sent her and the kidnapped children to die, in order to protect you."

"No," Karia said.

"Yes, dear. I'm sorry, Karia, but magic was the most important thing to him. He had ceased to love. He only wanted to protect you because of magic."

Karia felt hollow again. She looked down, not knowing what to think.

"I'm sorry, dear, but there's more. Shall I wait and tell you later?"

"No," Karia said weakly. "Go on."

"The first Tsilinakaya was the oldest of triplets, and every one since then has been as well. And back in those days, since triplets were so rare, there was a superstition that the third child was actually an evil spirit taking advantage of the birth of twins to force his way into the world.

"So they waited until the triplets were ten. They wanted to be sure the evil spirit was aware of what was happening, and send him back to the other demons with fear to keep it from happening again." She paused.

"They killed him?" Karia said, shocked.

"Yes, dear. But that's not the worst of it. They felt the demon had taken advantage of the girl, while they were in the womb. So they had her kill him. They even had a special knife for just that purpose."

Karia was horrified. "But … that's horrible!" she said. "They stopped that, right? Because it was just superstition, right?"

"That's what one family thought, one of our ancestors. They didn't want to put their girl through that, didn't want their son to die, either, and they didn't kill the third-born. That Tsilinakaya was weak, and did not advance magic, as each one had before. And all the Inamali felt their magic weakening, until the pressure was too great.

"The people forced her to kill her own brother, and the magic did not weaken any more. But it took several decades before the magic of the people was back where it had been.

"Irina was made to kill her own brother, and that's one of the reasons your Grandpa Jiki tried to end the whole thing."

Karia sat in stunned silence. "Mom, which one … who's the youngest?" she asked, though she thought she knew.

"Narek, dear."

"Thank you, Mom. Thank you for not making me do that, and thank you for saving Narek's life."

Tears came to her mom's eyes again, and Karia embraced her again.

"Golly," Karia said with a laugh, "is this what it's like to have a sister?"

Her mom laughed as well. Then she sat up from Karia's embrace.

"There's one more thing," she said. "Actually, there are dozens more, but one more thing I should tell you this morning."

Karia realized from the dim light on the horizon that her mom was correct; dawn was approaching.

"Karia, you cannot let what happened with Gerik send you back into the arms of Timbal," her mom said.

"Mom! Yuck! He's my brother! I'd never … ew!" She shuddered.

"Listen to me, Karia. In order to strengthen the magic, and keep it pure, every Tsilinakaya has married her own brother, the surviving male triplet. Grandpa Jiki's mother and father – your great-grandmother and great-grandfather, and mine – were brother and sister."

Seeing the look on Karia's face, she added, "And they've both married willingly. For the sake of magic."

Magic is gross, Karia thought. *Ew. I mean, ewwww!*

CHAPTER SEVENTY-SEVEN

"We should get back inside," Failean said. "But before we go, you must understand that even your dad should not know all that I have told you. And I need to ask you to keep calling me Mom."

"That's not hard. You are my mom," Karia said. "I mean, I know you're not my mother. And now I know you're my sister, or I guess my half-sister. But you're the only mom I've ever known." Then she hastily added, "And the only mom I ever want."

They hugged again and started walking back to their house.

"I guess this means I still have to obey you, doesn't it?" Karia said.

"Yes, dear."

"Gosh, I missed that opportunity."

"Yes, you did."

They were almost home when her mom spoke again. "This is Aunt Heather's day to make breakfast, so I'm going to see if I can help her. She's probably up by now."

"I'll go with you," Karia said.

Her mom stopped and looked at her.

"What?" Karia said.

Her mom seemed to gesture toward her waist, and Karia looked down. She blushed. She had completely forgotten what she was wearing. She simply said, "Oh."

"And the men will be up and on their way to the fields at any time," her mom added.

Karia blushed again. "I suppose I should go get a dress on."

"I suppose so. But why don't you go home and try to get some sleep? I'll come and get you when it's breakfast time."

"If it's all the same, I'd rather come and help."

"Fine," her mom said. "But let's not stand here talking. Go! Before the men see you like that."

Karia turned to go home and her mom swatted her behind. Karia turned and looked at her, surprised. Her mom just smiled and said, "Get going! You deserved it. Parading around like that."

Karia blushed. *I wasn't parading.* But she hastened home and went into her room. She got her dress on just as she heard her dad's door open. She went and gave him a hug. "Good morning, Daddy!" *Still can't quite reach.*

"Good morning, farm lady," he said. "You going to help your Aunt Heather this morning?"

"Yes, Sir. Then I'll finish cleaning, sharpening and oiling everything. I'm sorry I didn't finish yesterday."

"Oh, that's OK, Tsil," her dad said. He tousled her hair. "I understand. And yesterday Timbal said he was going to stay up until he got that done."

Karia knew that if Timbal said he was going to stay up until he finished the chore, he probably had. She wasn't quite so upset with him anymore.

It dawned on Karia that Timbal had no idea she was his sister. *One day I'm talking to him about marrying me, and the next I'm calling him a friend and there's a man from town courting me,* she thought. *No wonder he's jealous.* But she had no idea what to do about it. *I can't tell him that I'm his sister, can I?*

But she forgot all about that as the day became busy, like any normal day around the farm. The only thing different was the long nap she and her mom took after lunch. The next day was very much normal – no midnight talks with her mom – and though she kept glancing around, expecting to see the magician, she never did. Once or twice she thought she felt someone, sort of like she felt her mom or felt the presence of the house, but she shrugged it off as her imagination.

The following day Karia was starting to feel like perhaps she could actually live a normal life without magic intruding. She certainly wanted to believe that. She was also thinking that perhaps that life could include Gerik. Yes, he had hurt her. But she could not deny that she had feelings for him. And no matter what he said about social standing and whatever else it was, he admitted that he found her attractive, and she thought there was more to it, despite what he said. She even wondered what on earth a man like Gerik cared about social standing, or the fact that he was a couple of years older. She did not see Timbal, and did not give him another thought.

That evening at dinner her dad said the horse needed to be reshod, and he asked Karia if she wanted to go to town with him the next day. She saw her mom look up at him, then at her, with a concerned expression. "Oh, sorry," her dad added quickly. "That probably isn't a good idea."

"Actually, Daddy, I want to go," Karia said. *Gerik called me pretty. And he was definitely looking at me. I want him to see me again.* It was a spur-of-the-moment decision, and she wondered if she was being vain. But she wanted to try, and she needed a reason that would sound plausible. She thought only a moment.

"I want to see if Silla has some fabric like this," she said, gesturing to her green dress, "because I'd like to make Mom a dress. I think it'll look beautiful with her hair."

She saw her dad look at her mom and smile. "That it would, Tsil."

"Thank you, dear," her mom said. "That sounds lovely."

Karia knew that she couldn't make a dress quite as nice as the one she was wearing, and she knew her mom was well aware of that too. She just hoped her mom didn't guess why she really wanted to go to town. *Or maybe, if she does guess, she won't stop me.*

"OK, then," her dad said. "We'll leave after breakfast."

Ian Fallis

CHAPTER SEVENTY-EIGHT

After breakfast, Karia again got the chore of hitching the Great Smelly Beast. But as she and her dad reached toward the front bench to climb up, her mom stopped them both. She made Reva go around to Karia's side of the wagon to help her up.

"I can get in a wagon, Mom," Karia protested.

"I know that, young lady. But you need to learn to let a man show you respect and honor," her mom said. "And as for you," she said, turning to Reva, "You need to remember that Karia is not a farm girl, and treat her like a young lady."

"Yes, dear," her dad said. He helped Karia into the wagon, then got in himself and took the reins.

They rode in silence a while, and then her dad spoke.

"Tsil, I'm sorry that the advice I gave you about Gerik didn't work out," he said.

"No, Daddy, it wasn't your advice," she said. "I'm pretty sure he had decided to call things off before he even got to the farm that day. Even if he hadn't, that was my decision, and I don't blame you."

"Good," he said. "Because I also need you to forgive me if I sometimes forget you're not a little girl anymore."

Karia laughed. "I have trouble remembering that myself at times," she said. She thought a moment and then said, "Daddy?"

"Yes, Tsil?"

"If Gerik is at the smith's when we pull up, I don't want you to help me down."

"Karia, I'm sorry, dear, but he's made himself clear and I don't think …"

"Please, Daddy?"

"OK. But if he doesn't come over and your mom finds out I let you climb out on your own …"

"If he doesn't come over you can come and help me, Daddy."

"Sounds good."

They rode on in silence into town.

They crossed the bridge and went past the village green, and past the intersection where another road crossed.

If they followed that road to the left today, Karia knew, it would lead through another part of town, past Silla's shop and the apothecary and mill, among other things. Then it would take them to a couple of farms, including the one where Sikarra lived, before petering out at the edge of the rocky hills. But she knew from the map that at one time it led to a road through the rocky hills. To the right it led to a few more farms, though she only really knew one of the people out that way – Akamon – and he always gave her the creeps. For the first time she wondered if that was actually something she felt about him, like the way she felt her mom and the house in the Old Wood.

She looked at the northeast corner of that intersection – where the old map showed a small fort – and almost gasped. A raised wooden porch ran along the front of all the businesses, down the main road and around the corner along the road to the left. But she had never before noticed the three-foot-high wall of massive stones under that porch. It appeared to her that all the buildings on the corner were built atop the ruins of the old fort.

Just past the wall was an alley, and as she looked down it she could see that the old fort wall ran down the alley as well. On the other side of the alley on the left she saw the rough, unkempt wooden shop and house of the horse trader. The paint had long since peeled or flaked away, and the bare wood was gray and weathered. Just beyond that, before Gerik's stately brick house, was a large yard that served the trader and the blacksmith, with a barn at the back for each of them. Just as the houses were a contrast, so were the barns. The trader's barn was in worse shape than his house, with weathered boards missing here and there. But the blacksmith's barn was bright yellow, with red trim. Karia had always thought it was a bit gaudy, but today she noticed that it always looked freshly painted.

She had a new appreciation for the work Gerik's mom did to keep their home and business looking fresh and clean, and for the first time understood why she sometimes griped about the way the horse trader's house and barn looked. *If that becomes my house, I'd feel the same way*, she thought. She caught herself. *If that was my house, I mean.*

Karia's dad turned their wagon into the yard and headed for the far side, where the smithy was. As Karia had hoped, Gerik was at the smithy, helping his dad. Her dad pulled the wagon up and got out to talk with Gerik's dad. Long hours in the noisy smithy had left Gerik's dad hard of hearing, and he always talked much louder than was appropriate. Karia moved to the side of the wagon and waited. *Gerik looked. He saw me.*

"Gerik, assist me," Karia commanded loudly, slightly scolding.

Gerik walked to her side of the wagon and said, "Yes, Miss." He helped her down, and probably because they were both a little awkward and unused to it, ended up standing uncomfortably close. Karia looked up into his eyes, and she wanted to put her arms around him. *Oh gosh, not in public!* She almost forgot what she had planned to say. But only almost. She took a half-step back.

"Sir, I trust your manners will be better when we meet again," Karia said. "Good day." She turned her back on him and walked toward the road.

Gerik's dad spoke, probably intending for only Gerik to hear, but it was loud enough for Karia to hear as well. "That, boy, is a lady," he said. She smiled.

Karia turned right when she got to the edge of the yard, and walked up onto the wooden porch of the businesses there on the corner. At the corner was the pub, the most popular business in town, though it was quiet at this hour. She turned the corner to the right, walking up the porch along the other road and down the steps. She walked along the road past four or five shops or houses, then crossed the street to Silla's shop.

A tiny bell tinkled as she opened the door and stepped into the front room. She noticed a girl's red gingham dress on a form to her right, and several drawings of women in dresses scattered on a small table to her left, next to two cane-seated chairs. She heard movement from the back room, separated by a piece of fabric hanging in the doorway, and assumed Silla was back there. She turned to look at the dress just as Silla pushed the fabric aside and began to step through.

"Gingham," Silla sneered. "It's all that snotty little redhead from the farm up the road will wear, and now she's got all her nasty little friends wanting it."

Karia looked at her. She had one of those faces that seemed to be in a perpetual scowl, and her attitude right now didn't help. Her graying hair was pulled back tightly into a bun, and she wore – incongruously for a seamstress, Karia thought – a simple navy blue dress. Karia knew of only one redhead, her little shadow, Sikarra, and did not care at all for Silla's description of her. But she had no intention of getting into an argument. Anyway, as soon as Karia looked her way, Silla's face brightened.

She stepped close to Karia and touched the shoulder of her dress. "Oh, dear, this is just as lovely as the blue one," she said.

"Thank you, Ma'am," Karia said.

"Don't you Ma'am me, young lady," Silla said, her smile widening. "You can call me Silla."

"Thank you," Karia said, and stopped. She knew Silla meant that as a compliment, but she couldn't bring herself to call her by her name. It seemed so disrespectful to her. "I'm looking for a fabric like this, so I can make a dress like this for my mom."

"Oh, that would be lovely," Silla said. "Almost as lovely as this is on you. You are such a pretty young woman. Take after your mom, don't you? But I'm afraid I don't have any fabric nearly that fine, or in that color."

Karia was disappointed, and it showed. She really wanted to make her mom a dress that would go well with her hair.

"I could order some from the Central Plain, and it would only take a couple of weeks to get here," Silla added. "Or can I show you what I do have?"

Karia had time available now; she was all caught up with the mending. But in two weeks, who could say? "Why don't you show me what you have?"

Silla turned and walked toward the back of her shop, but she did not stop at the fabric on the shelves in the front room. She led Karia through the doorway into her workroom, to a table where bolts of fabric were stacked.

"These are fabrics I bought to use, fabrics I'd rather not put into the hands of a lesser seamstress. But I know you'll do them justice, dear," Silla said, drawing out a bolt of rich, deep blue velvet. "About four yards of this would do – or eight yards could make a gown fit for the courts of Talitakaya."

"That's lovely," Karia said, running her hand over the fabric. "But we're farm folk, Silla, and my mom isn't going to Talitakaya anytime soon."

"Good thinking, dear. How about this?"

Silla drew out a bolt that looked like plain tan linen. Karia thought it looked similar, but perhaps somewhat finer than, the basic linen you would make a chemise from, and disappointment must have shown on her face.

"Oh, but let's take it over here, shall we, dear?" Silla walked to a window at the side of her workroom, where sunlight illuminated her sewing area. In the light, the fabric shimmered like silk.

"That still seems too delicate for the farm," Karia said.

"Feel it, dear."

Karia felt the fabric, and it felt sturdy.

"Test the strength," Silla said. Karia pulled at the fabric, and found that it was as sturdy as it felt. "That'll make a lovely dress that your mom will be able to wear for a long, long time, dear."

OK, now the hard part. "It does seem very nice," Karia said. "And so I would expect it to be very expensive, but I don't have a lot of money."

"Well, now, I have an idea about that, Karia," Silla said. "A girl of your talent could do very well as a seamstress. If you will come on as my apprentice, I'll give you four yards of that fabric. That should be enough for a very pretty, sturdy dress for the farm."

Karia was flattered. Very flattered. She knew firsthand how particular Silla was about sewing, and had heard stories that made even what she had seen seem mild. She knew that was why Silla had no apprentices. She also knew she had nowhere near the talent Silla thought she had. And she didn't really want to be a seamstress.

"Silla, that is a very gracious offer – both the offer of the apprenticeship and the fabric," she said. "And I don't say this lightly, because I know you are a very good seamstress and I could learn much from you, but I'm afraid I'm needed on the farm."

Before she could continue, Silla added, "You could live with me, and you'd be closer to Gerik."

Gosh, does the whole town know? She blushed, then finished her thought. "I'm also not sure I can put up with any more changes in my life right now, so I am going to have to decline. I'm sorry."

"Nothing to be sorry for, dear. I'll tell you what, you take the fabric anyway. Your family's been a very good customer, and I'm dying to see what you do with this."

"Oh, Silla, I couldn't …"

"Nonsense," Silla said. "It's just business. People will see your mom in a beautiful dress, and they'll want to know where you got such lovely fabric, and after you tell them, maybe they'll come here and start buying some of the fancier stuff. Deal?"

Karia smiled. She knew very well that everyone around here had to get their fabric from Silla anyway. And seldom did they need anything fancy. It was Silla's way of giving Karia a gift. *Maybe she's not as mean as I thought.* She accepted the offer. "Thank you," she said.

"It's my pleasure," Silla said, smiling, as she tied a piece of string around the bolt to be sure the fabric didn't come off as Karia carried it home. Something about Silla's manner made Karia think there was more to this change in attitude than Silla thinking she'd make a good apprentice. *Is it because I'm fifteen now?* she wondered. *Is it because she thinks I'm pretty?* As she stepped out of the shop, she remembered Silla's words: *'You are such a pretty young woman.' Am I?*

She crossed the street, lost in thought, and was upset with herself because she could not even remember looking to see if any riders or wagons were coming. Thankfully it was still early in the day, and as she looked around now she saw that the street was mostly empty.

She also saw Rekon, crossing the street toward her. He smiled and nodded. She stopped. *Should I have stopped? Is he coming to talk to me, or did I just make an assumption? Oh, gosh, if I just assumed that, I'm going to look and feel like an idiot.*

She was relieved when he walked up to her and took off his cap. "It's a pleasure to see you, Karia," he said.

"And to see you, Rekon."

He reached for the package. "Allow me to carry that for you," he said.

She hesitated a moment. *I am not going to let gossip change the way I treat people.* She held the bolt out toward him. "Thank you. I'm just taking it to our wagon, outside the smithy." She thought she saw his smile grow slightly.

They walked together around the corner, down the street and across the yard to the wagon. Karia saw that Gerik was still at work there, and deliberately avoided looking at him. But she thought she could see him watching her. "Just put it in the back there," Karia said, noticing her dad holding the Great Smelly Beast as the smith took off one of the horse's old shoes. "Thank you, Rekon."

"You're welcome," he said. *He's glancing over at Gerik too. I wonder why.* "Karia, would you come to my house for lunch?"

Karia was surprised, and looked to her dad. *Say no.* He nodded yes. So in a voice she hoped didn't sound fake, but would be loud enough for Gerik to hear over the noise at the smithy, she said, "Why, yes, Rekon, how kind of you. I would enjoy having lunch with you."

Rekon offered her his arm. She hesitated. To take it would imply to Gerik – and to Rekon and the whole town – that she was at least receptive of Rekon's advances, and she realized that she was not. But to decline it might make Gerik think she was some silly little girl who was doting on him.

So she took Rekon's arm and went to his home for lunch. She was actually relieved that it was deadly dull and awkward. Rekon's mother seemed cool to her. And one thing she said may have been an insult to farm girls, but Karia was not certain. At any rate, she found it all quite odd. The miller's livelihood depended on farmers.

She and Rekon barely spoke as he walked her back to the smithy, and Karia was glad to see that her dad had just finished hitching the Great Smelly Beast. Rekon stopped and reached to take her hand. She withdrew it; she felt he was being too forward. "Good day, Karia," he said.

"Good day, Rekon, and thank you again for lunch," Karia replied, politely but a bit stiffly. He nodded, turned and left.

She walked to her side of the wagon, and when her dad started over to help her up, shook her head no. She looked at Gerik and cleared her throat. He came over and hesitated.

"Karia, I don't think you should be seeing Rekon," he said.

She took a step back from him. "Sir, in the first place, my choices are none of your business, though it would please me if you desired to make them your business again. Secondly, I should think that you of all people would not listen to gossip. I do not.

"Now, please, assist me."

Gerik helped her into the wagon.

"Thank you, Sir," she said.

"You're welcome, Miss."

Her dad climbed up and shook the reins to tell the Great Smelly Beast to start walking, then pulled on the right lead to turn her and therefore the wagon.

Again Gerik's dad spoke, and again she thought he meant it just for his son, but half the town probably heard him. "You oughta think again about that young lady, boy. Your mom ain't always right." *His mom? I thought she liked me. But ... it wasn't his idea. So maybe he'll listen to his dad. I'm very glad I came to town today.*

"What was that all about?" her dad asked.

"What?" she asked, smiling.

"All that stuff about Gerik and Rekon and all that?"

"That was nothing, Daddy. Nothing at all." Karia smiled the whole way home.

Ian Fallis

CHAPTER SEVENTY-NINE

Karia was eager to start on her mom's dress the next afternoon, and was disappointed when her mom asked her to go water and weed Nana's flowers instead.

"You and Nana puttered about with them all the time," her mom said, "and I'd hate for them to be dead when she gets back. And since you know I'd just end up killing them if I went over there, and you know what you're doing, well, I just think Nana would appreciate it, dear."

Karia knew she was right. As much as she loved her mom, it would just be wrong to let her touch Nana's flowers.

Karia went to Nana's and started digging weeds out from among the tender plants with the deep purple flowers that edged the walk. Then she got a bucket and fetched some water from the irrigation pond next to Nana's house. She was turning the corner to the front of the house when a small flash of light caught her eye.

She shaded her eyes and looked, and she could see movement all along the old stone bridge. *The flashes of light ... what is that? ... Horses ... Riders ... Spears ...* Karia was shocked when she realized there were cavalry, riding hard, all along the bridge. Some had already crossed. *There must be a hundred or more. And they'll be here any minute.*

Karia dropped the bucket and ran to her house. "Mom!" she yelled. "Cavalry! Mom!" Her mom ran out onto the porch. Out of the corner of her eye, Karia noticed movement from Aunt Heather's as well. "A hundred or more, Mom!"

Karia heard her Aunt Heather. "Failean! That many? They've not come to search, they've come for her!"

For me? What? Why?

"Karia, run to the Old Wood. Go to the house," her mom shouted urgently. Karia, stunned, just stood there. "Run, girl, run!" her mom screamed. "Don't even look back!"

The fear in her mom's voice terrified Karia. She took off through the fields, as fast as she could. Her legs burned. Her lungs burned. Just as she reached the small rise at the edge of the Old Wood, she stumbled and went down. It felt like she stepped on something wrong, and her knee hit something hard. She definitely heard something snap, but she could not tell what. Her entire right leg felt like it was on fire. She sat up and looked back. She vaguely saw movement in the fields to her left, where her dad had been working, and around the houses to her right. But her attention was caught by a group of horsemen coming directly toward her. *They must have seen me running across the field!*

She turned and stood to run into the woods, and felt a sharp pain in her right ankle and a dull throb in her right knee. With each step it seemed like the pain increased, and her speed decreased. She was moving as fast as she could, but she was mostly dragging herself forward with her left leg, and that was not fast at all. She could hear hoofbeats and shouts now; the riders were closing fast. She was amazed – and very happy – to come to the lane as soon as she did. She concentrated and focused and tried to will herself to sprint toward the gap under the hedge. Instead her right leg gave out and she fell to her knees. Pain shot up her leg from her right knee, and she cried out. She crawled and clawed her way down the lane, trying to ignore the way her knee throbbed and felt like something was scraping inside. Just before she reached the gap, she saw the riders reach the edge of the lane, heard them yell, watched their horses accelerate across the open ground toward her.

She dove under the hedge and almost screamed from the pain of pushing with her right leg. She felt like she was crawling on her aching knee for a long time before she reached the house. She tried to stand and fell again, so she pulled herself along her left side to the doorway by the parlor. There she leaned, watching the entry, hoping the magician had not been lying, hoping they could not follow. She realized she was crying and making little whimpering noises with each breath. *Stop it*, she thought, closing her eyes and concentrating. *Grow up.*

When she opened her eyes she saw a ribbon of blood leading from the wall to her right knee. The knee of her dress was shredded and bloody. When no one had come through the wall in a few minutes, she lifted her skirt and saw that her ankle was already blue and swollen, and her foot was at odd angle. Lifting it further – it was stuck to her bloody knee and hurt to pull it off – she saw that her knee was scraped raw and cut deeply. There was sand and dirt all over it, and it was still bleeding. She tried to move it, and it felt like someone had just shoved a knife into it. She cried out again.

"Oh, good. I get to use the amber ointment again. I hope it doesn't kill me." *Oh, gosh, stop whining! Stop crying!*

She rolled onto her left knee and struggled to stand, pulling herself up at the doorway. But she could put no weight on her right ankle. And she couldn't crawl on that knee. She slumped back to the floor.

"Generality!" she shouted.

He zipped to the doorway, but stopped well short of her. "Mistress!" he cried, and he began fluttering rapidly all about her, looking worried.

"Generality, hold still and help me out," Karia said.

"Yes, Mistress, anything, Mistress! What can I do?"

"How strong are you?"

"Well, doesn't that just take the cake. You know all faeries are very strong, but you have to take another jab at me for being so fat."

"I'm not taking a jab at you," Karia said.

"Well, maybe I'm too fat to do you any good."

She snapped, "Will you please stop being such a conceited little prick and give me a hand?!"

He stopped. He stared at her.

"I'm sorry," she said. "It's just that …"

"You called me little."

"Yes, so …"

"You didn't call me big and fat. For once you didn't make fun of me. You called me little."

"I haven't been making … oh, never mind. Do you think you can help me up and support me on the right side? I can't put any weight on my right ankle."

"Yes, I could. But where are we going?"

"To the waterfall room. That's where the ointments are."

"I can bring them to you," Generality said.

"Thank you," she said. "I hadn't thought of that. But I would like to rinse the blood – and the sweat and the dirt – off myself too."

"Ah, right, and that cut should be cleaned first," Generality said. He deftly helped her to her feet and then supported her right side as if she weighed nothing.

"You're very strong," she said.

"Thank you, but don't be too impressed. You're not exactly the biggest human I've ever seen."

Karia laughed. "I'll take that as a compliment, even though I'm not as pretty as a horse."

"Was that a compliment? I never know with humans. Especially human women."

Karia laughed again, but that made her ankle move slightly, and even that minor movement caused excruciating pain. She stopped and winced, her eyes tearing. She took a breath and went on.

They made it to the waterfall room and Karia said, "OK, help me sit on the floor, please."

Generality helped ease her to the floor. In fact, he did almost all the work.

"You can go now. Can you close the door?"

"Well, yes, but, excuse me, Mistress, I mean, please forgive me for disobeying you, but may I speak?"

"Yes, but please try not to ask a lot of questions. I'm hurting."

"Yes, Mistress. You need to clean that wound before you put ointment on it, and to do that you need to get into the waterfall. I suppose you could drag yourself across the floor to get in there, but I'm not certain you can even undress by yourself right now. Please allow me to help you undress, to help you in the waterfall, and to help you with the ointments."

"Wow. You didn't ask even one question." He was right, but Karia didn't really want to admit it. And she really didn't want to answer him.

"No, Mistress."

They looked at each other awkwardly for a while.

"Will you allow me to serve you, Mistress?"

"OK," she said. "You're right. I hadn't really thought that through. But this is very awkward for me."

"I wish I could say I understand, but I don't. And I only say that in hopes that you will feel somewhat less uncomfortable with me helping you."

They both stayed like that for a moment, Karia sitting on the floor looking up at him, and him hovering. Finally he said, "Am I supposed to start taking your clothes off you?"

"No!" Karia shouted. "I'm sorry; I shouldn't have yelled at you. No. Please close the door first."

Generality looked puzzled. "There's no one else here," he said.

"Close the door," Karia said. Generality did as he was told. *I have to stop being so polite when it's an order, I guess.* That made the whole uncomfortable process easier, and by the time he helped her sit down by the door again they were working well together. It helped that he didn't seem to be looking anywhere he shouldn't have, and Karia knew that because she kept checking. And checking.

"Get me the amber ointment and the thinner white ointment," Karia said. As Generality flew back holding one in each hand, even though each was about twice as large as he was, she looked down at her right leg. Her ankle and knee already looked better.

"May I suggest the white one first?" Generality said. "It has less of a kick to it, and then your ankle won't hurt when you use the amber."

"Thanks, Generality. That's a good idea. I can take it from here. Go now," she said.

He flew to the door and opened it, and went out.

"Close the door," she called, and he obeyed.

Karia used the white one first, as Generality recommended, and when her leg spasmed as she applied the amber, she was glad she had. She began to stand, gingerly putting her weight on her right leg. Her knee and ankle were stiff and sore, but they seemed to be working. She dried off, put the robe and her locket on, picked up her chemise and green dress, and limped back to the bedroom. She sat on the bed and looked first at the dress. The knee was shredded, and beyond mending.

Well, I suppose I could just cut it off just above the knee, she thought, jokingly. Then she blushed. *I'm not going to walk around and let everyone see my ankles, let alone my calves and my knees! What kind of a girl would do that?!*

Then she looked at the chemise. She had been wearing the fine chemise she had gotten from Gerik's mom, and she was very glad that it looked like it could be mended. So she had to get the blood out of it. She called Generality again.

Again there was a delay, but she waited a short time, and soon he was flying toward her face. "Sorry for the delay," he said.

"Bowling again?" she asked.

"No, just puttering about the flower garden."

Flower garden? She looked up at the canopy. *What all does he have up there?*

"They're very small flowers," he said.

"Right," Karia said.

Seeing the dress and chemise on her lap, he asked, "Would you like me to mend those, Mistress?"

"I was going to ask you to clean the chemise," Karia said. "I can mend that. But the dress is beyond mending."

"You could cut it really short like a faerie dress," Generality suggested, as he flew in for a close look at the tear.

"No, I don't think so," Karia said, slightly amused.

Now hovering right next to the hole in the knee of her dress, he said, "I can mend this."

"Well, yes, but a patch wouldn't look right on a dress this nice," she said.

"Who said anything about a patch? I can reweave it." He held up his hands. "Very small hands, you see?"

"I see," Karia said. "That would be wonderful. I was just glad the chemise was mendable, because it's such a nice one. But I was going to darn it. Do you think you could reweave that as well? It's very fine."

271

Generality flew to the tear in the chemise. "Oh, yes. I can do that." Then he flew to her face. "You like this better than the linen ones?"

"Yes," she said. "But don't get me wrong, the linen ones are quite practical, and very sturdy."

Generality thought a moment. "But you're a girl. And if you don't mind me saying so, you're not very practical. You want to be covered up, and then you say this very thin chemise is nice. You need my help in the waterfall room, but you don't want me to see you naked. And even though it gets in the way of nursing, you cover up your teats."

"Breasts," she corrected. *Why did I say that?* Then she blushed.

"Right. Sorry. Breasts it is then. Anyway, this chemise is not very practical, and you called it nice. So what I'm wondering is, do you want me to not only mend this one, but make you another?"

"You can do that?"

"Who do you think made the dresses and chemises in the first place?" he asked.

"I assumed my father did," she said.

Generality looked at with a quizzical expression. "A great sorcerer, making dresses?"

"I thought he used magic."

"No, the magic is just to hide this place. Everything else is made, a lot by me. For instance, he told me to make clothes for you. I had a lot of time on my hands," he said, gesturing to the elaborate dresses.

Karia smiled and laughed. "How long would it take you to make a chemise?"

"No time at all. Literally," he said.

"Oh. Right. But I mean, here, how long?"

"How am I supposed to know? Haven't you noticed how hard it is to tell time here?"

"I'm sorry. You're right," Karia said.

"But you know how you go to bed and sleep sometimes?"

"Yes," she said.

"In the time you sleep, I can get these cleaned and mended, and make you a new chemise," he said.

"That would be splendid," Karia said with delight. She leaned forward and tried to give him a little kiss.

"AAAAAAAAAAAAA!" he screamed as he moved away. "Don't eat me! Please!"

"I'm sorry, I was just going to ..." she started to say, then blushed. "I just wanted to give you a little kiss because you made me so happy."

"OK, fine, but think about it from my perspective a second. All I saw were these big huge lips coming at me. What was I supposed to think?"

Karia laughed. "Big huge lips? Now who's calling who fat?"

"Oh, there we go. I knew we couldn't get through a single conversation without a fat faerie joke." And with that, he snatched up the dress and chemise and flew back to the top of the canopy.

Ian Fallis

CHAPTER EIGHTY

With her injuries and clothes attended to, Karia sat at the dressing table to brush her hair and think. She knew she had all the time in the world here, so there was no rush to leave. At the same time, she knew that when she left, it would be the same instant she had come in – the same instant the cavalry had come to the lane in the wood – so she needed to think carefully about where she would want to come out and why. And once she had that sorted out, she decided, she could figure out what she needed to do to prepare for whatever she was going to do.

As she began to think about it, her Aunt Heather's shout rang in her head: *'Failean! They've not come to search, they've come for her!'*

If they came for me, they must have known I could do magic. How? Maybe the magician had told them. Even though he said he wanted to help her, she knew she could not trust him. *No, wait, he was here just a few days ago.* He would not have had time to go back to Talitakaya before or after that, and that was the only place from which a hundred or more cavalry could be dispatched.

Talitakaya. Of course. Narek. They must have discovered Narek had no magical ability, let alone the ability to make fire. And he must have told them what she had done. She wasn't angry with him. How could she be? He blamed her for his arrest, and she also felt it was her fault. But she was disappointed with him. *Gosh, is every man in my life going to turn out to be a disappointment?*

And if Narek told them she could not only make fire, but make it appear that fire came from him, they would have decided she was a powerful and dangerous sorceress. *No, you dummy. They know who you are. They know you better than you do, Tsilinakaya.*

She sat and stared at herself in the mirror. She traced her long auburn hair. She saw the small, sharp nose and the girlish freckles. She looked into her own oh-so-blue eyes. That's all she wanted to see. That's what she wanted to be. Karia, the farm girl who was becoming a woman.

275

She saw tears in her eyes. *Karia, stop feeling sorry for yourself. You don't cry, and you've got a whole world waiting to see what you're going to do.*

She knew she was right. She knew this was no longer about what she wanted, but about all those people who depended on her. And her mom and dad were among them. Soldiers were no doubt holding them, wanting to find out how to find her. She thought about making fire and burning the soldiers to free them, and then was disgusted with herself. She could not kill. She was not going to become a killer.

But what if that's what's required of me? What if that's my future and my destiny? To kill those who oppress and kill? Is it wrong to kill killers?

She was starting to feel overwhelmed when she remembered her mom's words: *'You're a smart girl, Karia. Put aside everything else. Focus on the important thing.'*

She took a deep breath. The soldiers knew who she was. The magician had taken precautions before coming up against her, so certainly the soldiers would have as well. She could not save her parents. That deserved another deep breath, and another reminder to herself: *I don't cry.*

If the soldiers knew who she was, the Dr'Zhak and their lackeys among the Teneka knew too. They would hunt for her. In fact, they had seen her go under the hedge, and they would probably already be trying to figure out how to get in.

No, she thought. *The riders are still just now arriving at the hedge. Soon they'll be trying to get in. But not while I'm in here. I think.*

She was starting to give herself a headache.

She took another deep breath.

Her father put all kinds of books here so she could fulfill her purpose. *OK, right, what he saw as my purpose.* She needed to take the time necessary, here, to study all she could. Maybe, within the books that her father intended her to use to master the gift of magic, she would find out how to break the curse of magic.

She wished her mom had taught her more about Inamali. *By Gnome's Arm, there's so much I wish she had told me. Wait, stop. That's not the important thing.*

She got up and limped to the study. She picked up a book from the bottom shelf and took it to the kitchen table. She sat down and opened it. *Animal husbandry. Wonderful.*

CHAPTER EIGHTY-ONE

Karia read and read and read. Her ability to read and understand Inamali was growing, and she knew it was more than just practice. That was somewhat frightening.

She was coming to realize that in order to truly understand what the Inamali wrote, she had to see it through the Inamali's eyes. In short, she had to remember the Inamali were *inamali* – proud because they were better. That way of thinking repelled her, but it was in everything she read, and she felt like it was slowly clawing its way into her heart.

She was also seeing that this was indeed the language of magic. She now knew, even from reading about mundane topics like farming and baking and sewing, this language had not come along with magic. This language belonged to magic. This was the language magic needed her to think in, in order to bend her to its ways. And yet this was also the language she needed to master if she was going to defeat magic.

Karia reached a point where she felt as if she had read all afternoon. After all, it was afternoon when she had gone to take care of Nana's flowers, and seen the soldiers. She stood and stretched, then picked up the book she had been reading about smithing. *I wonder if I could teach Gerik a trick or two now?*

She sighed. *I wonder if I'll even ever see him again.*

She carried the book back to the study and bent down to put it back. She was shocked to see that she had read nearly three-quarters of the books on the bottom shelf. She knew she could never have read that many books in one afternoon. She could not even begin to calculate how long that would have taken. *A day? Two days? Perhaps.*

Yet she was only a little tired and slightly hungry. She wondered if magic was sustaining her, in order to drive her on to its own goals. *It doesn't matter. I need to keep reading to reach my goal.*

She fixed herself some dinner, then went back to reading. She had gotten through two more of the books when she felt very dizzy. She looked

277

up and it was as if the whole room was being squished, then stretched, and now squished again.

"Generality!" she cried.

He zipped into view. "Oh great. This makes me look fat. No, that's not true. I was already fat. This makes me look fatter."

"What's happening?"

"Someone's trying to get in."

"Will they be able to?"

"Oh, yes, eventually," Generality said. The room went back to its normal appearance. "There, they've mastered the first step. We're back in time again."

"What's that mean?"

"That means that for every second that passes here, a second passes outside."

"How long do we have?" Karia asked.

"That's hard to say. I'm going to guess at least a couple of hours," Generality said.

A couple of hours. I can't even begin to get through the rest of the books in a couple of hours, and I must get through them. The answers are in there.

Generality apparently saw the look of worry on Karia's face. "Would you like a more precise estimate?" he said.

"Yes!" Karia replied.

He flew off and returned so fast it seemed almost as if he hadn't left. He was carrying a spherical brass machine about the size of her head, with spinning wheels and gears and orbs. At the center were five numbered dials, two with the hands spinning wildly, one moving more slowly, and two that barely seemed to move. He let the machine go and it floated in the air. He appeared to be adjusting it, slightly moving some tabs and levers, then flew straight into the center as wheels and orbs dashed past him.

Karia gasped, thinking he was going to be hit, and he came straight back out again. "Are you OK?" he said.

"Yes, I was just afraid you were going to be hit," she said.

"Oh, don't worry," he said, and dashed into the center again as she held her breath. There he hovered, reading the dials and shaking his head. He dashed back out and appeared to be checking his adjustments, then zipped back to the center again.

Now he came out and zipped right at Karia's nose. She closed her eyes. "Oh, sorry," he said. "Forgot you didn't like that. Anyway, it's strictly amateur hour out there. They pulled us into time, but they tripped the first trap."

"What does that mean?" Karia said.

"Well, it means that the sorcerer who worked the spell will have to recover from the spell that was the trap, and that should take about a day," he said.

Ian Fallis

CHAPTER EIGHTY-TWO

"What is that infernal sorcerer doing now?" Hinar asked. The sergeant was standing beside the hedge, watching the sorcerer jump from one tree limb to another. Moments before, the sorcerer had said, "Aha!" and then "Oh no!" before stripping off all his clothes and climbing the tree while wiggling his nose and making chirping noises.

"I'd say he thinks he's a squirrel," said the sorcerer's assistant, never taking his eyes off the hedge. He appeared to be concentrating. "He succeeded in breaking through the place's first line of defense, but apparently tripped a trap spell."

"Well, do something!" Hinar said.

"I am doing something, Sergeant," the assistant said. "I'm exerting all my abilities to hold the place in time. It's under an extremely powerful enchantment that is trying to take it back."

"Well, then, what about him?" Hinar said, pointing to the sorcerer, who was now nibbling at an acorn.

"It'll wear off by tomorrow evening. Perhaps as early as dawn tomorrow. All we can do is wait. Well, all you can do is wait. I need to keep focusing on this. But we're closer, Sergeant. And after he recovers, there are only two more lines of defense to breach."

"How long will that take?" Hinar asked.

"Depends on how squirrely the rest of the defenses are," the assistant said.

Ian Fallis

CHAPTER EIGHTY-THREE

"So I have a day?" Karia asked.

"Approximately, mistress. Could be a little less, or perhaps a little more."

A day. And I've not even finished the simplest books.

Generality saw that she was still quite worried. He pointed in the direction of the door out and said, "Mistress, do you not know that at any time you can go through that wall and be anywhere you wish?"

"You mean, go through the door."

"No, I mean go through the wall. There's no door there. That's an illusion. But illusions don't work on faeries. There's a wall, and just in front of the wall there's a spell that takes you wherever you are thinking about as you step through."

"But I opened the door," Karia said.

"No, you thought you did. Tell me, did you see a door on the other side?"

"No," Karia said. "OK. Fine. But that still doesn't solve my problem. Even a day isn't enough to get through all the books, and I need to read them all to figure out what to do."

"So take them with you," Generality said.

"I can't carry that many books," Karia said. "And I need to take food, and the ointments too. Just those things will fill up the haversack."

"No they won't," Generality said.

"Fine, maybe I could fit one or two books in as well, but not all of them."

"Yes, all of them," he said.

"What are you talking about? I'd need a wagon or something!"

Generality flew off and zipped back with the haversack. "Put that in," he said, pointing to the large volume on botany that she had been reading. Karia opened the clasp and put the book into the sack.

"Good," he said. "Now put in a wheel of cheese."

Karia, curious, got a wheel of cheese and put it into the haversack. It looked full. "There, you see?" she said.

"Get another wheel of cheese," Generality said.

"It's full," Karia said.

"Yes, so it is. But watch this." Generality flew to the pantry and grabbed two more wheels of cheese – one in each hand – and flew into the haversack with them. It did not expand. He flew back out. "Pick it up," he said.

She reached over to pick it up, bracing herself for the weight of the large book and three wheels of cheese. But it was no heavier than it had been when Grandpa Jiki's diary was the only thing inside.

"More magic," she said with bitterness, feeling like she would never be rid of it.

Generality missed her tone. "Yes, wonderful, right? You can take everything you want." He paused, and appeared to be thinking about something. "But there's only one problem," he said sadly.

"What's that?"

"Once you fill that haversack with more than it can hold physically, you'll find it's very difficult to reach everything from the top. You'll need someone to get what you need and bring it to you. And that someone would have to be very small, and very strong. Oh, and very quick, too, so they could just get in and get what you needed without you waiting a long time while they went and got it." He had a puzzled expression on his face.

"Someone like you, then?" Karia asked, smiling.

"Well, what do you know?" he said, his face lighting up. "I never thought of that. Yes, certainly, that would work. I'm small and strong, and quick. Well, that's very good thinking, Mistress! I suppose, if you'd like, I could come along and help you."

"Thank you," she said with a laugh. "But would you want to leave your home and live in a sack?"

Generality looked grim. "Once they get in, Mistress – and they will get in – they'll torture me until they know everything I know, and then they'll … they'll …"

"They would kill you?" Karia asked.

"No, nothing that nice. They'll cut off my wings."

CHAPTER EIGHT-FOUR

Karia knew it was time for another deep breath. She wished she had time to sleep, because she always awoke fresh and thinking clearly here, and because she was feeling quite tired. But time was no longer unlimited here.

What's the most important thing? she thought.

She decided that as much as she wanted to just go, run and get away now, and as important as that was, her first priority was to prepare to get away.

But every minute I spend preparing is a minute less I'm ahead of them. And I can't run far feeling this tired. She took yet another deep breath.

She looked at Generality. He was quick, he was strong – and he could work while she took a nap.

"Generality, how long do you think it would take you to pack up everything – books, pots, pans, food, clothes – everything but the furniture?"

He thought about it a moment. "To pack it up properly, so I could get to everything easily and quickly – and assuming you'd let me take my things as well – probably an hour or two."

"Good. Please do so, and do feel free to pack up your things as well. I'm going to go take a nap. Wake me when you're done."

"Yes, Mistress."

"Oh, wait. Please leave one of the linen chemises and – oh, did you get my green dress mended?"

"Yes, mistress, and I've almost finished mending your chemise. But I've had no time to make you a new one."

"That's fine. Leave out one of the linen chemises and the green dress, oh, and the shoes and the traveling cloak."

"Yes, Mistress." He began zipping and toting, and Karia – being careful to duck as he zipped toward the kitchen with two large books – went to the bedroom to lie down.

She climbed into bed and barely had time to think, *I'm really going to miss this bed,* before falling asleep.

It seemed to be only a second later when she awoke because she heard her name and felt something tickling her ear. Without thinking, she swatted at her ear, and hit something rather solid. "Ow!" she heard directly in her ear.

She sat up. "Generality, I'm sorry! Are you OK?"

"Yes, Mistress. I am both sturdy and well-padded."

"Are you done packing?" she asked.

"No, I was just thinking it would be nice to be flattened between your hand and your ear."

"I said I was sorry," Karia said. "But you are done, right?"

"Yes, Mistress."

"How long have I been sleeping?"

"Almost two hours," Generality said. Karia was surprised. On the one hand it seemed she had just gone to bed. Yet she felt as refreshed as if she'd had a full night's sleep.

"Any sign of the people trying to get in?"

"No change, Mistress."

"So we'll still have at least a day's head start if we leave now."

"Yes, Mistress."

"Good. Please wait for me in the kitchen."

Generality zipped away, and Karia got up and dressed. She picked up the traveling cloak, and noticed that it was closed at the neck with a dull bronze clasp like the pattern on the haversack and on bread she made, a vertical cross with a connecting line from the top to the right.

She touched it to open it, and found it was stitched to the left of cloak and hooked into an eye on the right. But she also was startled when this too glowed like hammered gold at her touch. She pulled the traveling cloak over her dress, hooked the symbol into the eye, and glanced in the mirror. She saw the clasp fade from gold to a dull bronze again.

That was when she noticed that the cloak was much more comfortable and lighter, and less bulky, than she expected. *Gosh, I hope this will be warm if I need it to be.*

She walked into the kitchen, where Generality was hovering over the haversack. "One moment," he said, and zipped toward the bedroom with the haversack. He was back as quickly as he'd promised. "Had to get the bedding."

Karia took the haversack from him, and asked, "Do you want to ride inside?"

"What? In the sack?" he asked.

"Well, yes, I just thought …"

"No, thank you. I'll fly along with you. I need the exercise. I'm fat, remember?"

"What if someone sees you?"

"Oh, sorry, I should have realized you'd be embarrassed to be seen with such a fat faerie," he said. "Why can't you just give it a rest?"

"No, that's not it," she said. "I just thought ... I mean, I've never seen a faerie before, and you hid when I first came in, and I just thought all faeries hid from people."

"I didn't hide from you. I just didn't make myself known until you spoke to me. And there were several times I was right in front of you, but like most people, you didn't even notice me."

"Really?" she said. "Such as, when?"

"Do you really want to know?" he asked.

She blushed. "No, I guess not. So you're just going to fly along with me?"

"Well, after we get out of the house. I don't know where we're going, so I'd better ride in the haversack until we get there."

Oh my! Karia thought. *I don't know where we're going either! I'm all ready for a journey but I don't know where I'm going. Great start.*

"Generality, there was a very thin book on the top shelf with a map inside. Do you know the book I mean?"

"I think so," he said.

"Please get it for me."

Generality ducked into the sack and emerged with a thin book. It looked like the correct one, and she took it and opened it. There indeed was the map, folded over and over.

"Well done," she said.

"You gave me time to organize it properly."

Karia carefully – tenderly, even – opened the map, trying not to tear the brittle paper any more, and looked at it. *It won't do any good to go to town. People know me there, and if there aren't soldiers there already, the ones at home will go through town on their way back to Talitakaya.*

So she avoided even considering anything along the road from the farm through town toward Talitakaya. She briefly considered Sikarra's farm. *No,* she thought. *No, I will not bring any danger to her or her family.*

The map showed three options, but she was certain none of those destinations still existed the way they were pictured on the map. There was the town on the lake where there was now marsh; there was another town on the bay where there were mud flats now; and there was the castle near the western edge of the mountains. She was starting to panic, and reminded herself she still had a day. She took a deep breath. *Think, Karia.*

She looked where the town had been on the bay. To get out of there, she would need to go past farms where people knew her. She also knew for a fact that there were no ruins there, nothing that could shelter her, and she was hoping to find someplace indoors to hide while she figured out what to do next. That would not do, not at all.

The castle looked interesting. It was depicted as quite large, and she guessed it was made of stone. The old stone bridge had lasted all these years, so perhaps there was still shelter there. But she was concerned about having roads leading in from the fields to the south – *to here* – and the mountains to the north. *I can't watch two different directions.*

As much as she dreaded the marsh, she decided that was her best option. Besides, who would think she would go into the marsh? It was said to be filled with deadly creatures, and not just ferebeasts, the great, cat-like creatures with huge fangs and a nasty disposition, that were said to be resistant to magic.

She had also heard that the huge redbears lived there – though as far as Karia knew no one had even seen a redbear in her lifetime. People said there were all manner of snakes too – deadly poisonous ones that killed in seconds, long muscular ones that crushed their prey, even huge snakes that had mouths full of teeth and legs and were as at home in the water as on the land.

Legs, she thought when she heard that. *Snakes with legs? Well, then they aren't snakes, are they?* But that didn't make them sound any less scary.

Worst of all, the marsh was another place said to be home to Saviki, who kidnap naughty children in the night. Karia had long ago dismissed that as tales to keep children in line. She realized she had also dismissed the stories about a wizard roaming the Old Wood near her farm, and accepted as fact the idea that women couldn't do magic. She caught sight of Generality, hovering patiently before her. *And I didn't believe in faeries,* she thought. *And how wrong was I about all those things?* She shuddered. *What do I really know for certain?*

No one would think she would go in there, she was sure of that. They would think she was headed for certain death. *And, gosh, they're probably right!*

Feeling herself getting scared, she took a deep breath. *Akamon's been in there, and he's still alive,* she thought. She was pretty sure that she had heard Gerik went in with him one time, and he was still alive too.

Gerik. If only he was going in with me now. She caught herself thinking about walking down a trail with him, and scolded herself. *Stop being a silly girl and doting on a man. You're a woman. You're Tsilinakaya.*

She took another deep breath. *Focus, Karia. What's the most important thing?* She thought a moment. *Right, shelter. I need to find shelter. And perhaps there are at least ruins there, in the marsh, that I can take shelter in.*

"We're going here," Karia said to Generality, pointing to the town on the lake in the map. "So all I have to do is think about this, right?"

"Well, you actually have to have a picture of it in your mind. You know, be thinking about a specific place there."

"But I don't know what that looks like," Karia said.

"Then you can't go there," Generality replied.

"Why not?"

"Well, you have to know the place – you have to have been there – for the magic to work."

Karia felt a flash of anger toward Generality, feeling as if he should have told her that in the first place. But she kept herself from saying anything and took another deep breath. *It's not his fault*, she thought. *He doesn't know how much I don't know.*

Karia looked at the map again. She had been to the ford, and knew what that looked like. And while she did not like the fact that now she would have to try to find the old road, travel north, and work her way through the marsh, she still felt that was the best option.

"OK, we'll go to the ford," she said. She gently folded the old map back into the book and had Generality put it back in the haversack. She put the haversack over her shoulder, and Generality flew in. Then, steadfastly ignoring the fact that she now knew the door was only an illusion so she didn't think about walking into a wall, she opened the door while picturing the ford in her mind, and stepped through.

She stepped out on the hard packed ground at the edge of the ford. Level fallow fields spread out behind her and on either side of her. Generality flitted out of the haversack and looked around.

"OK, where to now?" he asked.

"There," Karia said, pointing across the river.

Generality flew up right in front of her nose. "Over there?" he asked.

"Yes, across the river," she replied.

He glanced over his shoulder at the river, and then back at her. He crossed his arms. "So why didn't you think about the other shore to start with?"

Ian Fallis

CHAPTER EIGHTY-FIVE

She took off the cloak and had Generality put it in the haversack. It was unseasonably warm, even for early fall, and Karia feared that meant winter may be late, but sudden and severe.

She waded into the river, Generality flying alongside her shoulder. Almost from the start she could feel the water tugging at her dress, pulling her downstream, and she had to turn slightly into the current to keep going straight across. The farther she went, the deeper it got, until the water was up to her knees. She could feel her dress – made with a lot of fabric at the hem to look fuller and more ladylike – *and to make it look like I have curves I don't have* – filling with and billowing in the water, trying to drag her under.

There, at the deepest part of the ford, her right foot hit a rock as she brought it forward for her next step, and her left foot lost its precarious hold on the sandy-silty bottom. As she fell, being pulled to her right by the current, she put her hands up without thinking. Suddenly she felt pressure on her left hand, then felt herself rise, and settle back onto her feet. She looked up at the faerie. "Thank you," she said.

"At your service, Mistress," he replied.

I'm glad this is fall. This would be impassable on foot in spring, when the water is higher. Especially in a dress.

She also thought about how handy it would have been to have the Great Smelly Beast.

Reaching the top of the other bank, she looked south and west, toward the farm, and was saddened but not surprised to see smoke rising from that direction. She stood there watching the smoke rise higher and higher, long enough, apparently, for Generality to become concerned.

"If we're supposed to be hiding, this is not a very good place to stop," he said.

"Oh, gosh, you're right," she said. She walked along a trail that she now knew was an old road that headed toward town. Her family had been this way before, but had never gone far down the trail. They had gone far enough to have seen the other road on the map, the one leading north and south, but she never recalled seeing it. So she was worried as she walked toward town that she would not spot the road.

She need not have worried. Now that she knew what she was looking for, and about where it was, it seemed obvious. She turned north on the dusty trail, and a slight breeze out of the north brought the smell of the distant marsh to her nose. It wasn't an altogether unpleasant smell to her. It reminded her of spring on the farm – damp and moist and, well, truth be told, rotting. But that was just a part of life to Karia, a farm girl.

As she walked she saw something blue beside the old road. It was a pure, clean blue, and as she drew closer she realized it was a flower. She took a single stride off the trail to look at it more closely. Standing over it, she could not help but think it was the same color as her eyes.

She bent over to smell it, and the fragrance caught her off guard. It was heady. She did not simply smell it; she felt it all through her lungs. It felt invigorating and fresh. She also knew that fragrance. It was very similar to the smell of the blue ointment from the house in the Old Wood. She stood up again, gazing down at the flower.

"Akinasta," Generality said. "They say it grows wherever a fairy died."

She looked up at him. "How beautiful, but how sad," she said. *Akinasta*, she thought. *Where have I heard that before?*

She stepped back to the trail, pausing to look across the plains. From here, the marsh looked like a hazy forest at the base of the Dentanal Mountains. Once more she wished she had the Great Smelly Beast with her. She sighed and trudged onward.

CHAPTER EIGHTY-SIX

In the center of a cavernous dark stone room, illuminated only by three candles in a gold lampstand on a heavy oak table, one of the twelve men broke the silence.

"We knew Lukaliva had failed to report to us. It is distressing to now know how profound his failure was."

One of the six men on the other side of the table stood up. He scowled as he first surveyed the large gilded throne opposite him, topped by a painted and jeweled carving of an oh-so-blue flower. He turned next to the smaller throne next to that, to the left of the man who had spoken. Then, anger burning in his eyes, he surveyed in turn each of them, all attired as he was in deep brown robes edged with red.

"We waited. Because of you, we waited," he said, jabbing his finger toward the man who had spoken first. "Instead of verifying that the third was dead, we waited. Instead of acting on her fifteenth birthday, we waited. Instead of acting when we felt magic stirring from her, we waited. And now she is lost to us!"

"Sit down, Vulakili," came a soft but strong voice from the man seated at one end of the table.

The man who had spoken did not sit. Instead, directing his anger toward all the others, he said, "You did not listen to me when I warned you that the heart magic was fading. You forbade me from working the deep earth magic ..."

His words were cut off, and he put his hand to his throat as if trying to ward off an attack. "I said, sit down, Vulakili," the man at the end of the table said again. The angry man sat.

"She is not lost to us," the man at the end of the table said. "Even now, we track her. And we know the magic is at work in her, drawing her. We will feed that, and she will rise. And with her, the Inamali will rise out of the shadows."

293

"What about the third?" asked an elderly man at the other end of the table.

"That will be seen to as well. Soon."

A preview of …

Karia's Path

Book Two of *The Day Magic Died*

IAN FALLIS

Ian Fallis

CHAPTER ONE

Dust sprayed into the air, shrouding the young man in a choking haze, when the large horse skidded to a stop. The man pulled the reins to the right, wheeling the horse in a tight circle as he vainly tried to scan the rocks around him. The dust was too thick to make out the weathered carvings. Turning was just stirring up more dust.

He cursed, pulling on the reins without realizing it. The horse reared, and surprise combined with the weight of the bulky pack on his back almost flung him to the ground. He wasn't sure how he managed to stay in the saddle, but as the horse settled back he patted its neck.

"Steady, Nebok," he said.

He silently cursed again, and sighed. He was impatient with worry, but there was nothing to do but wait until he could see clearly. He blinked his eyes and coughed. In a few moments it was clear enough that he could tell he had left the trail – again.

He turned his horse and followed his own tracks carefully back, scanning until his eye caught something. He stopped, then spurred Nebok closer. Yes, there it was. A small carving that looked like an obelisk set in a circle. It was ancient, so worn by time that it was barely visible, but still there nonetheless. He wheeled and spurred his horse forward, believing he had found the road again. He scanned ahead for the next carving.

The beast was made for heavy work, not speed, and Gerik was a pretty good load. He was only nineteen but he already stood over six feet tall. His shoulders seemed almost that broad as well. Despite his size, he was still getting a pretty good pace out of the draft animal he had recruited to carry him.

Regardless of his pace, he was trying to watch for the carvings. His eyes scanned from side to side. Some of the markings appeared at first to be simply features of the rocks. And sometimes the natural shape of a rock mimicked what was left of a carving. If Akamon, the hunter, had not pointed out the markings to him, he never would have noticed them. These were the only signs of the one safe way through the rocky hills. If he lost them, he would have to backtrack – as he already had done four times – or he could end up lost forever in the maze they called the rocky hills. Even a compass was unreliable here; something in the rocks sent the needle wildly spinning.

So he was forced to try to follow the faint signs of the ancient road, which he missed every so often. And every second he lost was a second less that he had to save Karia.

He set out a little more than an hour ago, and that was less than ten minutes after the disturbing visit from Akamon. Gerik was busy at the smithy. The town was still in an uproar after what seemed like scores of cavalry came through from east to west the day before.

Drical, a farm boy in town with his mom for some supplies, claimed to have counted one hundred twenty-four, before his mom hustled him back to the wagon and out of town to their farm. The apothecarist, Gabric Minter, who was so obese and so pompous that he needed two names, made some people believe he may actually have been telling the truth about once being a cavalryman. He identified the troopers as hussars – fast, light troops intended for quick strikes.

A few of the hussars stopped at the western edge of town and kept anyone from leaving in that direction. They would not say why. Rumors of an invasion began to rumble. The name "Inamali" was whispered; had they come back?

The talk became more urgent when, a few hours later, more troops arrived. These, Gabric Minter said, were dragoons – heavily armed elite cavalry. Some took the place of the light cavalry on the edge of town, who then sped off westward. More dragoons commandeered the inn, and a small detachment under a lieutenant took over the miller's house and turned him and his family out into the street. They looked nervous there; the apothecarist hurried to take them into his shop and home. It was neither charity nor hospitality; he saw it as a way to elevate people's view of his social standing.

Just as some were beginning to debate whether they should rebel in the face of an invasion – which cooler heads pointed out was a bit premature – four wagons arrived. One was a prison wagon, enclosed with bars in the back. But these were not the iron bars of a typical prison wagon. These were different from anything anyone had seen: bright, white-silver. Next, two covered wagons carried about a dozen Dr'Zhak each into town. All of these pulled up to the pub at the intersection – the only intersection in town. The fourth wagon, also covered, pulled up to the miller's house, where five hooded and robed men got out. Crimson peeked out from the bottom of their tan robes.

Not long afterward a single rider rode hard up to the dragoons at the western edge of town, stopping to ask something. His haste was clear in the fact that his horse was spent, and there it fell. The man ran on foot to the miller's.

Shortly after that a wagon and a squad of dragoons headed off to the west. For the rest of the day and all through this morning, all seemed quiet. The people of the town stayed indoors except for a few folks who had work to do, and a few brave busybodies spreading rumors. Gerik and his dad opened the smithy, knowing there would be work for them. His dad surmised that pushing wagons and horses over the old roads in the area meant repairs would be needed. He was correct.

Another messenger sped into town a little before noon, and soon after that another wagon and a squad of dragoons started down the small road south of town. They returned an hour later with Akamon in tow. The others went to the miller's while Akamon came to the smithy.

Gerik noticed as Akamon approached that he was dressed for hunting. He wore a rugged leather coat that used to be black, but now was mostly charcoal gray and in many places worn to a brown almost the same shade as his weather-beaten face. His low, broad-brimmed hat came right down to his eyebrows, providing enough shade not only for his deep blue eyes but also for his long, sharp nose. He wore his tall leather boots, and carried a ratty old pack and an immaculate longbow and quiver. Akamon may have let other things go, but he was always careful with his bow and arrows. Though he was ostensibly a farmer, hunting was how he made a living, hunting and tracking, and no one knew this region better than Akamon.

"Reshoe my horse, boy," Akamon said in the odd drawl that Gerik could never seem to place.

"Didn't my dad just …"

"Shut up and reshoe my horse, boy," Akamon interrupted, and then, leaning closer and speaking more quietly, "We need to talk."

Gerik picked up his clinch cutter and hammer, and went to work on the front right hoof. As he worked, Akamon spoke softly almost directly into his ear.

"Listen good. Yellow-skinned bastards say they'll kill my wife if I don't help 'em. So I need you to mess 'em up. And I think you're gonna want to.

"Came and told me I was gonna track something – that's what they said, thing – and then said it was a girl. About fifteen. Five-foot-seven, eight or so. Auburn hair. Pale and skinny. After that, the funniest thing – almost like poetry after all that – 'eyes so blue they make the seas jealous.' Sound familiar, boy?"

Gerik nodded. He knew why Akamon had come to him. On more than one hunting trip he had told Akamon of his intention to pursue Karia, and described her to him. What he didn't understand was why they wanted Karia. And apparently they wanted her quite badly. He also didn't understand why it seemed to matter so much to him.

Akamon continued. "Said they lost it – it, they called her – in the Old Wood, and they needed me to find it. Made a big deal that this was very valuable to them, and they'd reward me well. Also made a big deal that I was to find her and then stay back, because she was dangerous – very dangerous.

"I asked 'em what made a fifteen-year-old skinny girl dangerous, and they told me I didn't need to know."

Gerik was puzzled. Karia? Dangerous?

"So here's the deal, boy. I'm gonna take 'em, at wagon speed, over the road to the farm where that girl lives, and then I know exactly where to go. They've got soldiers watching the bridge, and the only other way she can get out of there is the ford. You remember where that is, boy?"

Gerik nodded. The farm of Karia and her family, and two other families, was the only one west of the Heldasfar River. West and south of her farm was ocean, mostly a rocky, inaccessibly coastline. Northward lay rugged, impenetrable mountains. One old stone bridge crossed the Heldasfar, and well north of that was a ford, where the river was wide and shallow.

"Good," Akamon said. "If you take the old road through the rocky hills at a gallop, you can be there hours before me. Find her tracks and cover your tracks and hers. And find her and get her out of there. You got it, boy?"

Gerik nodded, but uncertainly. *The old road at a gallop?* It was hard to follow the weathered obelisk-shaped markings at a walk.

Akamon saw his uncertainty. "You listen to me hard, boy, hard! These red-eyed *hrukikili* are vicious, and that girl needs you."

Gerik had no idea what a hrukikili was, but he guessed it wasn't a nice word. He was also confused, because he had never heard Akamon sprinkle Inamali words into his speech before.

"Don't waste any time. Pack like you would for a long hunting trip. Anyone asks, that's what you're doing. Want to get out of town while it's all astir."

He saw continued uncertainty on Gerik's face.

"What is wrong with you, boy?! That girl needs you!"

"I … I broke it off with her," he said.

Akamon got right in front of Gerik's face, and hissed, "Then do it because I asked you to, and because any girl is worth saving from those speckle-chested snakes."

Gerik nodded, then said, "I can't hide our tracks well enough that you won't find them."

"You don't need to. In fact, I'm counting on that. They won't see them, and I'll know where you went so I can lead 'em elsewhere."

"Now, finish up with the shoes, then go, get your things, boy. You've got three hours on me. At most, four. And she may have as much as a day on you."

When Gerik finished, Akamon slowly walked from the shop. Gerik hurriedly tidied up and nodded to his dad. His dad was hard of hearing from years of hammering on metal in the smithy, and – to keep from yelling so loudly the whole town could hear – most of their conversation consisted of nods and smiles. Gerik was thankful for that now as he hurried home.

He gathered his hunting gear and had just opened the back door to step back into the yard of the smithy when his mom called out to him.

"Gerik, what are you doing?"

"I'm going hunting, Ma'am," he replied. He decided it was best to not tell her what he was actually doing.

"But with the troops in town, there's likely to be more work at the smithy," she said.

"I just have to get out of here, Ma'am," he said.

"I'll be fine at the smithy," Gerik's dad said, loudly, from right behind him. Gerik was surprised. He had not heard his dad approach. He turned to look at his dad as the man said to his mom – or actually, hollered, "Elestra, your boy just needs to get out away from all this ruckus. Let him go."

His dad smiled at him, and Gerik, in the moment before he started briskly walking to his horse, smiled and wondered just how much his dad had actually heard or figured out.

Ian Fallis

ABOUT THE AUTHOR

"Words are playthings to him," one of Ian Fallis' co-workers is fond of saying.

After earning a journalism degree from Northwestern University, he spent fifteen years at daily newspapers in Southern California, in almost every editorial role: reporter, photographer, copy editor, assignment editor, features editor and night managing editor.

From there he went into New Tribes Mission, learning about languages and linguistics and culture and worldview. In his subsequent fifteen years with NTM, he has been to tiny hamlets and villages across the Asia-Pacific region and in Latin America, gathering stories, taking photos and helping film documentaries.

You can find:

- More about Ian Fallis (too much, most likely)
- Behind-the-scenes looks at his writing process (it's kinda creepy)
- News about current and upcoming books (oooh!)

at his blog: **ian-fallis.com**

Made in the USA
Charleston, SC
26 September 2013